MW00856231

THRILLED TO DEATH

ALSO BY LYNNE TILLMAN

NOVELS

Weird Fucks (1980, 2006)

Haunted Houses (1987)

Motion Sickness (1991)

Cast in Doubt (1992)

No Lease on Life (1998)

American Genius, A Comedy (2006)

Men and Apparitions (2018)

SHORT STORY COLLECTIONS

Absence Makes the Heart (1980)

The Madame Realism Complex (1992)

This Is Not It (2002)

Someday This Will Be Funny (2011)

The Complete Madame Realism and Other Stories (2016)

NONFICTION

The Velvet Years: Warhol's Factory 1965–67 (1995)

The Broad Picture: Essays 1987–1996 (1997)

Bookstore: The Life and Times of Jeannette Watson and Books & Co. (1999)

What Would Lynne Tillman Do? (2014)

MOTHERCARE (2022)

THRILLED
TO DEATH

Selected Stories

LYNNE
TILLMAN

With an Introduction
by Christine Smallwood

With an Afterword
by Lucy Sante

Soft Skull
New York

THRILLED TO DEATH

This is a work of fiction. All of the characters, organizations,
and events portrayed in this collection of stories are either products
of the author's imagination or are used fictitiously.

Copyright © 2025 by Lynne Tillman
Introduction copyright © 2025 by Christine Smallwood
Afterword copyright © 2025 by Lucy Sante

All rights reserved under domestic and international copyright. Outside of fair
use (such as quoting within a book review), no part of this publication may be
reproduced, stored in a retrieval system, or transmitted in any form or by any means,
electronic, mechanical, photocopying, recording, or otherwise, without the written
permission of the publisher. For permissions, please contact the publisher.

First Soft Skull edition: 2025

Library of Congress Cataloging-in-Publication Data
Names: Tillman, Lynne, author. | Smallwood, Christine, writer of introduction.
Sante, Lucy, writer of afterword.
Title: Thrilled to death : selected stories / Lynne Tillman ; with an
introduction by Lucy Sante.
Description: First Soft Skull edition. | New York : Soft Skull, 2025.
Identifiers: LCCN 2024044528 | ISBN 9781593767198 (hardcover) | ISBN
9781593767204 (ebook)
Subjects: LCGFT: Short stories.
Classification: LCC PS3570.I42 T48 2025 | DDC 813/.54—dc23/eng/20240930
LC record available at https://lccn.loc.gov/2024044528

Jacket design by Nicole Caputo
Jacket photograph: Lynne with Mums *by Heather Stern*
Book design by Wah-Ming Chang

Soft Skull Press
New York, NY
www.softskull.com

Printed in the United States of America

1 3 5 7 9 10 8 6 4 2

For my father

Nat Tillman
1908–1984

Everything starts in doubt.

ANNE CARSON

You rest at the end.

KOBE BRYANT

CONTENTS

INTRODUCTION

by Christine Smallwood

The stories in Lynne Tillman's *Thrilled to Death*—fictional, though a couple might be based on actual events—date from the 1980s to the present, but unlike many career-spanning books of stories, they are not arranged chronologically. Which isn't to say there's no logic at work (or play). "I wanted it to be more associative," Tillman explained when I asked how she ordered the pieces, "thematic perhaps, and to deny the idea of 'progress.'"

As readers of *Haunted Houses* or *American Genius, A Comedy* or *MOTHERCARE* or any other of her wholly original, utterly canny/uncanny works know, denying progress is one of Tillman's major preoccupations. It's not just about saying no, though it's telling that she's said she feels closer to Bartleby, who would prefer not to, than Molly Bloom, who says yes yes yes. Denying progress, whether your frame is a story or a life, can be a way to keep moving. In the case of Tillman, the chosen direction is often inward rather than forward. We turn pages (I think of her recurring character, Paige Turner) as we live our days, one at a time, and though we can't help moving into the future, we're often looking behind. We drop what we pick up (Tillman's characters are more inclined to pick things apart); we return, then turn another way. Things don't always get better, though sometimes they do; people don't always change, though sometimes they can; lessons not learned can still be toyed with.

Progress implies that things are going toward a destination, that they are getting better, more perfect, as they close in on the end. (*The end*—that promised narrative utopia where threads come together, order is restored, secrets are revealed, and meaning is made.) When we read an author's work in the order it was written, there's the additional pressure on how the work stands for the life, with each story a station on the journey from birth to the other thing. Perhaps making the order associative isn't only a way of moving in or on; it could also be a way of moving backward—staying, or again becoming, young.

It could be. But keep in mind that Tillman has no interest in innocence, or innocents. Like the sagest children, she's an experimenter. Her subjects here are various—art and sex, death and ghosts, bad parents, bad friends, bad lovers, and animals (cat lovers, beware the sad tale of "Boots and Remorse"!)—and her deepest passion is for the rhythm and cadence of thinking, for her characters' busy minds.

To deny progress when the subject is the mind is to court comedy as well as tragedy. Tillman is one of our most unsentimental and yet playful writers, which makes me think that the two must somehow go together—that it's only when we take the measure of the absolute shit we are in, here in twenty-first-century America, and when we reject the pablum that's supposed to make it go down, that we can get involved in the serious business of creativity. Her prose is like a disco wrecking ball, noisily smashing conventions of character and plot, and merrily strewing beams of crazed (cracked) insight all over the house of fiction. Here I note that the phrase on the cover is "selected stories," not "collected stories." This is a sampling, not a sum, and anyone who tries to sum it up will find themselves a little short.

Many of Tillman's characters yearn for freedom, though never from thoughts and dreams; there's no drive here toward dissociation or nihilism. But they also recognize that freedom has its limits. "At dinner with so-called intelligent people," begins the story "Contingencies,"

> during our discussion of the Marquis de Sade, I recognized a common lunacy: the fairy tale of absolute and complete freedom. People don't know what to do with the freedom they have, I announced, and trounced off, as if insulted.

There's something of a non sequitur in this sequence—the fact that people don't know what to do with the freedom they have doesn't follow from the fact that absolute freedom is a fairy tale—but that's not so strange; non sequiturs hold Tillman's thinkers together. (At the opening of "Thrilled to Death," Rose Hall looks out a train window and, after a bit of mental wander, concludes, "It was strange how one thing didn't follow another.") Her sentences and paragraphs veer off in unexpected and unpredictable and yet perfectly right, never random directions. The non sequiturs are invitations to associate, to read closer; they'll slow you down, if you let them. In the case of "Contingencies," the speaker's leap in logic might imply that there is something funny about the same people who are impressed with the freedom exhibited by de Sade's characters using their own to sit around after dinner; they *do* have freedom, and what they choose to do with it is . . . talk. The narrator, on the other hand, knows exactly what to do with her freedom: She ends the session.

Much of "Contingencies" takes place on a bus that's moving through a city. Like many urban dwellers, Tillman's characters want to be close to others while preserving their privacy. "They appreciated the distance between things," is how one character describes another's paintings, and the same could be said of the stories themselves. Points of contact emerge and then suddenly recede. What is being close, anyway? Is it being understood, or touched? Can you join with another without disappearing yourself? (If you disappear, where do you go?)

The freedom to move, to mix it up with like and unlike, to determine where one goes and what one does, to arrive and leave on one's own time, feels, for Tillman, deeply connected to the freedom that most matters to her—the freedom on the page. Unlike most of us, who don't know what to do with freedom when we find it, and so get into the habit of taking shelter in confinements of one kind or another, Tillman seizes the freedom to put any word after the next, and makes a kind of insane hay with it. She isn't only curious about the activity of thinking; she's curious about thoughts themselves, the phrases and notions that get into our heads. She holds words to the light, examining them for defects and testing what they can do.

Like any good Freudian—like anyone trained in surrealism, or, as she would say, Madame Realism—Tillman loves puns and wordplay. "This is a wit's end, he told himself," says Tiny in "Tiny Struggles"—but it never is. You may know the old story about Kafka laughing out loud while reading *The Metamorphosis* to his friends. It's easy to picture a similar scene with Tillman reading from "More Sex," in which a character sets a timer so she can think about sex every seven minutes, like men are said to do, or from "A Simple Idea," in which the narrator, to calm a friend who has received a phone call from someone claiming to be the police, has a bizarre conversation with the local precinct. The story ends suddenly and sadly, like a road that runs into a wall, or a rug that's pulled up beneath you.

"That's How Wrong My Love Is" concerns a woman who watches mourning doves. Maybe calling it funny says more about me than about the story, but there is wonderful comedy in the narrator's list of the things she eats—less meat than she once did; roast chicken; fish; crustaceans; never bacon, horse, cat, or dog— and the declaration that follows:

> If I were starving, caught in a war, desperate to survive, like the Donner Party, who ate their dead colleagues, like most people I would ultimately succumb, with remorse and disgust.

It's the syntax that makes me laugh, the compounding over-explanation, and how that rhythm is juxtaposed against the dark, matter-of-fact disclosure. After the list of foods, the clauses themselves seem to list, to lean so far to the side that they threaten to fall over. (That diction, too—referring to the pioneers as "colleagues"!) Or maybe it's the sheer assertion of self that makes it funny. "There are things I like to do, and I do them, and, as much as I can, I don't do what I don't want to do," the narrator concludes, simply and absurdly. Few would say it like this, but who couldn't relate?

Tillman's constant attention to language is a clue, or maybe it's the solution. Her world is a game, a world of language, of writing itself. As Cólm Toibín put it: "Writing, for her, is like writing, if it is like anything, and it probably isn't like anything; words, for her, come from words, they have their own shape and sound." And yet also—or maybe because of her attention to words—her fiction is compassionate and emotionally vivid. She has the playfulness of an Oulipian and a heart for the suffering. There's a moral core to her world, a passionate hostility to power. Many people today believe that language is like a machine or a computer program, or, rather, that because computers can spit out sentences, language itself must be machine-like. Tillman reminds us that playing with words, collecting and rearranging their meanings, is a pursuit of the heart. We are fantasists, dreamers, and builders. "Imperfect knowledge accompanied him across the field to a big tent," begins the story "The Shadow of a Doubt." It's a very typical Tillman image. Her characters are accompanied by their pasts, their memories, their minds—they seem to exist next to their minds rather than being located inside them. They are assemblages of memory and thought and body, going through the world alongside the things they know. These things they know (and don't know) have as much life as they themselves do.

The situations and scenes that Tillman collages and constructs are how she remembers, puts us together. (I almost said "back together," but I'm not sure she would say that there was ever a time we were whole. Maybe in utero, though if you can only be whole by being entirely subsumed in another, that raises a bunch more questions I can't resolve in a parenthetical. One thing I love about Tillman's work is how it gets you asking these kinds of questions—how it urges you to take apart your words, to think harder and longer about them—and reminds you that when you do, you won't arrive at anything but another question.) That's why she's always writing about smell, especially the experience of running into an old lover and smelling them. Smell connects us to the past, and it connects us to animals. We *are* animals, of course.

Tillman has something of a reputation for writing prose that's provoking. This is especially true in the novels, where the sentences stretch out and luxuriate in the folds of the brain. But short stories are—if you will permit me to state the obvious (Tillman would, I believe; she once wrote a poem, "Do the obvious"— short. Tillman's stories don't test the reader's capacities as much as they demand the reader's attention. She plays multiple hands in every game. She is a genius of the immediately engulfing weirdo voice, while also always reminding you that the voice is the creation of an author—that writing is artifice, art. Many of her stories feel personal, even hermetic, like the voice is working something out for itself, something private. And yet the stories are spoken *to* the reader, so the feeling I have is never that I'm eavesdropping—it's that someone particular, who I don't know very well but is intent on making herself known, is speaking right to—even just to—me.

Thrilled to Death is chockablock with references to films and Hollywood. In addition to the narrator of "Other Movies," who understands life only through film stills, there are references throughout the volume to Hitchcock, especially *Rear Window*. Sal Mineo and Marilyn Monroe even show up as characters. More typically, Tillman's non-actors are shaped by screen dreams and screen stars, and sometimes brush sleeves with celebrities while being resolutely unfamous themselves. The real proximity/ estrangement is not between Hollywood actor and New York writer, however, it's between fantasy and tragedy, stardom and death. One narrator is a guest at a costume party, dressed in her dead father's clothes. "No one at the party knew what man I was, and, like so much of life, it was only in my head." A few pages later, Clint Eastwood arrives. The narrator is not surprised. "I'd been expecting him for years," she says.

> Sometimes I conjured him after watching one of his movies, and then in dreams I knew him intimately. Dreams, the mind's gifts, can be sweeter than anything reality offers, and they satisfy me more than sex. Or, they are sex.

It doesn't make sense to ask if Eastwood is "really" there, any more than you can explain what "really happened" in a dream. And Tillman's characters are always talking about their dreams.

It's easy to fixate on the question of narrator, of who tells the story—a worthy inquiry, and something that the writer can (mostly) control. Tillman also requires us to ask who listens, or reads, or looks. We can't help sending messages, we emit them all over the place; does anyone receive them? It happens more than once in *Thrilled to Death* that a narrator or character believes someone is listening, looking, or speaking, when in fact no one is there.

In "Hung Up," the narrator is furious that her friend keeps ending their phone calls, until he declares himself bemused that someone keeps calling and not saying anything; whether the line is broken or the narrator is nuts (must we choose one?) is not clearly resolved. But my favorite moment in the whole collection is hardly even a story—it's more of a bit. (Skip ahead if you don't want it spoiled.) A near-sighted woman walks into a bar and makes eyes all night with a man who never gets out of his seat; when she finally goes over to him, she realizes that she's been flirting with a stain on the wall. The mere fact of her mistake isn't what gets her. "She wondered who saw her making eyes with a stain on the wall. That cracked her up, later."

There are some writers who don't ever think about readers, because it's too terrifying. Is anyone really out there? What's scarier to contemplate—that no one is, or that someone is? *Making eyes with a stain on the wall* describes how it feels, some days, to write. (If Tillman's stories are the woman in the bar, let me be the stain on the wall!) But the self-consciousness—the wondering who sees her failing to see—is what transforms the joke into a work of art. Getting outside of one's own experience, being out of one's head, standing a little to the side, looking back in—what can it do but crack us up, in every possible sense?

The art of the short story, like the art of so much else in life, is knowing when to stop. In the sprawling title story, "Thrilled to Death," characters unknown to one another descend on a carnival, where they meet a dominatrix, a hunger artist, and assorted freaks. "Nothing dies here, everything's alive," says a fortune teller. "It's also a tragic place, a cemetery for things that aren't dead." The story doesn't tell us if things ever die in literature, or if literature is a cemetery for what can't die. What we know is that people fall in and out of love. They go round the Wonder Wheel, and round the carousel. They are entranced by light and shocked by violence. Paige Turner, whose life is changed by what occurs that day, describes it like this: "That carnival deranged me, rearranged me maybe." That's what Tillman's writing does—it deranges and rearranges. You keep going back and it's never the same.

THRILLED TO DEATH

Come and Go

What does it matter what you say about people?

—FROM ORSON WELLES'S
Touch of Evil

PART I

It must have been the movie. Afterward, New Yorkers did a dumb show, and the city was silent, except for its special effects. But she heard the sinister soundtrack. Especially the hissing. Everything, everyone, was out of sync. A man with two lit cigarettes in his mouth gazed ahead, stupefied. He must've seen the movie, too.

Now it was noisy. Her head hurt in the late afternoon, when she walked up Broadway to the green market at Union Square. The fruit and vegetables looked good, but she knew she wouldn't buy any. They'd just rot. She waved her hands in the air, fending off an imaginary object or punctuating her unspoken utterances with a familiar futility. Her right hand hit a man in the shoulder. He had a stud in his ear and was carrying flowers, one of which fell to the ground. He bent to pick it up.

Charles shoved the flower into the bunch, embarrassed as hell, and the woman, whoever she was, also seemed embarrassed. He said he was sorry, though it wasn't his fault, but he always said he was sorry, and she said she was, and it was her fault, so that was right, and he walked out of the market, abandoning the profusion of ruddy people and green and yellow vegetables. Carrying flowers embarrassed him, also, as if he were in an ad for romance or Mother's Day. He touched his earring, took it out of his ear, shoved it into his pocket, annoyed about everything suddenly, noticed a cute guy on the street carrying flowers also, wondered who for, and hailed a cab.

Emma had never seen him before. He seemed to recognize her—he looked at her in the skewed way people do when they think they know you—and was gallant about being hit hard in the shoulder. But her sense of ridiculousness overcame her, and with even this brief, awkward attention, she plunged into the imaginary conversation she could fashion at the drop of a flower.

You're Emma, right?

Emma Green. Have we met?

At a party. Real name: Emerald Green?

My father was a painter and an accountant.

Weird.

Yes, Emma said, he sometimes stained his accounts.

Don't we all, she continued to herself, while the man walked off too quickly. She was a little hungry, or peckish, her English friends would say. She had not even a crumb of fantasy, not of hell or heaven, to sustain her.

Hospitals are diseased. Charles stood at the elevator, inhaling and exhaling heavily. Any elevator in a plague, he thought, and noticed three elegant male junkies—Armani suits, good haircuts—encircling a fourth, a beautiful girl they guarded like perishable treasure. The almost-dead protecting the near-dead, he thought, what Poe wished for—drop-dead gorgeous. The elevator took forever. You could die waiting, someone said to someone else. Death was a grotesque punch line to this hairy ape story, an endless joke. It had a name, but he couldn't remember it. No one ever told that kind, except his father. A shaggy dog story. He remembered the ancient phrase now, as his father's face plummeted before him, an apparition or a curtain. Next to it, a fat, wet dog shook itself violently. His father's face was wet, transparent. Rain, sweat, tears; blood, sweat, rain. The elevator arrived and two people wrapped in bandages—heads only—got off. He laughed stupidly. Couldn't help himself.

The beautiful junkie couldn't hold herself up. Without her friends, she would have gone spineless and collapsed on the floor. Third floor—drug rehab. Her friends said she had to turn herself in, be an inpatient. Hang with the in-crowd, one said dryly. His eyes were tiny points. She couldn't focus. She nodded. Her body was weight. She wanted to die and had, nearly, yesterday. Or maybe it was before, in bed, but then she didn't know what time it was or care. She wasn't thinking, she wasn't actually anything. Each one of the men holding her up, pushing her body along, had been the object of a frail feeling, like lust but not as energetic. Lust was dust. She hated the thick, windowless doors that divided rehab from whatever wasn't.

Emma had seen two movies in two nights, sort of the same movie, and afterward thought the same thought: I need a drink. This afternoon, she went to a local bar, but a different one because she didn't want to be seen as a woman-alone, an alcoholic, or any of the variations or alternatives, when there were none, really. She smiled and ordered a meal of peanuts, pretzels, and Stoli on the rocks. A second drink produced the sensation she wanted, a dull happiness or absence of affect, and she left, singing, not loudly and more or less to herself, she believed. When she reached her corner, she stepped down from the sidewalk onto the street and into a hole. She heard a pop, began to fall, found herself on the ground, and had to be lifted off the street by a man she didn't know. He accompanied her to her door. Put ice on it, he advised, keep it in the air. Maybe he was a doctor.

She didn't feel any pain, but momentarily her foot and ankle throbbed, along with her bothersome head. Her ankle blew up. She struggled out again, down the stairs, to the street, and pathetically hailed a cab. NYU, emergency entrance, she told the driver.

The doctor's waiting room itself wanted. Anything might enliven it, but probably not for long. A confession from the lips of someone in much worse shape than Charles. That always gave relief. But the air was heavy with anxiety and a damp, communal sweat. Green walls and orange furniture. Magazines about health or fame. He had been waiting for two hours—his doctor had been called to an emergency operation. But when the doctor walked in, finally, he'd tell Charles, I have good news. Your test result was negative. Then Charles would smile, laugh, maybe cry too. He practiced his reactions, unaware that others followed his face crumpling and relaxing. In a kind of revolving-door fantasy, the other verdict spun out: Charles, the result was positive, but don't give up hope. There are many treatments. Charles would cry then, and the doctor would offer him a tissue from a box on his desk. Charles would read the brand name and look to see if they were single or double-ply tissues. He noticed those things.

Emma hated people more today than she ever had. Her ankle pulsed, throbbed, and her heart didn't, it sank, and she was surrounded, in an ugly emergency room, by unexciting strangers. Triage meant that she wasn't a most-favored candidate for treatment, and while in most cases she'd want to be low on that list, Emma envied, in a perverse way, the startling emergencies who were taken quickly by semi-anxious professionals in white. Emergencies like the woman who'd fallen face down on a crystal vase. Most of the professionals wore sweaters or something with a color so that the uniform wasn't uniform, and there wasn't even order to admire. Emma hated any disorder that wasn't hers. Meanwhile, with mean thoughts her company, she listened to the TV's drone; sometimes it screamed, and people paid it that curious inattention the smaller screen fosters, which, when she was feeling better or more herself, which might not be better, she liked. The new, old man next to her smelled, so she limped over to a chair near a talkative younger coot. She liked his cowboy boots.

Maggie's doctor wanted to know how she had let herself sink so low. The doctor was bald, avuncular. He followed orders and a technique meant to shake her to her senses. Boring. She looked down. Her sweater was filthy, it stuck to her body like a snake's shed skin. She was a snake. Did she really want to die? he asked. She didn't know. Probably not, she said. She didn't think she could kick, she didn't want to. Her friends were hanging around somewhere, she figured, for some news, or until it became too disgusting or sad, or they became too depressed or sick to stay. They'd split, cop, return, split, cop, return. Her parents might show up. Her mother, anyway. The same boring, angry story. She heard herself talk: I like drugs, and I'm not exceptional.

Cancer-free, Charles had himself now and no disease to battle or worry about to make his shallow life precious. He rubbed the earring he'd replaced, once he'd had the good news. He couldn't leave the hospital. It was where his father had died of cancer. Charles had an awful compulsion to stay inside the scene of his former fear and misery. He entered the dismal cafeteria, because he was hungry, he told himself, and grabbed some junk food, because he was going to live, he told himself, and sat at a table with the three elegant, druggy men, who weren't speaking and looked shaken. Stirred not shaken, he thought. Charles was content or calm. He could study, at a small distance, the faces of people like himself, who were condemned to more life.

The cowboy wasn't a cowboy, he worked in advertising, probably on that Ralph Lauren campaign, she thought. Emma's broken ankle was only a bad sprain. She was given an Ace bandage, bought an aluminum cane, and her sole desire was to have her hair washed and cut. She wanted to enter the salon, don a black robe, lie down, and hear Yoji say how important hair is. Listless, she reflected for a while, then gathered her strength, rose, and, balancing incorrectly on the cane, hobbled out of the hospital.

What's my name? Maggie repeated the nurse's question but thought, Turkey, cold turkey, though said, Margaret Adams. She was lying in a fog on a bed in a yellow room. She had to leave. Her friends had told her she could not sing in their group, she could not live in their loft, unless she cleaned up her act. Her mother would pay for it. Hypocrites, all of them. The nurse gave her something for the pain, and Maggie floated someplace. She noticed another person on another bed, shut her eyes again, and saw a bloody hell through her eyelids. Showtime, she thought.

For a hospital cafeteria, the food wasn't bad. Charles was glad to be eating. The druggy guys interested him, as did drugs, moderately, all things in moderation. He hadn't done the hard ones, hadn't injected himself, anyway. But the lanky men barely acknowledged each other and didn't look at him. One of them finally muttered something about the beautiful, near-dead one. She was something—he couldn't catch the words—waxy, wasted, wack, worked up. The other two grunted or nodded. He supposed he wouldn't ever be even a nodding acquaintance. That amused him. Charles rubbed the ring in his ear, shook his head, and hoped to appear exotic. When no one glanced his way, he stood up, lifted his tray, as if he were partnering a great ballerina, and laughed. Then he made a slow exit. What's he on? one of the guys asked, almost interested.

It was raining hard, everyone wanted a cab, desperately. Emma didn't have an umbrella and, temporarily crippled, couldn't race for any that pulled up. She waved her cane in the air, standing on one leg like a wounded bird. It was 7:15. Maybe the salon would be open. They did models. Her hair was wet, her clothes soaked, but it didn't matter; her slight infirmity was no selling point, compared with the stricken in wheelchairs whose attendants vied near her. Suddenly a man sidled up, nodded at her with a kind of recognition—the man from the market, she remembered almost instantly—and said, I'll hail us one, how about that? Charles raced into the street and plundered the next, indifferent to the maze of wheelchair-bound. Bright eyes, a ring in his ear, he might be all right. He carried a gray attaché case and told her he made films sometimes and did PR. She'd begin with her sprained ankle.

Maggie's mother called and woke her. Though half-dead, Maggie heard the drug-induced non-anxiety coating her mother's voice.

I'm okay, Mom, she said, alive and kicking.

Very funny, her mother said.

Maggie's mother doctored film and TV scripts, especially comedies. She was not fun to live with, even when she was funny.

You mean, Maggie said, I'm not your heroine du jour.

You're not funny, her mother said.

And I'll have whatever you're having.

Her mother said she'd call later when Maggie could control

herself, and Maggie rolled over, wondering if the next call would be from her father, whoever he was. Her mother, ever independent, claimed it was the man who called himself Dad, but Maggie didn't believe her. He was just her putative pop. Pop goes the weasel.

There was an air of perfect, impossible contentment in the salon. No sound or Muzak sullied the salon's minimal aesthetic. Emma and the others—men and women—received not just the salon's great cuts, but also its persuasive, osmotic sensibility. Beauty and style, like stillness, were in the air. Japanese men and women shaped and colored hair, blessed hair, of which Emma now had little. She was shorn like a sheep. Yoji colored what remained aubergine, while she contemplated Charles and their cab ride. She'd told him she was a horse trainer and had hurt her ankle in action; he'd accepted this and talked about his experience in the hospital, his relief, the junkies. Terrible crosstown traffic allowed for a long, even intimate, cab conversation. When Charles dropped her at the salon, he said he'd call—after all, they'd bumped into each other twice accidentally, didn't that mean something? She nearly said no. Now they might see each other on purpose, if he liked women, or her, which was more complicated. And now she had aubergine hair. She looked like an eggplant. Maybe he was partial to vegetables.

Maggie's father didn't call, until later, when Maggie was inside private hospital hell. He didn't like the idea, he told her, that she was in any institution, didn't she have friends to help her . . . He hated hospitals, he was sick about it, her, sick sick sick. She learned he'd called her mother to complain that Mom had driven her to drugs. Their usual fight, she told the shrink, making some inane comment about Mom having shrunk her first. Pop's involvement made her think he really was her father, but who knew.

She disliked the psychiatrist, structurally speaking, but less than she had. She told him a friend of hers had ODed, slipping into that indefinite sleep, and she longed to have nothing to worry about, too. Her mother would say, What have you ever had to worry about?

Charles's father had been a shrink. But no talking cure for Charles—there was no talking to his father when alive, impossible dead. He threw his earring onto the dresser and lay down on the floor. He stretched idly. He masturbated and thought afterward about the first time he'd had an erection—sitting on the chair his mother loved. That was such a dopey memory, he wept. He ordered Chinese food, watched Bill Murray in *What about Bob?* and fell into a comfortable nostalgia. His father had never had a stalker patient like Bob. But to his father, Charles could have been a Bob. He'd never know.

Emma's hair, in the light, was even more purple, but it would fade, everything fades. Yoji had done the best he could, his best was better than most, but he didn't understand lavender. She didn't understand people's love of purple prose, she preferred porn, but there was none in her apartment. The light by her bed was not strong enough, the phone by her bed did not ring enough. It sat on the table like a dumpy Buddha. Her older sister had told her, all her life, that she had a big mouth. Emma didn't think that was true. She wasn't nasty, just frank, candid as a camera, which also, like her, lied. She looked different in every photo she took.

PART 2

The next morning, when Charles went to work, he was determined to overcome a recalcitrant melancholy. Charles was a publicist, and he worked hard to sound on top of things. I'm on top of things, don't worry, he'd say. He handled a range of clients from foundations to individuals and was moderately successful, giving good phone, demanding without seeming obsequious or needy. Sounding needy was bad, only for the last resort, and some of his clients were. This morning, when he hailed a taxi, he remembered the horse trainer from the hospital and their weird ride together. He decided he'd call her, she seemed sympathetic if neurotic. Charles phoned immediately. Otherwise he might not. Sometimes he was impulsive. His impulses were, he thought, the best thing about him.

Emma woke to his early-morning call. They should be banned, she thought, except that they might contain early warnings and be necessary, but then that was why they were horrible and should be banned. Charles was in a taxi again.

You get around early, she said.

Don't you go to work? he said.

Work comes to me.

She yawned, purposefully.

Want to explain that? Charles asked.

No, Emma said.

He laughed, which was okay, and she agreed to meet him at the Oyster Bar. Thinking of oysters made her sick, but she superimposed Charles's face on the slimy creatures. Maybe he wasn't as slimy.

Maggie's dream life worked overtime to produce excessive colors and danger. She slept as much as she could. Though given to dramatic sighs and moans, she was no nineteenth-century heroine. She cursed her fate, her so-called life, and filled it now with an aggressive, contemptuous self-pity. She was in a room with three people, all of whom were, like her, withdrawing and in the program. She felt compelled to muffle herself. She was withdrawn, anyway, and withdrew further, to stay inside herself. The drug was out of her system. But her brain kept its vivacious memory to which she, her body or her brain, achingly returned. Shit. Each day her roommates became less loathsome to her; and she wasn't sure why. She feared she might be turned, like a trick, into a loathsome Pollyanna. Her best friend assured her that was impossible. That's what best friends were for.

"Even though," Charles contended, fixing the earpiece of his phone, "even if you did all the work and he's taking the credit, it doesn't matter, because you'll still get paid." Assuaging a client's hurt feelings, encouraging the wounded ego to roll with a career's punk punches, was what he was paid for. Charles sometimes believed the lies or relative truths he insisted upon. How crazy everything is, he'd sometimes declare. And it was. Everything. Crazy. Still, when he hung up the phone and looked out of his office window at other office windows, Charles's body collapsed a little, let down by something he could never name. The light was leaving, and something with promise was snatched away, or it was the beginning of darkness and the start of unnameable feelings. He should work late, but he had a date with Emma, whatever she was or did, at six. Her work came to her, she had said, mysteriously. Analyst, personal trainer? Oysters on the half shell with a strange woman might be just what the doctor ordered, although he couldn't remember any doctor saying anything like that.

In group therapy, following a hostile silence, Maggie told everyone what she thought of them. They in turn told her. No one liked her. She didn't care. The opinion of one woman affected her, mostly because it was offered with discernment and haughty disdain. Maggie decided to win her. It was a junkie's form of sublimation—to score the love or good feeling of the most truculent, the most obdurate. Someone like herself. Someone desirable for all the wrong reasons, who suffered as she did from helplessness. No one liked her, but she wasn't going to eat worms. She could be charming. She'd turn it on.

Titillated by the evening's possibilities, Emma energetically, or libidinally, she might ironically put it, threw herself into her job. She was a social worker and psychic. Emma had wanted to become a psychoanalyst and determinedly entered into training after receiving her MSW. Along the way she developed an unfortunate transference to her training analyst—she thought he was trying to destroy her. Much as he tried to convince her this was a projection, when one of his other analysands committed suicide, Emma's fears were confirmed. As a social worker, she was licensed to treat individual patients; and her psychic powers were something that, over the years, she'd come to use and trust. Slowly she had brought them into her practice, with the right patients, and slowly word spread among the unhappy and the chic that Emma absolutely saw right through you, as if you were glass, to the inside or the other side. It was peculiar to Emma that she herself was unlucky in love, but like the esteemed editor who can't write, Emma spotted the problem because it wasn't hers.

Maggie's obdurate woman—the woman least likely to succumb, to her—had skin like mother-of-pearl. Like my mother's old compact, Maggie thought. The woman's pearlescence was the first reason Maggie stared at her. Then it was her airy disinterest. Maggie soon wanted the woman's good opinion, though it signaled a corruption of her usual state of mind. But Maggie was out of her mind, out of it. One of the nurses repeated several times that quitting junk was easier than stopping smoking. Her stained fingers and teeth were a burnt testament to that truth. The obdurate one, smoking in a corner, coughed and laughed. Bitter humor smoothed Maggie's serrated edges. She took it for sophistication. Being sophisticated, Maggie felt, established a respectable distance from the unhappy pursuit of happiness.

When Charles and Emma met at the Oyster Bar, Emma didn't see right through him and he didn't understand her. It was the source of their immediate attraction. She admitted she didn't train horses and didn't explain why she had lied initially. Her refusal to explain was itself seductive; Charles never wanted to and thrilled to those who didn't, imagining they possessed an inner grace. From Emma's viewpoint, Charles's hunger to be liked and his cuteness—the earring he kept tugging—were undercut by his reticence. She took shyness for truthfulness. Disingenuous herself, she was susceptible to people who hadn't given up on honesty's promise. They usually were promising. The next time they met, Charles kissed Emma, after two bottles of Taittinger. He opened his mouth completely, his wet upper lip clinging to the tip of her nose. If he was gay, she thought, he was very generous. The more they touched each other, the more they liked each other, a feeling neither could remember having had in a while. Aroused, Emma asked him what he liked best. When Charles said, Honestly, sweetie, I don't know, she almost fainted.

Nothing nothing mattered. Nothing. Nothing nothing mattered. He was on top of the world, his world. Nothing mattered, he was shattered. What about Charles, Charles? he bellowed in the shower, lathering again and again, getting clean clean clean. Skin is thin, sin is fat, it's like that. He pinched himself. He wanted to cancel every appointment, because nothing mattered, but then he buttoned his jacket, picked up his keys, and strolled to the subway. Mass transit. He hadn't had sex—say LOVE, Charles—since he thought he was dying. Now he knew he wasn't—say LIFE, Charles—nothing really mattered, nothing nothing. He'd send

Emma flowers and buy a new bed, throw out the old, full of sorrows, toss out every Tom, Dick, Harriette, and Charlene who'd rolled there. A firm bed. FUN, Charles, nothing mattered so much you couldn't have fun. And weren't Metro cards great, too. Dr. Bones, Maggie named him, was gaunt, like a user, except some junkies were fat. Bones expected her to talk and talk five times a week, which was how you knew she was in a watering hole for wealthy abusers and other rich, dependent types. Women who loved gross men and forced them into dresses, men who chased women who despised men. It catered to the best of the worst. Bones was handsome, in a tortured way, with rings under his eyes, one for every sad story he heard. She liked that. He was perceptive, or maybe there wasn't much hidden. The obdurate one wasn't talking in group, just staring, still pearly, and sometimes laughing through her opaque eyes. Maggie talked to Bones about her. He said Maggie's fantasies were analyzable. Analyze that? Maggie sighed.

Emma's dilemma wasn't Charles, not in the purest sense, though nothing was innocent. She hadn't liked someone in a long time and was unused to it. Charles was returning tonight—"I can't get enough of you"—and she was glad, she thought. But her life already had a shape she liked, its dimensions assured her. She could make a list and follow it. Apart from an accident, when she landed in an emergency room and met a man like Charles, life conformed to her expectations. Nothing extraordinary. That might seem strange given her psychic powers, but it wasn't to her. There were no great surprises. People were unhappy and wanted confirmation they were right; that the pain wouldn't last long, and in the end they'd be loved and rich. Happiness would discover them as if it were a talent scout, and doesn't everyone have talent. Charles had sent flowers twice. His enthusiasm overflowed.

Emma wondered what his story was. Last night he phoned once, then twice, but later she turned off the ringer.

Maggie didn't answer her calls now.

Charles didn't want to speak to anyone except Emma.

Emma was exhausted.

PART 3

They didn't want to be themselves, they wanted to be someone else. If they weren't themselves, they weren't anyone else, either. Who they should have been, they never imagined they could be. And then, as if by magic or the stroke of a sword or pen, they vanished.

With that, I came into being.

I wanted them to go, and I have my reasons. The disappearance of Charles and Emma resulted from a fast, ferocious pull toward each other that could have just one end—as strong a repulsion. Maggie withdrew from drugs and entered therapy like Alice falling through a hole in the ground. She had grown so little, her withdrawal was complete.

I had seen myself, or expressed myself, to be old-fashioned, in them, since Charles, Emma, and Maggie were excrescences of my needs, evidence of my frailties. I used them, too, but because I can be frivolous and intellectually promiscuous—I flirt whenever I can with whatever I can—their usefulness stopped. My interest in them as extensions of myself has, too, and now I don't want to need them. I'd like to be myself. I'm not sure what that means, but I think it signifies an oppressive self-centeredness.

I left them before they left me.

I shift between wishing to control what I can and being afraid

I will, only to become bored, and vacillate between a dislike of constancy and consistency and the fear that I will inevitably be betrayed by others who lose interest and float away. We are things bobbing in the water, things to be discarded when advantage has been taken and regard lost.

I'm not inured to myself, but on some days I think I am. Hating yourself is a thankless job, and others can relieve you of the obligation. People are more easily defined by those who hate them than by those who love them. Sadly, the people who hate me are weak and vile. But I don't court disaster; it visits me. I don't flaunt, I don't shout on streets or on buses. I've been a good dog in the back seat of the big family car. My tongue never hangs out, I don't slobber and drool, I don't piss on the seat. I curb myself until I can't stand it anymore.

Charles, Emma, and Maggie are figments, elements. I couldn't bear to be them, and maybe I am them. I'm not everyman. I'm no one in particular, and they're not just clutter, my trash, or dust bunnies. But I do sweep, collect, and hurl bits and pieces into the whirly world.

I miss them already.

Yesterday I was determined to remake myself into any appealing image. I watched TV. *Dances with Wolves* was on, and I wanted to be the Indian woman when she was slashing herself after her mate's death and also the wolf on the plain. A combination of their passion and fierceness, with the wolf and Indian woman emblematic of my person, would form the design for the fearsome, inviolate character of my dreams. In dreams begin what?

Everything challenges the tenuous world order. Every emotion derails every other one. One rut is disrupted by the emergence of another. I began drinking white wine, had a thirst for it, and now demand it at 6:00 p.m., exactly, as if my life depended upon it. That was a while ago.

What does a life depend upon?

Maggie is a handy composite of some people I've loved whose narcissism was once irresistible. When you fall out of love with a narcissist, life is emptier. The real M and I have known each other a while. If she opened any of my notebooks and saw how I see her, she would be displeased—but also glumly appreciative. At least I thought of her. M thrives on the way I help her, on how I support or serve her, and I lean on that.

What am I serving, and who, I ask myself, a glass of white wine—it's 6:00 p.m., the light's leaving—in my hand. The wine's subtle, from Umbria. Take umbrage, I tell myself.

Whose will do I bend to, and from whom do I beg forgiveness so quietly I'm never heard? With its remarkable colors and after-tastes, the wine, dry as wit, urges me to forgive myself.

Life's aim, Freud thought, was death. I can't know this, but maybe it's death I want. Life comes with its own exigencies, like terror.

The notebooks I mentioned don't exist. I wish I kept a running account of my life—then the complaints and pleasures wouldn't be forgotten, by me. I'd like, at the end of a year, to be able to read a detailed ledger of time past, to be able to linger in, even relive, all my days, one by one, and by paying attention to time, also obliterate it.

I don't have this kind of attention, I don't live a life of calm reflection, I don't add up the days, I don't make good use of time, I waste a lot of it, and it wastes me, and I'm not sure each day counts, although I also think it may, with frightening conse-quences. I have a memory that usually doesn't fail, unless record-ing pain involuntarily is a failure.

The actual Emma prides herself on her memory. She often flaunts her great gift. In an argument about the past, recent mostly, she details an incident with a flourish, displaying it like a precious jewel from a former lover. She has a good memory, and she has many souvenirs.

These days are Emma's. Memory is what everyone talks about. Will we remember, and what will we remember, who won't be mentioned, or who will be written out, ignored, obliterated.

I didn't decide to forget.

People make lists, take vitamins, and exercise. It's reported that brain cells don't die. I never believed they did. The tenaciousness of memory, its viciousness, really—witness the desire over history for revenge—has forever been a sign that the brain recovers. I remember too much and too little.

Try to hang on to what you can. It's really going. So am I.

Someone else's biography seems like my life. I read it and confuse it with my own. I watch a movie, convinced it happened to me. I suppose it did happen to me. I don't know what I think anymore, and I don't know what I don't think.

I'm someone who tells things.

I'm more or less like Charles. He makes me giddy with possibility, the sense that nothing is impossible. Cocaine also does this. Charles didn't have cancer, so I will never have it. I am a man unsure of himself with women. Every flight and fancy is riddled with openings to vaults storing unacknowledged or hidden lusts. But I'm not sure if desire is naked. Grifters seduce suckers so fast; they know how to dress up their leechlike plans. Some days it's all I can see—the scheme residing on the surface, or located in a gesture, the terrified glance, or the traitorous word not spoken.

But where does all this lead, where does this suspiciousness get me?

I wanted to locate movie footage of tidal waves. They occurred in typical dreams. But an oceanographer told me that a tidal wave was a tsunami, it moved under the ocean and couldn't be seen. This bothered me for a long time. I wondered what it was that destroyed whole villages, just washed them away.

Maggie might think that. Maybe she did, and I stole it. There are people who think they're being stolen from all the time. Generally, they have nothing anyone wants. Maggie's absorbing addiction to heroin—I almost wrote "heroine"—is a physical attachment and an embodiment of neediness, repugnant because of that. She is also romantically engaged with the underground, unseen creature in her that moves through the world and crashes on someone else's floor, destroying everything around it and her.

That's dramatic. Maybe I'm trapped in a new romanticism. After midnight, there are parties, the music's thunderous, and we perform excessive, heartbreaking dances of sex and love. I fly across the floor, leap into the air, and catch myself. I have to rescue myself everywhere.

This morning's decision: let life rush over me. The recurring tidal wave is not about sexual thralldom, not the spectacular orgasm, not the threat of dissolution and loss of control through sex—that, too—but a wish to be overcome by life rather than to run it. To be overrun.

Running away, I make things up—Emma, Charles, Maggie. I want to have them again, I want to live with them. I don't believe any response, like invention, is sad. The world is made up of imagining. I imagine this, too.

Things circle now, all is flutter. Things fall down and rise up. Hope and remorse, beauty and viciousness, and imagination, wherever it doggedly hides, unveil petulant realities.

I live in my mind, and I don't.

There's scant privacy for bitterness or farting or the inexpressible; historically, there was an illusion of privacy. Illusions are necessary.

The wretched inherit what no one wants.

In the beginning, the woman in the green market became Emma, but naming her was a dubious activity. She was a thought, who had to be called something in order to exist.

What separates me from the world? Secret thoughts? I produce a lot of garbage, and I'm not alone, I see it piling up on sidewalks. It could, one day, overwhelm the city. I can picture it. But sometimes I dismiss my fantasy life, and then I can't fantasize. This augurs a terrible constipation—a walling in, holing up, dropping out of sight, believing stuff must be kept inside, held there, wherever that is. It's too disgusting to release. Let go and what comes out is shit.

Maggie has just left rehab, riding the same elevator down that she took on her way up. Two of the guys are waiting in the lobby. They're clean, they say.

Emma phones Charles from a taxi, where she always thinks about him, when she thinks about him. Each time she decides she's over him, she realizes she's not. There's something about him.

Charles hears her voice coming out of a small black box. He tugs on his earring. He reaches for the phone. His hand wavers over the receiver.

Everything is a decision now.

What Americans fear is the inability to have a world different from their father's and mother's. That's why we move so much, to escape history.

Margaret Fuller said: I accept the universe.

I try to embrace it. But I will leave it to others to imagine the world in ways I can't.

I leave it to others.

Out of nothing comes language and out of language comes nothing and everything. I know there will be stories. Certainly, there will always be stories.

There's a Snake in the Grass

I'm on my way, one of four NYC college girls, heading for Bar Harbor, Maine, to spend the summer as a chambermaid, waitress, or piano player. Bar Harbor is on Mount Desert Island, linked with the mainland by one bridge only and, we are warned, if there is a fire, we might all be caught on the island. Only two lanes out, they caution in dour Maine tones, and the only way out.

Bar Harbor is full of Higginses. There are three branches of the family, no one branch talking to the other two. We took rooms in Mrs. Higgins' Guest House. Willy Higgins, a nephew to whom she didn't speak, fell in love with me. He was the town beatnik, an artist with a beard and bare feet. He would beat at the door at night and wake all four of us. I'd leave the bedroom Hope and I shared to be embraced by this impassioned island painter who would moan, "I even love your dirty feet."

I was in love with Johnny. Johnny was blond and weak, his mother an alcoholic since his father died some years back. Johnny drove a custom-built racing car that had a clear plastic roof. He was a society boy.

The days for me were filled with bed making and toilet cleaning. I watched the motel owner make passes at women twice my age who couldn't read. We had doughnuts together at 6:00 a.m. I would fall asleep on the beds I tried to make.

At night Hope would play cocktail piano in bars and I'd wait for

Johnny. Mrs. Higgins watched our comings and goings and spoke in an accent I'd now identify as cockney. She might have been on the front porch the night Johnny picked me up in his mother's station wagon. We drove to the country club in the middle of the night and parked in the rough behind a tree. We made love on the front seat of the car. I actually thought of F. Scott Fitzgerald. He asked me to put my arms around him again. He whispered in my ear that, although he knew many people, he didn't have many friends. He asked if I minded making love again. This would be my third time.

The rich boys who were sixteen and devoted to us NYC girls robbed a clothes store in Northeast Harbor. They brought the spoils to our apartment. Michael, a philosophy student and the boyfriend of one of us, insisted the stuff be returned within twenty-four hours or else he'd call the cops. The next night Bill returned the tartan kilts and Shetland sweaters that hadn't been missed. But he dropped his wallet in the store while bringing it all back and somehow or other the cops were at our door the night after. They spotted me as the ringleader. We went to Bangor for our trial and got fined twenty-five dollars each as accessories. They called it a misdemeanor. The newspaper headline read "Campus Cuties Pull Kilt Caper." I didn't really want to be a lawyer anyway, I thought.

Johnny never called back again. I dreamed that Mrs. Higgins and I were in her backyard. I pointed to a spot in the uncut lawn and said with alarm: There's a snake in the grass.

A guy who hawked at carnivals wanted me to join the circus and run away with him. I was coming down from speed and learning to drink beer. Some nights we'd go up Cadillac Mountain and watch the sunrise. Bar Harbor is the easternmost point in America, the place where the sun rises first. I pined away the summer for Johnny and just before heading back to NYC heard that his mother had engaged him to a proper society girl.

Coming of Age in Xania

I was sitting on a sidewalk in Athens, sitting on the curb in front of a shoe store. Jack saw me and called out, "Are you an American?" and I answered, "Yes," and told him I was looking for a hotel. "Share mine," he said, "a dollar a night."

Jack was from Chicago, a spoiled and wealthy Irishman who wanted to write. He had just gotten to Athens from Tangier. He had reddish hair, pale skin, and eyes Carla would have called "sadist blue." He was recovering from an unhappy love affair that, having ended badly and to his disadvantage, made him vindictive and self-righteous. I didn't want to travel alone and he looked like a lifesaver. We went to Crete and he hated me, or at least it seemed that way. "Look, Jack," I told him, "you can stay in the house I'm renting but our being together is insane since you criticize me constantly." He didn't argue this point and we agreed to be housemates only. But Xania is a small city, and a small Greek city at that, and a young woman doesn't leave a man simply. Or at all. Friends of Henry Miller littered the island, and all would later descend on me for my unfairness to Jack, who was drinking so much now.

I had fallen in love with Charles, who arrived with Betsy and her child. She was separated from her husband. He had remained in their native land, South Africa. Charles told me that he and

Betsy were friends. They seemed like adults to me, the big time, and when Charles looked at me longingly, I returned the look. At first we were secretive. Betsy, who was older and probably wiser, seemed to take this in her stride and Charles moved out, into his own room near my rented house. Jack still slept in my bed, and every night I would leave my house and go to Charles's bed. He wanted to be a writer, too. Jack and I would have pleasant talks together on the terrace. We'd smoke some grass and he'd talk about his broken heart. Things seemed okay and in fact they were extremely bizarre.

The first week in Xania I was cast, in my naïveté, as the young thing who arrives in town and enters a world she doesn't understand. This was my screen role in Charles Henri Ford's film *Johnny Minotaur*. I had been given Ford's address by a Greek called Stephanos. He approached me on the Spanish Steps, urging me to go to Crete and look up Charles Henri. He said Charles would want to put me in his movie. Luckily for Charles Henri, who left Xania shortly after filming Jack and me in a classic beach scene—I wore a skirt and held a black doll in one hand, a pinwheel in another—he never saw his second heroine descend into her role.

Xania is made for secretive strolls, its lanes curve from house to house. I took these turns recklessly, leaving my house every night, strolling a curved lane to Charles's bare room, where we would lie together on his skinny cot. Morning would come and I'd stroll back to my house. Breakfast at the Cavouria restaurant and a swim before lunch. I took to going fishing and the fishermen would smile as I walked down the pier to the tower and cast my line into the sea. I never caught anything.

Betsy continued to be civil to me. We went dancing at a

taverna where the Greek sailors did their famous carrot dance. Charles didn't come and I sulked. Betsy was understanding and her graciousness made me uncomfortable. We watched a sailor place a carrot at his crotch and another sailor hack away at it with a sharp knife. I went to sleep outside the taverna in Betsy's car and woke to find Greek sailors peering through the car windows. I was driven home.

The strolls continued. Charles was good-looking, moody, given to short-lived enthusiasms and other things I can't remember. Jack and I socialized with Greek waiters. Waiters have always been partial to me—my mother has always said I had a good appetite. One such waiter took us for really good food in a place where men who looked like officers cracked plates over their heads, even though this was then against the law.

The waiter took us to his home and fed us some plum booze that's thick as a hot night. Jack and I went home and I went for my usual stroll. Several weeks later it was common knowledge that the waiter's common-law wife wanted to kill me. Alfred Perles, his wife, and Betty Ryan—the friends of Miller—all accused me of destroying Jack. It was the right time to leave.

The woman who took care of my rented, decrepit house and lived just across the lane offered to wash my hair and bathe me. I hadn't had a hot bath in two months. She heated the water in a huge black cauldron over a fire in front of her house. She sat me in a plastic tub. She even scrubbed my back. I felt she had some sympathy for me, and had watched, from her position in the chorus, other similar young women.

There was no love lost. Charles slept at my house on my last night in Crete, Jack having sailed away, alone, almost nobly, a week before. I refused to make love with Charles, complaining of the heat and the bugs, and as a final indignity kept my underpants on and slept over the covers, while he slept beneath them. Charles and Michael, who had played Count Dracula in Ford's movie, drove me to the airport. On a similar ride one year later Betsy's husband, who had come, I imagine, to win her back, would be killed in a car crash. I made it back to Athens.

No Object in Mind

London was quiet. Soho. Covent Garden, quiet then. The pubs, wine bars, cafés, clubs, restaurants—tourists didn't like the nights, they weren't as safe.

She was moving through the city on a quiet night, with a clear black sky, and she may have seen some scars, though it was a city, and electricity hides even galaxies.

She liked the stillness, the quiet. She didn't think she ever would, but there's so little of it, she thought.

The sounds of traffic faded into the dark night, or they seemed to, and she walked along, seeing hardly anyone on the street, a boy here, a woman there, a man in a suit. They looked disconnected, out of place, and none even glanced at her.

The man wore a bowler hat—she imagines him now—and that man reminded her of another Englishman, one she also didn't know, not long before on a bright summer day, when she stopped and asked him what time it was, because she didn't wear a watch, and cell phones hadn't been invented, and the man looked at her, a young, pretty American, without any sexual interest, this chap in a bowler, starched white shirt, ordinary tie, ordinary black suit, and said, "I don't know what time it is." He was startled. Then he said, "I don't even know what day it is." He stared at her, and she stared at him, letting him know she had absorbed his meaning— he didn't know what day it was. Then he walked on. It was in

Piccadilly Circus where he disappeared into the crowd on Oxford Street, a thinner crowd than there would be now, but still there were tourists, excited, excitable, waiting to see the next great thing they'd only ever heard about or seen in pictures. The red double-decker buses always looked happy, to her; though mostly they were standing still.

She kept walking through the quiet night, and now she felt she was absorbing the particular solitude of a great, old city, often said to be sleeping, but cities don't, why would they.

Sidewalks become broader at night, streets wider, people not filling them with their needs, not agitated—to do this, go there, to get back to work, to look good. Streets are different for anyone who has something to do. She had nothing in mind to do, she really had nothing to do, except try to be someone who had something to do.

She walked closer to the theater. She was going to a play written by a friend's friend, based on Kafka's diaries. The theater was not a normal theater, it was an alternative theater, and its temporary home was in an office building. The office building shot up, tall and erect, from the street whose buildings were mostly four stories, but this must have been twenty, and a theater was on the tenth floor or fourteenth.

She couldn't remember, or maybe she wasn't ever told by her friend what floor it was on. It's strange how you go from place to place and have scant interest in, or knowledge of, what may happen, or what you're getting yourself into. She didn't want to know where she was going, what would happen, because she thought surprise could undo some of the damage that had been done to her, or that she'd inflicted on herself, during youth, which she was still living; Americans have extended youths.

She slid into cars of people she barely knew, or sat, sliding, on the backs of motorcycles, for adventure. To adventure required her not to think ahead, she could imagine, but she didn't, because she didn't want to be disappointed about what she might find, what might happen ahead. It was weird to think that the future was ahead, in front of her, she could ride to it, as if the past were in the back, and a road led from one to the other. She didn't believe in that. Besides, adventure was meant to be an abstraction.

When she entered the lobby, which had a marble floor, was well kept, but still dingy—it may have mattered once, such a tall building—and probably why the owner rented space to small theater companies, she looked for a sign to show her where to go, where the play was happening. There was none. No one was in the long hall, an arrow indicated that elevators would be toward the back of the lobby. She took her time walking toward them, and hoped she'd remember the floor number.

It was an old-fashioned building, because the elevator had an operator. Everything was old. The man was old, tall, and thin, and looked weary. She was on time, not too early, and felt relatively okay. The man acknowledged her with a headshake. Then he waited some, probably for other people.

"What floor do you want, Miss?"

She told him she didn't know. "The floor where the play about Kafka is, Sir."

He looked down at the floor, then directly at her. No one had looked that directly at her, she felt, in a long time. He pressed the button. Nine.

The elevator traveled up, she felt it go up, which was reassuring, the night being so slow. The man hesitated as he slid open the elevator door at her floor. He paused before moving out of her way. Then he said, solemnly and with deliberation, "Everybody talks about Kafka, but no one does anything about him."

He studied her, bothered, and she knew it wasn't a question. Or if it was, she couldn't answer it. "You're right," she said. "No one does."

The play wasn't memorable. She can't remember much of it, or what season it was. It wasn't raining.

Now very late, the streets emptier, single wanderers like her scrolling in an artificial desert, the dark blacker, the quiet more quiet, a promise of promise reverberated in her. She lived in London a long time, testing herself in a strange world. Time was strange, expanding and contracting, long and short days and nights, empty and full, seemingly endless.

MYSELF AS A MENU

appetizers

Sometimes I wake up and I can't remember who my friends are. Then I can't
remember where I am. I try to remember my friends. I think about where
I am. And why. I'm in NY and my friends are....And are my friends in
Europe my friends? So, I make lists in my mind of my friends, new and
old, different colors, different angers, different dilemmas, different
loves. I carry the list in my mind; it's my pledge of allegiance. I
wonder who has allegiance to me. I look for signs. I consider that no
one feels loved all the time. I expect that each of my friends will betray me. Or has. I have masochistic fantasies about the betrayals. When
I'm betrayed, in my fantasy, I approach the traitor, say everything I've
wanted to, and end the friendship. I am victorious in defeated love. It's
the only real love I've ever known. I make friends easily.

soups

And who knows what to believe. People want you to take sides, have opinions.
I think about that man in the nuthouse, when H. was there I visited him often,
in a London nuthouse far from London's center, and this man would quote G. K.
Chesterton: "For views I look out the window, my opinions I keep to myself."

steaks

Ernie was three people before they fried his mind. He was He, Tony and Ernie.
Ernie told me once that the ladies had a surprise for him at the cigarette
store. Tony told me there was a golden silence for men and a golden silence
for women. The GKChesterton man continued to quote:"The position is ludi-
crous, the expense damnable..."....he was talking about sex. The inmates all
got fat on valium and endless pieces of white bread and jam and tea. A constant tea in the nuthouse. After they fried Ernie's mind, he didn't talk to
me again. I sat with the men and watched TV. Nutty men in one ward. Nutty
women in another. Crumb's comicbook Fuzzy in the Nuthouse made me laugh later.
The women visited the men at afternoon tea. One young woman sat on an older
man's lap. More tea, more white bread.

seafood

I left England and returned and left. In Amsterdam I saw people on the street
and knew that their faces were London. I kept on forgetting where I was. I
woke upside down. My shrink had once told me that when you awoke upside down,
you knew that you had been masturbating in your sleep. I never understood that
piece of information. I wasn't spying on myself, or was I? Anyway I know when
I'm masturbating, so now when I wake up upside down and don't know where I am,
I know I'm not spying on myself. I really don't know what I'm doing. You can
believe anything and most people do.

cold buffet

It's always a wartime situation as far as I'm concerned.
I don't want to have any secrets. When you have secrets, you keep yourself
from having other thoughts. Your whole mind is taken up in concealing, you
become devious, you have to plot strategies endlessly in order to keep your
secret. Hidden. There are no secrets;B. told me that everyone knows everything anyway. I felt as if enlightened, for a moment. If everyone knew
everything, I had nothing to hide. Mystery is not deception. So I have
nothing to hide and I have no secrets.

BANQUET FACILITIES AVAILABLE FOR PRIVATE PARTIES

I made a film of the man who sits in his window across the street. Everyday he was the first person I saw. The red brick wall, his shape in the window;he reads the newspaper waters his plants, looks onto the street.A few frames every day.I was afraid to be caught filming.I was spying.Sometimes I thought he saw me. He'd leave his window or stand behind, just out of sight.I felt criminal, like a cop with a guilty conscience.I couldnt stop myself.One night I dreamt he was filming me. I awoke frightened. The film I shot is beautiful, serene, as if I hadnt had these feelings.It's a certain kind of lie.He's sitting in the window right now, with his glasses off.I know him a little.I began to imagine that he would become a voyeur because of me.I felt I was poisoning him.

specialties

It's very strange communicating like this, but experience teaches that what is strange is lasting. Talked with Daryl and Bob about secrets. Told them I had none. Began to discuss nature of secrets, sitting in a restaurant, by the end all spaced out about secrets. Later I realised I lied- I have one secret.

Mashed potatoes reminiscent of nuthouse life. White passive lumps. Binghamton: I volunteer to visit an inmate. She is blind, retarded, 25. We go for walks. She tells me the same stories over and over. She is not an interesting madwoman. I am her only visitor-her parents put her away. I don't want to visit her anymore. I tell her and we say goodbye. She touches my hair.

desserts

He has become a voyeur. I did poison him. Just now I walked to the window to pull down the shade and I noticed his blind down and half his bidy visible beneath it. Then my eye drifted to the side of the window and I saw the blind pulled slightly away, his hand gripping it, his eye behind the opening. I pull my shade down fast. The bath water continues to run and I write this down. Do not believe it but it is actual. .... I leave and return home, walking east, west, north south - imagining: the man in the window. He is angry; next time I can expect a gun at the window. He becomes a vicious killer trapped in his window due to his past as a hood. He thinks I've found out and that's why I watch him. Every action has become suspect. My intention, to make a film, is percieved through his eyes. I am dangerous to him now.

beverages

Tony had an affliction which kept him in the nuthouse and he kept on getting worse. There is no progress. His affliction began in history and continues into the future. Ernie said to me "I've been to the Ladies Ward. They call me 'dear' when I buy cigarettes." What does that mean I asked. "I think they have something in store for me." The surprise at the cigarette store.

Lynne Tillman

HUNG UP

We were about to move. The next day, in fact. Which I think gives one some right to be deranged. I called my friend, the man I live with, to complain, or explain, I can't remember which. He said, "Hello," and after my first few sentences, there was silence. Then he hung up. I instantly called back. He said, "Hello," I said his name and asked what happened, and he hung up again. Perhaps I'd been too demanding in the first phone call. I dialed again and realized that I was shaking. It was cold because it was January. "Hello," I said, and even faster, he hung up.

I always carry dimes for times exactly like these. And no junkie on Ninth Street was more desperate than I as I stuck my hand in my bag for another one. "Hello," I asked, "is there anything wrong?" No sooner than I'd said that, he hung up. Why was he doing this to me? I dialed again. This time I got angry. "What do you think you're doing?" I demanded. He hung up. I could see that that approach just didn't work. I was beside myself. I decided to call one more time and then take a taxi to see him. To confront him. This time the answering machine was on. That was the last straw. Now I felt like I was standing beside myself. I left the phone and headed toward the avenue, where I waved my arms or rather jerked them upward several times toward the sky, hailing nothing. I forgot about a taxi and walked in the direction I should've gone—to work—I was already late.

He didn't want to move with me. I'd heard that signing a lease together, moving together, was a form of recommitment, a modern marriage of sorts. An apartment is more difficult to get than a marriage license. But if we broke up, where would he live? It wasn't reasonable. And who would get the apartment? Of course, this had nothing to do with reason. I had to calm down and believe that things might work out. There might be some other explanation. It didn't seem likely, though.

I walked past several phones, wondering if I should give it another shot. I passed another one, two, at the third, I thought, Yes, why not? I'd kind of resigned myself to the inevitable, wanted to be adult about it, and this phone booth was an old-fashioned one, enclosed. I wouldn't freeze to death, an injury to the insult. "Hello," I said, "I'm calmer now." He didn't say anything, but he didn't hang up. Obviously I'd hit the right approach. I continued in the same vein. I talked about the work that was being done on the place, our place, as if everything was all right. My voice sounded deeper than usual, probably the sound of resignation. "Why don't we meet for lunch?" he asked. "All right," I said, "that'd be fine." I figured he wanted to talk to me about the breakup and his feelings. He certainly sounded blasé, considering.

We were to meet in front of a Greek luncheonette at 4:00 p.m. Three hours later I walked toward it and noticed him walking toward me. He can't wait, I thought. I set my expression to grave, to suit the occasion, and decided not to be the first one to speak. Let him bring it up, I thought, he wants it. As we entered the restaurant, he said, casually, "Some crazy person kept calling me today." Ah, I thought, that's how he talks about me, the me he's dissociating himself from. Or perhaps he's going to act just like a man and pretend it didn't happen. "What do you mean?" I asked disingenuously. "I'd pick up the phone and there'd be no one there." "No one there?" I asked. "No, the phone kept ringing, I'd answer, and there'd be no one there. Finally I put the answering machine on." "You didn't hear anything?" I asked. "No," he said. I drank a little tea and looked him straight in the eye. "That crazy person was me," I said. "You?" he said. "Yes. Whenever I called, I'd hear you say 'hello' and I'd say a few things and then you'd hang up." He looked at me over his coffee cup. "Didn't you ever consider that the phone might be broken?" "No," I said, "I thought a lot of things, but I never thought of that." He lit a cigarette. "Why would I hang up on you?" he asked. He said this in a kindly way, much the way that the psychiatrist examining Paul Bowles as to his fitness for the army spoke. "No one's going to hurt you," he reassured Bowles, having already moved a pair of scissors out of Bowles's reach. Why, indeed, I thought. Why does anyone do anything?

On my behalf I'd like to say that I am capable of learning, and the next time something like that happens, I will immediately think that the phone is broken. And I'll go on to the next. Flexibility is one of the signs of mental health.

CONTINGENCIES

At dinner with so-called intelligent people, during our discussion of the Marquis de Sade, I recognized a common lunacy: the fairy tale of absolute and complete freedom. People don't know what to do with the freedom they have, I announced, and trounced off, as if insulted. Today I took a bus, a random bus, no particular number, a white-and-blue bus, or pale green. No matter, it was a bus, and I took it. First I stood in line, with everyone else, a citizen of a city standing peacefully, waiting for public transport, a condition of urban life. I heard two men, no particular men, or maybe very particular men, but not to me. I took the bus anyway. The men were discussing their office, where they seemed mad about a woman, and I listened because I could. They described her in broad terms: "She's got big tits . . . OMG, that ass. Shit!" I entered the bus, paid my fare, the driver said nothing, and unencumbered, except by my hopes and dreams and desires, I walked to the back of the bus, my eyes roving, checking for free seats, and there were good reasons why I kept moving and took the seat I chose, but these are insignificant reasons except to me. I found a seat all to myself, sat down, exhaling freely, and happily, because I celebrate public buses, especially when I have my own seat next to a window, but then the two men, still exclaiming about the woman's ass and tits, took the seats behind me. Now I felt hindered also by their bulk and hulk, as well as their boisterous voices, bellows about asses and tits, and if I hadn't known myself as myself, if I didn't understand the invisible boundaries in which I existed, with my freedom, I would have assaulted the men. I was bigger than both, and freer, and a black belt in karate. Before I had the chance to pummel one or both, because I was at liberty to do what I wanted, even if it meant imprisonment for a day or two, the two men stopped their bellows, and instead turned to watch two other male passengers nearly come to blows, one jostling the other for a seat. Now the three of us, the tits-and-ass men and myself, alarmed by this altercation, became a community of sorts. Suddenly I heard a rip, certainly a rent of some kind, that made a decided sound in the air. The man who had jostled the first for a seat, now watched by the newly formed society of the three of us, took that prized seat. Oh, I thought, oh, and wondered what my two companions thought. It was a strange day, and one has such strange freedoms; for I could have ridden that bus the entire day—until it ended its journeys, or until the bus driver informed me that I had to get off. Any number of possibilities presented themselves to me; I could even have fought him to remain! But thinking it over, I watched all the people I had known, in a sense, on the bus, as they removed themselves from it. I was alone again with my thoughts, not bothered by anything, and, when the bus stopped near a park, one I had never visited, I leaped off violently. Again, the driver said nothing, but now I took his silence to mean assent and even understanding, and walked toward the park and into it through its wide gates, and sat down, this time at a café, where I discovered that the man who had been jostled on the bus, earlier in the day, was being advised by another to patch his overcoat, a dark-brown parka, the same one he had worn on the bus. A piece of fabric hung from its hem. It may have come down during that altercation. Now, I thought, he's having an alteration, and wondered if this linguistic association occurred to him as well. Here we are, I remember thinking, in a great chain of being, and he could think whatever he wanted. I pretended not to notice him, naturally.

MAYBE

He stood in a corner of the large room, hoping not to be seen and also wanting to be, his usual ambivalence, the party racing, the booze going fast, a cool desperation, he thought. If he tried, he could imagine her at the party dancing sinuously, throwing her head back, her movements flighty and also deliberate. She knew what she was doing, and standing here, stuck in a corner, he could visualize her the way she was back then, when she was with him, and of course she wasn't anymore, and might never be; she could be anywhere and with anyone, or content to be on her own, stunningly independent. It seemed interminable, though, the time he was kept waiting, hanging on until she declared . . . what, though, her undying love. So he cut . . . the umbilical cord, his analyst said, which, back then, twenty years ago, felt inappropriate. This isn't funny, he said to the analyst, who went silent, but now it was funny, though he usually regretted any retrospective-mindedness, it didn't help. Prosaically, he had traveled in one direction, she another, insufficient reasons that would do, he told himself, because the heart has four chambers, each with its own rhythm, and feelings are way more complicated, and sometimes so mixed they can suspend your life, even paralyze you.

She bothered him in a silly way, she didn't interest him any longer, or he didn't feel he could hang on to what she offered him, a paltry dish. Her new life, what she said she hoped for, discomfited him and didn't align with who he thought she was, so maybe she wasn't what he thought, but do we know anyone else. Maybe she no longer wanted or needed his attention, and he didn't wait around to find out, didn't pursue her the way a fervid lover might have, instead he hung back. Anyway, we lost our momentum, he thought, holding his empty tumbler of scotch, if love needs to keep time. He refused to be the one to make decisions, he wanted to know he was wanted. She was anxious about getting somewhere in life, where he wasn't sure, where is there to get to, really, he said to her. She called it a better place, to do something worthwhile in life, find her passion, all of that California stuff, he thought, and moved incrementally toward her and away, in too different a way. She wandered off, he felt, even though she was present when she wasn't.

Surprisingly, in the gap of lost time, he entered medical school to become a heart surgeon, which she thought was amusing, but again he wasn't laughing, people in his family died young from heart disease, it was a good reason, but then she said he hadn't waited for her to make up her mind, he was too hesitant about her. He wondered if she would be a good life partner, he thought that way then, and time was his to take, wasn't it.

He was imagining her at the party, was there someone who incited these old memories, someone who looked like her or said something she might have. He stood in the same place, one hand over his heart, waiting for orders to change his position, but didn't know where he could go except to the crowded bar, drink more, forget to remember. You have got to decide, she said once, or maybe twice, sometimes you just have to take a chance, not look around to see if others agree with you.

Some people had left, most stayed, they didn't know what to do, either, where to go afterward, while the host began gathering dirty glasses, but the party was full enough, people talking, loosening up, nudging one another intimately, some kissing, swallowing tongues, so likely his lassitude or antisocial behavior, as she had called it, wouldn't be noticed. Quiet, he blended in to the darkening sky in the window behind him.

He might have asked, Do you want to live with me, should we move in or on, will you marry me. Something had stultified him, the prospect of commitment, she said, but he might not understand her, maybe she didn't love him, or maybe she did in her way. Maybe even now he existed in her spell, in an abstract way, after she went her way, far away. His memories remained the same, resolute, they didn't change, frozen with the years, and there must be something wrong about this, he felt. Their time, the past, their past, pictures just images, blurrier with time, still unreeled almost relentlessly.

He pictured her as if the day before, the last time he accidentally saw her on the same line for a movie, which had formed into two lines, a popular movie, what was it? the lines were dragging and, when he saw her in the other line, all dressed in black leather, her face rounder, her broad cheekbones fierce still, her dark-blue eyes, he moved toward her to embrace her, but she repulsed him, she wouldn't give him a stupid, phony hug, there was no them now, nothing, she had rebuked him. Some apologies come too late, when loving again is ridiculous, she could have said that, and yet it couldn't be. She was fixed in him, he must be in her, she must still love him, how could that have gone.

He looked around the room, emptier now, his third wife was talking to a man he didn't know, looking intent upon whatever he was saying. Maybe he should go over and introduce himself, break up their little conversation, assert himself, though he was content to watch, an onlooker who didn't possess her, his wife could do what she wanted, even complain about him, how he let people walk all over him, not bold enough, not enough for himself, and, worst of all, she said, he was slow to understand her needs. She was, he noticed, enthusiastic, listening, laughing, captivated, then, awakening to a sudden recognition, he thought, she's going to divorce me, when did we last have sex, but maybe I'll leave her, I might, I could. Something was missing in his life. Maybe it was always her.

His friend Gene once told him, People surprise you, never forget that. He didn't expect surprise, life had a regularity, his hours regular except for emergencies, though his wife might surprise him, shake him up, and maybe that's what he needed, maybe they needed surprise, or escape, or to get a divorce. Maybe she was holding him back, maybe he could become—people are always becoming—happier, a different man. And when he was that, different, even if his transformation was slow, it would happen, and he, unencumbered, would contact her, and she would have had a change of heart, realized it was him, she loved him, then the time would be right.

Emerging from his reverie, he looked out at the room, emptier now, his wife smiling, talking to the same man. He studied her. But still, he thought, maybe, he thought.

AKA MERGATROYDE

When I was first asked to write about my family, the Mergatroydes, I thought I'd disguise them, make them characters in a story. Revealing your family is a little like revealing yourself. I mean, even my best friends haven't met my mother. Then I thought, make it hard for yourself. Tell the truth. I don't mean the real or only truth. Only network news has the gall to say what they're doing is telling the truth ("We're here to tell you the truth"—*Eyewitness News*). But I've decided to write as myself, Patricia Mergatroyde, only child of a wealthy and somewhat infamous father, Mark, the stockbroker cum jockey Mergatroyde, and mother, Marilyn Miller Mergatroyde, an ex-showgirl who has spent her life living that down. And why do I even mention it? I who have spent a good part of my writing life designing characters so unlike my family that people actually think my pen name, Lynne Tillman, is my real name. Frankly I have exhausted my own interest in disguise.

The earliest Mergatroyde, or known Mergatroyde, discovered when Stephen, the intellectual Mergatroyde, had the family tree done, was a master builder in Scotland. Our family had a violent beginning. As a fiction writer I'd like to make the analogy between the start of the world, the big bang theory, and the start of our family history. But in our case the big bang was the lethal hammerblow to the head executed by the master builder upon his apprentice. It appears that this early Mergatroyde felt ill prepared to build a column modeled on one standing in Rome. So he left for Rome for further study, and while he was away, his apprentice went ahead and built it. And right in front of that very column, the master builder in a jealous rage hit the precocious apprentice on the head with a hammer, killing him instantly. The master builder was tried and hanged not far from the church. In the corners of the church, Rosslyn Chapel, are carved reliefs of their faces, including two of the master builder—one dead, one alive—one of the apprentice's mother crying, and one of the apprentice. That was in Scotland in the fifteenth century.

Though I'm fascinated by this bit of history, it's the modern-day Mergatroydes, my immediate family, and a few more distant relatives that I intend now to chronicle. And at this point I'm going to drop my first-person voice and tell some stories, stories as I've heard them, or as I imagine they might have occurred based on information culled over the years, the way oral history is ordinarily carried, especially in families.

Scenes from the Lives of the Mergatroydes

Mark Mergatroyde liked to say he was a gambler at heart. And marrying Marilyn was taking a chance. Starting to ride was a chance. But then he loved competition, being in the heat of battle. And what's more he never felt anything less than proud of his winning spirit. There are winners and losers, his father told him, and Mark adjusted his life accordingly. The only game he couldn't win, he complained to his wife, was the death game. Though he'd put money into research, he knew he would probably die before DNA was sufficiently decoded so that life might be prolonged infinitely. He was anyway going to have himself frozen and had made specific orders that no funeral be allowed, since one day he might be brought to life, and if anyone else was smart enough to be around, too, he didn't want to feel as if he were coming back from the dead. He said that would be socially awkward. Marilyn humored him and secretly wondered if that meant she couldn't have a death certificate made up and if she wouldn't ever be allowed to marry again. It would be just like him, she thought, to win even after death. Or after becoming an ice cube.

Wallace, the inventor Mergatroyde, was always jealous of his brother, Mark, the stockbroker, not only because he had taken the family money and multiplied it many times, but also because he was so successful in everything else. Wallace's inventions kept his family in clothes and college, but he had alienated the affections of his wife, Charlotte; his son, Michael; and his daughter, Greta. Greta's feelings for him would always be confused. Somewhere between revulsion and guilt, some of which he shared. Wallace kept having the same dream. He's twenty-two and Mark is twenty-five. Mark is traveling the wide world, on his honeymoon. Mark and Marilyn visit the Scottish church and send a postcard of the Apprentice Pillar. The Rosslyn Chapel, the card says, is one of Scotland's loveliest. The column looks something like Mark and Marilyn's wedding cake. Three bands of ornate decoration swirl around it, kind of like vines. The column behind it is bare of decoration. There is no spotlight on it. Just the way Wallace felt as best man, a shadow. Mark writes: Too bad you can't be here with us to see it, too. Marilyn and I are having a wonderful time and want to thank you for your understanding. She especially appreciated your blessing on our union. We do hope you forgive us completely. Mark. Miraculously, as it is in dreams, Wallace is with them in the church. He takes a hammer, not a real hammer, but a hammer he might have invented, something that could also be a gun. He kills his brother in such a way as to appear as self-defense, and goes off with Marilyn, his true love. Wallace awakens from this dream slowly. His wife, Charlotte, wonders why he's in such a bad temper.

Greta Mergatroyde, the actress Mergatroyde, has just turned off the stove, stepped back from it, and stared at the grease on the burners. The camera moves in to a tight close-up. The cinematographer, someone Greta can't stand, wants to pan from her face down her neck, to her breasts and then her ass. The director says he doesn't need it, he's got a lot of her breasts and her ass. The director tells Greta to project a strong will, a woman of determined mind who's vulnerable at the same time. She hasn't lost her femininity, is what he says to Greta. Greta takes a breath and imagines her father standing at the edge of her bed, naked. She says, Daddy, what are you doing here? She makes her face as stern as an eleven-year-old knows how. He retreats. But he returns. Greta conjures the scene, moving the muscles in her face, thinks she might cry, but doesn't. The director says perfect.

Greta's brother, Michael, the accountant Mergatroyde, had always wanted to travel like his uncle Mark. Instead, he took trips to the refrigerator. His family was at the dinner table. The nuclear family, except Michael changed the letters around in his head. The unclear family. Wallace berated him on having lost yet another job, and Charlotte complained about his cooking, since he had cooked and not his girlfriend, Sally, which his mother considered would have been proper. Greta was tired from the shoot and avoided his eyes as well as her father's. She was unusually quiet, but Michael put that down to work. Sally, who had refused to marry him and would only live with him as something more than roommates, to the shame of his mother and hers, made steady, uninflected talk, especially to Wallace. He was always eager to explain an invention. Sally brought a big chocolate cake to the table. She could eat chocolate endlessly and not gain a pound. It was almost eerie, because, Charlotte would say, she moves so slowly with a metabolism like that. Sally set the milk down on the table, and since she hadn't put it in a pitcher, something Charlotte found unforgivable, Greta took hold of the carton and read aloud the name of a missing child: Viki Lynn Hoskinson. Greta said the thing that made her really sick was to think how they were probably all molested before they were killed. Charlotte told her to please shut up.

Harris Mergatroyde, the social worker Mergatroyde, was the person who thought up putting the pictures of missing kids on milk cartons. Harris was unmarried and childless. He was a poor relation Mergatroyde, one of the few of that branch of the family still located on the East Coast. The family assumed Harris's work for social causes came from his own sense of disadvantagement. He turned over in bed, nearly crushing the cat who trusted him so much. Last night's romance was still asleep, and although Harris had a hard-on, he didn't grab the guy. He walked to the refrigerator and took out the milk and coffee beans, and was glad he didn't have children who could disappear. He thought, They were disappeared, a term used for political kidnapping and murder in Central and South America, a term used in a warlike or wartime situation. Yet these children were disappeared, too, and if people didn't think America was at war, they were crazy. He looked at the picture of Rosslyn Chapel that Greta had taken two years ago, on her ironic journey home. She had called it an ironic journey. Harris had enlarged the picture of the Apprentice Pillar, and it hung over his bed. Ironically, too, he thought, as he climbed back in bed, intending to get his money's worth.

Harris's sister, Laura Mergatroyde Williams, liked to smell her husband's underpants. It was something she started doing only after reading a story where the main character, a woman who didn't seem crazy or anything, did. She'd pick the dirty underpants off the floor, where he always dropped them—just like her husband—raise them to her nose and breathe in deeply. That's how the writer phrased it. Then she'd throw them in the laundry basket, smiling. At first Laura felt strange breathing in deeply, but after a while it kind of made her day, having this little secret. God knows she needed a secret, to make her interesting or keep her interested. Laura turned on *General Hospital*. The kids would be coming home soon, and the place was still a mess from last night. She hoped things would go easier tonight. Maybe he wouldn't be in such a bad mood. Harris said she could always divorce him if he tried to hit her again. There were a lot of single mothers these days. She still thought that Harris shouldn't have put those pictures of missing kids on milk cartons. She was going to tell him that it was sadistic to scare little kids like that. After all, who is it anyway who reads the backs of milk cartons. When Laura phoned him, she angrily told him that only someone without children would do that. Harris said, So don't get divorced.

Mary Mergatroyde, the anthropologist Mergatroyde, had attended the wedding of Stephen Mergatroyde and Bette Bloomfield, the parents of Harris and Laura. Stephen, the intellectual Mergatroyde, had encouraged Mary with her scholarly pursuits, and she had a great deal of affection for her second cousins. Even at the age of fourteen, Mary had been interested in family rituals, like weddings, and kinship systems, getting a copy of the family tree from cousin Stephen. She wouldn't have called it kinship systems then. In Tswana, she typed, the words for money and rain are the same. The group before which she would deliver this paper was very different from her family. The extended family consisted of members she had only heard about—the Paris Mergatroydes. The Hells Angels Mergatroydes. The Spanish Mergatroydes of New Mexico. The Black Mergatroydes of Alabama. A meeting of the clan would be so interesting. Mergatroydes scattered everywhere, not that most of them would come—they wouldn't. The immediate family itself had hardly come to her father's funeral. But Mary wouldn't scatter. She'd hang on to her name. Her father had played his final joke on her, putting it into his will that she'd get the house only after she got married. She'd thought about marrying one of Harris's lovers but hadn't been able to go through with it. Her mother had been great about it, Mary's lesbianism. It turned out that mother and daughter had more in common than a daughter might ever expect.

Floyd Mergatroyde was disgusted. It wasn't the first axe murder he'd seen, but this one was really nasty. His family's eccentricities were nothing compared to Ed Gein's, who wore his mother's skin as a suit. The story behind that movie you like so much, *Psycho*, he told his niece Doris, who one day wanted to make films. Floyd's work, policeman in Dubuque, brought him in touch with lives that weren't the sort of thing you talked about at dinner. At least he didn't. And he didn't want to go to any dinners, either, even if it was a meeting of the Mergatroyde clan, planned by a distant relative from the rich side of the family, who called herself an anthropologist. Fucking gravediggers, Floyd muttered. He had enormous disdain for his upper-middle-class relatives and their little deviations. And even if his wife wanted to go to that clan meeting, he sure as hell wouldn't. But his wife had social aspirations and gave him hell every once in a while for preventing their kids from moving up in the world. He said in his best policeman-like voice, The only movement in this world is out, and don't you forget it.

Doris Mergatroyde was very excited when she received the invitation to the Mergatroyde family get-together, the first ever, and immediately phoned Mary, whom she'd never met, to ask if she could film the proceedings. Mary instantly thought of Birdwhistell films, and said why not. It might be very amusing. Doris was thinking more of Sam Fuller and Diane Arbus. She had to construct an overriding, if not overwhelming, narrative in which the family could figure as characters. She didn't want it to be a documentary, and it couldn't really be a fiction film, either. Doris also liked nature films but didn't imagine that that kind of narrator's voice would be right for a film about human beings. She wanted a lot of attention paid to relatives meeting for the first time. Almost everyone there would have Mergatroyde as their last name, or second-to-last name. Maybe it'd be a docudrama. She could call it "A Roomful of Mergatroydes."

The clan met in a centrally located city, Cincinnati, at a large hotel that caters to conventions and the like. What distinguished this hotel were the elaborate columns, four of them, at its entrance. Harris, Greta, Mary, and I entered the hotel, climbing its ten or so marble stairs, when Harris noticed that one of the columns had vines coiling around it. He turned to Mary and said, Which one of us is going to do it? We all laughed, of course, not being fortune tellers.

And as I was there—note the entry once more of my first-person voice—let me report that this get-together free-for-all was one of the most thrilling and devastating experiences of my life. As a writer and as a person. A fight broke out between family members I'd never met before who turned out to have a long-standing feud. One of the men, Elvis Mergatroyde, a gem cutter, took out his gun and killed Matthew Mergatroyde, bank manager in a bank that had once refused Elvis's father a loan for his farm. And it went under. Anyway, that's what Floyd said, the only person there who remained calm. Although Harris recalls hearing Floyd's voice becoming quite strident at one point. When people were yelling and screaming "Call the cops, call the cops," Harris says Floyd shouted, "But I am a cop." Elvis Mergatroyde is trying to get a lighter sentence on the grounds that his crime was something like a crime of passion, as it happened in the family, where most murders do. Doris wants me to work all this into a script—she shot over two hours' worth before the shooting itself—because she thinks it would make an incredible, almost unbelievable film, what with so much weirdness and violence in one family. But, frankly, I'm not certain I'd want to collaborate with a family member, given our history. Still, it is a good story, and Harris, Greta (who naturally wants to star in it), and Mary are right behind us, and have encouraged even this little exposé, such as it is. As Mary succinctly puts it, Let's face it. The American family is no picnic. Why should the Mergatroydes be an exception?

PLEASURE ISN'T A PRETTY PICTURE

When she was fourteen, there was this boy, he was seventeen, he liked girls, sex, she knew it. He was passionate. She could tell just by looking at him. And she knew he meant it, and she knew it was the best thing about him. He wasn't afraid. Mostly what she knew was that he liked it. When she stood near him, she could tell. It drifted off his body, like a smell she could almost recognize.

He looked hard into her when he looked at her. She could feel his intensity, see it in his eyes, in how his eyes didn't leave hers when he looked at her. He was inviting, there was an invitation. Other boys were shyer, maybe they didn't like sex, or girls, or didn't know if they did, they were afraid and awkward, furtive about what they wanted. Those eyes would leave hers, lose hers, glance away, not look into her, not dare her, the way his did. He stared, glared, dared, he kept staring. It wasn't really arrogance. He was knowing. He knew something. She didn't know what he knew. She was eager and unsure.

Later, she could always tell who knew how to kiss, how to use his mouth, how to bite, how to hold her, by looking into his eyes and keeping the look and waiting for the glance into or away, she always knew. Her body was unruly. She was tremulous. She wanted to be lighter, fearless, and heavier, lustful, and freer, unburdened of an indeterminate weight she walked the world carrying. Her sexed body, unattended, sought attention. Attraction was received and sent ambivalently. She ached and tensed and didn't know why.

When he was sixteen, he didn't know what to do with his hands, where to put them, how hard to dig into her skin, did she like that, and he was mostly thinking about himself, his first time, and when he came, it was over and they'd done it, he'd gotten into her, her vagina was warm, kind of wet and velvety, and she didn't bleed that much. He didn't know if he loved her. But his friends said he didn't have to. He couldn't look at his mother, he knew she knew, and he wanted her to know, but he didn't want to tell her. He didn't see the girl again because she moved away. Maybe he wouldn't have anyway.

Later, he remembered the smell of her hair and the way she moved under his body and the way she didn't move. She made a sound, a little whimper. He didn't know what that was, pain, pleasure. He never stopped worrying about how heavy he was when he was on top of a woman. He never knew exactly what he expected from sex, women, from her, now. He wanted to feel good for longer than he did. He demanded stealthily. He suffered the loneliness of his own body.

She wasn't flying. She knew where she was. His hands and arms motioned down. Their gestures fell on the ground. Ecstasy's available, he laughed. Then he wanted to touch her. He was grimacing and smiling. He pointed again. She looked down. She was adamant. Literal minded. Blood rushed in her brain and pushed crazily through her body. It made thinking and orgasms possible.

He watched her. Her back was a ribbon of flesh, a river of flesh. He wasn't sure. He wanted her.

Someone else was another world.

Later, she wanted him.

She liked to lust, loved the sensation, the thrill, only when she could have what she wanted. She took a few chances. Sometimes she threw it away, let it go, risked everything, which wasn't much, she didn't care. She wasn't her body, she was. She couldn't tell about him yet, how he felt, how she felt about him.

He couldn't tell. He wouldn't tell.

Later, he entered her.

He said: You feel good.
He said: Do you think you could love me?
He said: Was that good?
He said: Did you come?
He said: I won't hurt you.
He said: Are you safe?
He said: Is this the right time?
He said: I don't go down on everyone.
He said: I don't know what's wrong with me.
He said: Are you bleeding?
He said: I think I could love you.
He said: Are you okay?
He said: Why did you do that?
He said: How do you like it?
He said: Did I hurt you?
He said: I really like you.
He said: Not now, give me some time.

He said nothing. He said a little. He said her name. He said everything he could. He couldn't talk.

She surrounded him. She took him in to her, let him in. The outsider's inside her, she thought and stopped herself. She didn't want to remind herself to forget. She looked at her body, his body.

They were angling for position. They were imperfect pictures of people having sex. She bit him on the cheek.

He made love to her. She made love to him. She dangled above him. He fucked her, she fucked him, he relieved her, she frustrated him, he teased her, she tempted him. She waited. He moved. She grasped. He grabbed. She touched. He held. She clasped. He released. She contracted. He kneaded.

He closed his eyes. He opened his mouth wider. Wider and wider. He wanted to take her into him, swallow her. He looked funny to her, unfamiliar in his pleasure. He wondered what he looked like to her. He blanked the thought out, erased it. Fuck. His body jerked.

She wanted to bite him harder, even make him bleed, just a little. This won't hurt him, she thought. She didn't. She licked his shoulder, tentatively.

She was strange to him, a stranger. He was new to her, but she could get used to him.

She said: You don't have to say anything.
She said: I like that.
She said: Do that again.
She said: No, not yet.
She said: Yes.
She said: I have a condom.
She said: Wait.
She said: I like you, too.
She said: It's been a while.
She said: I wish I knew you.
She said: That's all right.
She said: Are you crying?
She said: Again.

She said: Almost.

She said: You tell that to all the girls.

She said: Do what?

She said: Do it again.

She said: That doesn't hurt.

She said: That hurts.

She said: That feels good.

She said: Kiss me.

She said: Now.

In the universe of things she didn't know, sex was at the top of a long, unwritten list. Momentary, temporary, ever present, absent, disruptive, expected, it fled scrutiny. She didn't know if she'd ever find out. What wasn't named, named it.

A whisper, a moan, a stifled groan, lips parted, mouths opened and shut, like doors and windows. With sound. Without sound.

Talk to me, he said, say anything. He bore down on her. She didn't know what it meant. She was open to him. She confused him. He was alive and easier, heady. He was full. He didn't want to be empty. Later, it might make sense.

In the universe of things he didn't know, sex was a series of questions with good and bad in the answers. How good was he supposed to be, how good was it supposed to be, how bad is bad, how often is good, how long is good, how hard is good, how gentle is bad. It was always simple and immediate when he wanted it, and when he got it, it wasn't, and he wasn't, adequate or inadequate.

She looked at his face. His eyes were closed. His eyes were narrowed. His lips were clenched. Now they were curled. His hands were open, palms up. He was raw. His teeth showed. He chewed her lips, his lips. His upper lip stuck to his teeth. He muttered wordlessly. He threw his head back and forth. He rocked.

He put his hand under her thigh and flipped her over as if she were a leaf. She felt weightless, inconsequential. She wanted to be just a body. She didn't know if she could be. She didn't know what just a body was unless it was the idea, just a body. She tickled his back. She was lazy. He placed both hands under her ass and turned her again. She let him and threw her leg over his hip and made it impossible for him to move. She was stronger than he thought she was. She held him tight. He liked that. He thought he liked that.

He looked at her face. He didn't see her pleasure. He took his in violent spasms. She snatched hers from the wings of defeat. Her pleasure was a mighty trophy.

He was freezing. She was looking away. He didn't know what she saw.

He said: Are you cold?
He said: Want something to drink?
He said: Next time we'll go to your place.
He said: I have to sleep.
He said: Want to go out?

He pulled up the blanket and covered himself. He didn't know what she wanted next. She didn't, either. He didn't know what he wanted next. She didn't know what came next. The aftermath was awkward and familiar.

She said: What time is the clock set for?
She said: I have to piss.
She said: I need a drink.
She said: I couldn't sleep now.

Naked, alone, or with him, she wasn't unencumbered, didn't feel natural or unnatural. It was weird, lying there, bare and not stripped of anything important. She felt blinded, blinkered, by her nakedness, less capable, more vulnerable and less. If she had muscles all over her body, like a bodybuilder, muscles like small, implacable breasts, she'd be impregnable.

Naked, with her, he was modest. Then he was unconcerned about his nakedness. He studied her. He liked her body, then he didn't. He wanted her to admire him. He wanted her not to care about his body. He hoped she'd take it and him for granted, almost. Embarrassed, casual, he rolled around in bed clownishly. She was harder, he thought, tougher than he liked. She wasn't perfect. He changed position. She changed in front of his eyes.

She changed position. She avoided his body. Then she stared at him, it. His penis was coiled, recoiled, returned to him. He blended into the bed sometimes. She might not really like him. He was softer than she thought he'd be. He was different from the way he seemed outside.

What happened wasn't visible.

What wasn't apprehended stayed defiant, resistant. It was obscene, how they felt and thought, and the obscene ran with the ecstatic, raced away, right out the door, right out the window, right out the frame, on a road to nowhere.

She said: I have a lot of work.
She said: Maybe tomorrow.
She said: I'll call you.
She said: I don't know.
He said: Later.
He said: When will I see you again?

He said: I'm really behind.
He said: No rush.

Being on the street was strange. It was hard to talk. They walked away from each other. The absence of sex, a fast intimacy, could become the source of a dirty joke or despair. Everyone wants to be happy.

A Dead Summer

The coffin was never opened. The soul, she recited to herself, selects its own society . . . They wheeled the dark wood casket down the aisle of the church. It came to a halt next to her. The priest said that her friend had prepared for this day since his baptism thirty-two years earlier. He was returning to God. She touched the side of the coffin furtively, then it moved past her. People congregated on the street in front of the church. The coffin disappeared into a gray hearse. She thought, Where will it go, where will he go? Another friend, known for his dark humor, whispered, "Elizabeth, he's out of here." She smiled then and walked with friends to his mother's apartment, where everyone drank and talked of other things than death. His mother was brave, but every once in a while Elizabeth caught her staring into space, a helpless frightened expression on her face. Or Elizabeth found her staring at a photograph of him when he was a child, a healthy delighted child with no trace of disease, not even the idea of disease, touching the image. That perfect past would never allow a death like his, Elizabeth thought.

It was a hot summer, the summer of the ticker-tape parade for Nelson Mandela. Elizabeth had trouble waking up. Perhaps it was because the city's heat, with its ever-present malodorousness, lingered like a sullen fog in the streets. She slept deeply, as if drugged, and gave her nights over to a dealer who meted them out for days.

I am on a tour in a mansion, where I decide to curate an exhibition of images of women in mental hospitals. On the tour a man and a woman, who live in the building, become attracted to me and follow me. I cannot understand their attraction, but it is extreme, even obscene. The man begins to lean on me. The two fight over me. It is supposed to be about me, but it has nothing to do with me. I run away from them, but they are rapacious, desperate. They tell me they are sex-starved and lonely. The woman beseeches me, Please love me. Love me. I need you. I will die without you.

Elizabeth's dreams had always been vivid. She wrote them down every morning and filled notebook after notebook. At the new year she reread the old year's dreams. It was her diary, a veritable autobiography. But lately her dreams seemed too real. They were like movies she would never have made. When asleep Elizabeth felt invaded. During the day she stayed at home as much as she could. She turned down jobs—Elizabeth worked as a film editor—and hoped to pass the summer on what she had saved all year. Elizabeth thought the lonely woman in her dream looked like someone she knew.

The streets slithered with discontent and malcontents, unhappy creatures desperate for painkilling potions and numbing smoke. Arguments erupted, sudden and sharp, under an intense sun that irritated skins of all colors. Elizabeth avoided groups of young men who hung out in doorways and whose apathetic expressions could only hide something much worse than she could feel. She avoided seventeen-year-old Debbie, out of jail again, her scarred coffee-colored arms and thin face a kind of flag of the hidden nation. Elizabeth felt too white. She walked quickly past Benny, Prince, and their girlfriends, who never had names, and handed them quarters without saying anything. She bought milk and *The New York Times*. She turned first to the obituary page. She wondered if the good die young, or the young die good, or even if it is good to die. She read that Castro "accused President Bush of having a 'sick obsession' with Cuba. 'Neither asleep nor awake can Bush forget about Cuba.'"

I am in the country. The time is the early part of the nineteenth century. A train comes to a cottage in the mountains where a group of people are living. They may be revolutionaries. The women are waiting for men, who alight from the cars of the train. They are sickly, though, and need help walking. Now it is the twentieth century. I watch a woman leap through an open window. She is followed by a man, who calls her name. I am just about to hear her name. I strain to hear it.

The telephone rang harshly in the nearly empty room. It broke into the dream. The sound made her cringe. Were they Cuban revolutionaries? Who was the woman leaping through the window? She supposed it was herself and she buried her head under the pillow and burrowed farther beneath the covers. It was the way Elizabeth wanted to be buried when she was a child—with a blanket and a pillow, with her arms under the covers so that evil spirits wouldn't pull at her when she was gone, dragging her down and down, to hell. She had begged her father: Daddy, please bury me with my blanket and pillow. Though she was only five, she was obsessed with death. He reassured her as best he could. He promised he would bury her just the way she wanted. But he was dead. She placed her friend's picture next to her father's. The machine answered the telephone, but she didn't return the call.

Her boyfriend grew tired of her moodiness. His lackluster treatment of her was now an indication of great perversity. She could not speak of it to anyone. He told her she was inconsolable. It didn't seem important what happened between them, anyway. And how could she explain what she let him do to her? His sadism not only mirrored her masochism but was also perfect in its reflection of her inner world, which was already a mirror to the outer one. She considered that he might be the devil. He was too good-looking. The TV news reported that the funeral of a Vietnamese man, a member of Born to Kill who'd been assassinated at the age of twenty-one, was interrupted by machine-gun fire from Chinese gang members who shot into the crowd of mourners. Some of the mourners fired back.

I am feeding worms. They are growing larger and larger. I realize that they are living creatures and if I continue to feed them, more will be born and grow. A man appears and sings, The worms crawl in, the worms crawl out. They eat your guts and spit them out. I want to laugh, but I realize that this may happen at any moment. I scream. The man, she decided, was telling her that not all life is worthwhile.

The Mets were doing better, but with so many new players on the team, she didn't have the same relationship to them. Her dead friend had loved the Mets, too. Sometimes she watched a game just for him, as if he could use her as a medium. She was sure his spirit was hovering near her, especially at those times. But she did not speak of this to her boyfriend, who was talking about breaking up. That night she let him gag her. She didn't have anything to say anyway, not anything worthwhile. She read that the Ku Klux Klan had marched in Palm Beach.

I am a young Black child. I am in a school bus driven by an angry white man. He is obviously a racist. He may want to kill me. We are trying to cross the Brooklyn Bridge. But the bridge is being reconstructed. The bus careens across the bridge, going much too fast. I am afraid we will crash. I'm afraid I'll never get to school.

Her boyfriend finally broke up with her. She felt nothing. Friends tried to be sympathetic, but she knew they didn't really understand. There was a sheet of glass between her and them. She didn't return their calls. She watched TV and cut out articles from the newspaper. The stench in the streets nauseated her and she ate less and less. She stopped washing the dishes and wore dirty clothes. Elizabeth turned her underpants inside out and wore them twice and knew no one would notice. Her mother, when she was alive, had never been one of those mothers who said, "Always wear clean underpants, because what if you get hit by a bus." Elizabeth didn't expect to get hit by a bus, though she knew that death could come at any time. On a talk show she heard a man in a wheelchair say that the difference between health and sickness was negligible, that sick people know sickness is just the other side of wellness. In the hot apartment a cold shiver pierced her body. Her skin seemed too thin to be a protective covering.

I see my friend. He is dying. He is lying on a bed, thin and stiff. He dies in front of me. I am helpless. I know he is dead but somehow he is not dead. He sits up and walks. He walks grimly and is looking for something, someone. But you are dead, I say to him. Still he continues to walk, and then I see he is carrying the corpse of a woman. She is thinner than he is. She has thin scraggly hair. It falls onto her face, which is a sick greenish color. She is truly dead. He is dragging her beside him. He is like the grim reaper. But you are dead, I say to him again. His hands reach out for me. He cannot rest. He cannot sleep. I must help him. I run to find his mother. I must find her so that she can let her son die. Let him rest. I bang on a heavy wooden door, but no one hears.

On her occasional walks around the neighborhood Elizabeth first noticed, and then became fascinated by, an older woman, a blond woman in her fifties, who walked with a limp and spoke with a German accent. She looked poor but proud. The woman's fat old dog struggled to keep up with his limping mistress. Elizabeth began to follow her, because she felt the German woman, whom she named Ursula, had an answer. The older woman's singularity and dignity amazed her. It meant survival at any cost.

Ursula went into a neighborhood bar at about 5:00 p.m. every day. Her dog accompanied her, first panting and then lying still at the base of the barstool. Ursula's feet didn't touch the floor. Her gray cotton sweater hung loosely over her breasts. Her straight linen skirt, always clean but worn, hiked up to reveal well-developed thighs that age had not yet rendered to itself. Elizabeth took a seat at the bar and tried not to stare. She wanted to listen to the woman's stories as if she weren't. But the woman talked little and when she did, she spoke in hushed tones to the bartender or other customers whom she favored with her attention. Elizabeth wrote about Ursula in the notebook reserved for dreams.

She wanted to be the woman's friend. She was obsessed with the idea of making contact with her and learning her secrets. But Elizabeth couldn't relate to people as she once had. She didn't feel entirely alone, as she knew she was receiving messages in her dreams that she couldn't possibly convey to anyone else. Though only thirty-two, she felt terribly old, as if her life were already over. The German woman, who was many years older, seemed not to need friends. Elizabeth never saw Ursula with anyone but her dog.

Ursula strolled the streets as if she wasn't looking for anything in particular. She seemed to lack nothing. She bought the newspaper and carried home cups of take-out coffee. Sometimes she talked to neighbors or shopkeepers, but Elizabeth could tell that Ursula kept a distance between herself and them. From across the street she watched Ursula approach the door to her building, turn the key in the lock, open the door, and enter, glancing behind her in case someone was about to mug her. Ursula always waited patiently for her fat dog to follow her in. Then the door slammed shut and Ursula disappeared. Elizabeth could picture Ursula in her apartment, reading the newspaper, looking out the window, or watching TV.

She decided that Ursula was fearless in the face of life and death, not at all like Elizabeth herself, who lately feared stray bullets. Some had already taken the lives of several small children while they slept in cars or in their beds, in the supposed safety of their homes. Elizabeth went to the bar at 5:00 p.m. every day. She waited for Ursula and ordered a scotch and soda, which was Ursula's drink. Elizabeth liked the bar—its anonymity, that no one expected anything from her, that she could watch TV and sit for hours and hours without saying a word. She went home with a bellicose old man who bought her drinks and touched her thigh. She hated his smell and his body, but she felt sorry for him. When he fell asleep, she got out of bed and walked home.

I am about to have sex with a very young man. He may be old, too. We are in a bedroom. I am very excited. I am afraid someone will walk in. I go into a dark hallway. My mother, who's dead, is standing there. Her decrepit body is barely hidden by a diaphanous black nightgown. She is shriveled and skeletal. She is bent over. She is angry. She screams at me.

Elizabeth decided to approach the German woman, to make conversation with her. She rehearsed the conversation as she walked along the streets. "I have noticed you for some time. You seem wise. I'm sure your life has been very interesting." The young guys she'd been afraid of looked less deadly. They were just selling grass, maybe crack. She was fairly certain they weren't carrying guns, but if they were, they probably wouldn't want to shoot her. She wasn't anyone for them to worry about. Now she smiled at them because she wanted them never to fear her. She wouldn't ever call the police. Florida's electric chair, she read, might malfunction, so some executions were being held up while they tested it. If she were given the choice, she'd choose an injection and die in her sleep. Her friend had told her that he wasn't afraid to die. Late at night she thought of that as she watched movie after movie. She didn't want to fall asleep. She didn't want to dream. If life were so fragile, she might easily drift away in her sleep. But finally she did fall asleep.

I am with my mother. She looks like Ursula. We start to have a fight about politics. My mother makes many right-wing statements. She thinks the poor don't want to work and that's why they're poor. She is for the death penalty. How can you be for death, I say. Death stands nearby. He takes my hand and I strike my mother. She dies. I can't believe that I've killed her, but there is nothing I can do. I am sentenced to death. But I am not allowed to have an injection. The judge says my crime is so heinous, I must suffer.

Elizabeth didn't remember the dream completely. She thought her father may have been in it, too. What if he were the judge? And she didn't hear the telephone ring. It was perhaps the first time in her adult life that, when she tried, she couldn't invoke her unconscious life adequately. It took many cups of coffee to wake her. She dressed carefully. Today she would approach Ursula in the bar. At five she walked over there, but Ursula wasn't in her regular seat. The bartender poured Elizabeth a scotch and soda, and she felt that he knew her in a special way. She waited for Ursula. Men who were also regulars talked with her. She spoke to them in hushed tones.

Elizabeth looked down at her feet and thought she saw Ursula's dog. He was brushing against her leg. She looked down several times because the dog's fur tickled her. After her third scotch, even though the bar was air-conditioned, her cotton sweater and skirt stuck to her body. She was sweating and wiped her forehead again and again. She was restless, waiting for Ursula. The dog licked her ankle. He licked and licked. Elizabeth laughed out loud. At least she thought she did, but when she looked around the bar, no one seemed to have noticed her. That's why she liked it there.

My Time, My Side

During college, I had to invent or reinvent myself every day, create a person who awoke, dragged herself out of bed, and went to class. I was morbidly depressed; life was futile. I had to move from despair and apathy to the shower, then find clothes to put on my naked body, even though for three years I wore a self-fashioned school uniform: baggy chinos and a long-sleeved, all-cotton black T-shirt. A friend living near me on West Ninety-Sixth Street drove a Ducati, and when I could catch a ride on the back, getting to class was easier. She was depressed, too, but more manic, and sometimes she shouted above the engine and wind, "I want to kill myself." I hugged her waist tighter then and felt my own desire to die tested.

I met my other best college friend in a required Introduction to Sociology class. She had a bad attitude like me, she was two years older, not a freshman, very cool, but then she disappeared for a while. "I dropped out," she told me when she returned. She also told me to take studio art classes, and I did. I listened closely to everything she said, because she knew what was really happening; for instance, she knew the night Linda Eastman and Paul McCartney slept together for the first time.

The Beatles were cute, but they were too fresh and sunny for my dark, youthfully jaded, sort-of-hip character. The Rolling Stones existed for me and my friend, bad boys for bad girls.

The Stones were anti-everything and suited my sensibility. My psychotherapist had asked me, "What do you want to do?" I said, "I want to rebel." "Then," she said, "my job is to make you effective."

The Stones were rebels—at least their songs sounded rebellious—and they appeared effective. They could have whatever they wanted: sex, drugs, cars, houses, more sex, drugs. I didn't question the implications of their being middle-class boys, the Beatles working-class boys, or what rebellion worked in them. I lived inside my troubled mind, and each day had to awaken in the same bleak and unchanging world and do what I'd done yesterday or something a little different.

Every night for dinner I broiled chicken wings and heated up canned, sliced beets. Like wearing the same shirt and pants to school, I ate the same dinner for three years, unless my knowing friend said, Come on, let's eat out, or hear a band, or see a movie. Later, we shared a railroad apartment in the East Village. She fixed up her rooms reasonably, while I ripped plaster from a wall in one of mine, to uncover the brick, but it turned out to be the outside brick, so I stopped. The plaster lay on the floor of the room. I never cleaned it up; I couldn't use the room anyway, because cold air blew in through the cracks.

My friend found out when the Rolling Stones were doing their second concert in New York: May 1, 1965, at the Academy of Music. "Satisfaction" wouldn't come out in the States until June 1965, but we were already hard-core fans. We had to be at the Stones' triumphal entrance into our city.

The Academy of Music was on Fourteenth Street between Third Avenue and Irving Place, where the Palladium would be in the eighties. The first Academy of Music was a grand opera house, built in 1854 on the northwest corner of Irving Place and demolished in 1926. The Stones played the second Academy, erected in the twenties across the street from the original. This one showed movies from the twenties on, but by the sixties, it was mostly a concert hall. Its marquee letters broken, its seats uncomfortable and seedy, its brilliance and glory faded, the Academy of Music was the right theater for the Stones, who were uncomfortable to parents, and seedy and glorious in their own way.

We sat in the balcony, or we sat downstairs; wherever we sat, my sight lines weren't impeded. I'm short and saw everything that happened, and a lot did and didn't. Opening for the Stones, Patti LaBelle and the Bluebelles, which was how she was billed, as a girl band. In their ice-blue space-age costumes and feather headdresses, with Patti's big voice and their choreographed moves, they rocked. But the audience was indifferent. Stones fans were sullen like the band, and also we were there only for them. Patti must have been onstage an hour, and the audience grew restive. When the set ended, the group received some applause, but they didn't get an encore. They were really fine; we were just lousy for the Stones.

Then nothing, and nothing, and time went by, and no one came onstage, and nothing, and we were waiting and waiting. After a while, someone in the audience roared something, or there was an outbreak of off-the-beat white people's clapping, and a few dispirited, feeble calls for the Stones. Waiting, we turned more sullen.

Where were the fucking Stones.

Forty-five, maybe fifty minutes passed. I don't know how long it was, but still nothing. We were angry already; it didn't take much to make us angrier. Where were the Stones. Where were the Stones. The question was our breath.

People had slumped and settled into their lumpy seats, passive and aggressive both, because there was nothing to do but wait or leave, so we were trapped because we wanted the Stones. Wanting was hell, and while existentially waiting is all there is to do, we didn't like it. There was no clapping now, no sudden shouts for the Stones, just enraged sedentary bodies.

Then they walked out. They just walked onto the stage as if they were going to the men's room. They had no affect. There was no jumping or dancing or mugging. They walked onto the stage and plugged in their instruments and took their positions. They didn't look at us, not once, except for Mick. Mick came to the front of the stage and sort of said, "Hello, New York." He tried a little, but the rest of the band didn't care. They didn't want to be there, and they ignored us. Mick made another pathetic effort, that's all it could be: "Hello, New York." Brian Jones sat down on the floor. He was stage right, his head down, blond hair splayed over his face, obscuring him further, his instrument lying in his lap. Maybe it was his Vox teardrop guitar or a Vox Phantom. He never looked up, the group didn't look at us, they looked bored, and only Mick exerted himself a little, threw off some energy, but he didn't try long. We were angry, deadened, too, and quickly Mick accepted defeat. Listlessly, the Stones started their first number. Probably they were very stoned.

A matron stood at the edge of the stage, on the same side as Brian, but at the top of the stairs, which was the only way up there, except for leaping. She was a heavyset Black woman, about thirty—I don't remember any Black people in the audience—and she wore some kind of theater or usher uniform. She faced the audience, grim and solemn, with her arms crossed over her chest. The Stones were playing, and Mick was singing, Brian was sitting on the floor, head down, and I don't remember what Keith was doing, but he wasn't crouching the way he does now and uncoiling like a rattlesnake to strike. Charlie Watts was Charlie Watts, steady, imperturbable, playing the drums the way he's always played the drums, and Bill Wyman was himself, unmoving and dour.

There was a kind of stasis onstage, and in the audience. Into the third song, a hefty, dark-haired girl made a run for the stage, and up the stairs. But when she reached the top of the stairs, the matron blocked her. She gave her the hip. The girl flew down the stairs. One move, down she tumbled. The girl landed on the floor, stood up, and walked back to her seat. That was it, that was our resistance. The matron crossed her arms over her chest again and glared at us. The audience became more frustrated. The Stones hadn't even noticed, and nothing happened again, and not one of us yelled or stood up, either, and soon the atmosphere turned solidly against the band.

The Stones played eight songs, the songs were three or four minutes each. They were onstage less than half an hour. They finished their set and walked off the way they'd walked on. They just walked off. No one clapped or shouted, everyone was fed up, pissed off, let down. We'd become the anti-audience, and rose, grabbed our jackets, left our seats, and filed out. There was no fighting, no talking. We'd all been rebuffed, like the hefty, dark-haired girl. The audience spilled onto Fourteenth Street, a morose confederacy of rebels. It was early evening. I suppose my friend and I went out for something to eat. Or maybe I went home and ate sliced beets and broiled chicken wings. Life continued, but something had changed: the Rolling Stones had played New York.

By now, the Stones have changed a lot. Brian drowned, murdered, it's alleged, by his assistant; Mick Taylor quit, so Ronnie Wood plays lead guitar; Darryl Jones plays bass, since Bill Wyman retired; and Mick's, Keith's and Charlie's faces are crosshatched and filigreed with event and experience. I've changed, too. For one thing, I have stopped eating wings exclusively, though I eat chicken. I still love beets, but now fresh and roasted, and order them whenever they're on a menu. I still like to wear a uniform of sorts, but now I buy six or seven pairs of the same usually black pants, about that number of the same all-cotton, long-sleeved T-shirts, and many of the same linen, rayon, or silk blouses. I buy everything in different colors. Life isn't as bleak, with some variety.

MORE SEX

There were many men she wanted to have sex with, some days more men than other days, though she'd already had sex with many men, but those were the ones who were easy to have sex with or to find for sex, since they lived in the neighborhood; she could meet them at parties or in clubs, even in grocery stores, especially near the beer, wine, and cheese displays, probably because they're often served at parties. It was easy to find men for sex, because she knew that men think about sex all the time, or every seven minutes, so they're always ready for sex. She had read the seven-minute statistic in the *Times* science section some years back and wondered about it. Then she experimented with herself. She set a timer for seven minutes throughout five hours, when she was home, and, whatever she was doing, reading, eating, washing dishes, looking at the ceiling or out of the window, when the alarm went off, she thought about sex. Every seven minutes, she realized, was very frequent, and, if she were feeling sad, it was hard to think about sex, and also she realized she didn't think about sex, maybe she didn't know how, and she managed poorly or inadequately to concoct an image or something or someone to fantasize about. Every seven minutes was hard, she didn't know how men did it, because she didn't have that kind of imagination, and also she didn't know for how long men thought about sex every seven minutes. And what did they think up? Their penis entering a woman's vagina, if they were heterosexual, while she's moaning, Fuck me, fuck me hard, and was it always the same? Her lack of sexual imagination was one of the reasons she liked going to the movies. There was usually sex in the movies she saw, sometimes lots of it, if it was unrated or X-rated, and sometimes there was soft-core porn-like sex in movies, in so-called love scenes, which activated her dormant, lackluster, or empty fantasy life, but then she often became infatuated with the lead actor and, for a while, she pictured having sex with him. Many of the men she wanted to have sex with were actors, especially those who were good lovers in movies and sometimes on TV. They appeared to be good at sex, although that was hard to define, she didn't know if it was similar to being good at tennis or some other activity; anyway, to her, inexactly, it was the way they held a female actor, the way they looked into her eyes, the kind of passion they exuded, and, manufactured or not, the sex or passion seemed real to her. She hoped they were really good at sex and not just acting, although actual people do act when having sex, too, though why they do and for what purpose, she wasn't sure. It wasn't only faking or-gasms, which women were said to do to make men feel better or just to get them to stop, since they really weren't having any plea-sure anyway. Men acted during sex, too, she knew several, some were worse actors than others. But the men she wanted to have sex with, the actual actors, were not available to her, they were in Hollywood, or London, or they were sometimes on the streets of New York City, like Sean Connery, but he was old when she saw him, and Michael Imperioli from *The Sopranos*, but she had never wanted to have sex with him, he was weaselly, even if she felt sorry for him in his part, and Al Pacino, she'd seen him in an Italian restaurant where he walked around in dark glasses as if he didn't want anyone looking at him but made such a show of it everyone recognized him, though no one said hello or anything to him, because few do that in New York, mostly people don't. But none of these actors she had seen in person appealed to her. She wanted to have sex with Daniel Day-Lewis, but only as he was when he played an American Indian/Caucasian in *The Last of the Mohicans*, not in any of his other roles, he was never again a bare-chested, mostly silent Indian, and now he didn't want to act, she heard, and was a shoemaker, and then for a while she wanted sex with David Caruso, when he was on TV in *NYPD Blue*, because he could do tenderness and seemed gentle and also lusty, but then he quit the show, and she heard he was the opposite of that role, an egomaniacal asshole, and she did not want to have sex with George Clooney, Sean Penn, Tom Hanks, Ralph Fiennes, countless others, even McDreamy in *Grey's Anatomy*, because everyone wanted him, and that made him much too common, and in her fantasies, when she could cook one up, she would have had to compete with too many women—and men, probably—for him. There were so many she didn't want to have sex with that sometimes going to the movies was as disappointing as real sex with actual nonactors—though, on occasions—acting men. But wanting to have sex with men she couldn't have, because they weren't around ever, and would ignore her in favor of another actor, male or female, was also all right, because she could easily have sex with men she didn't necessarily want, and they weren't so bad, really. She could ask them about what pictures they had in their minds every seven minutes, and she didn't think she could do that with movie stars.

OTHER MOVIES

Along Tenth Street, it's pretty quiet. The beginning of the night and the taxi people opposite my building have four limos out front waiting, probably, to drive to the airport, but no one's gunning his engine. The motorcycle club is out of town, the ten bikes that are usually parked next to each other and which take up one and a half car lengths, they're probably rolling along a highway somewhere, or they've pulled over to the side of the road and the bikers are drinking beer and listening to the radio, something I know about from road movies like *Two-Lane Blacktop* or *Easy Rider*.

Roberta's walking her dogs. She's got three of them, two very small poodles and one big mutt. At first I couldn't stand Roberta. Along with her dogs, she owns three cars, all of them in bad shape, and she moves them daily. In this way she participates in a major block activity, car parking. There are people who sit in each other's cars, or move them, or just look after them. Roberta spends about three hours every day waiting for the time one of her cars will be legal in the spot it's in. Alternate side of the street parking means nothing to you unless you have a car in the city. Then, if you don't have the money to park your car in a garage, it controls part of your day.

As I say, I took an instant dislike to Roberta, because she raced her engine, turning it over and over late at night under my window, and because of the way she looked. She has a huge mass of dyed-black hair, eyebrows tweezed into startled half moons, and she wears sausage-tight pants stretched over a big stomach and ass. But by now we've taken to saying good morning to each other and she doesn't look so bad to me anymore and I guess she's all right. She probably never suspected that I had put a desperate and angry typed note on her car window, saying I'd report her for noise pollution if she continued racing her engine at 2:00 a.m.

That was a while ago, around the time Richie got put away. Now he's down the block, drinking coffee from a Styrofoam container, not worried that those containers cause cancer, just calmly looking at the setting sun. Richie's out of the hospital again and on lithium. The new people on the block didn't know about him then, didn't know that his screams weren't serious, and he probably woke them the way he wakes everybody at first. You learn not to pay attention. You learn to distinguish his shouting from anonymous and dangerous screams or from calls for help, and you fall back to sleep. But these new tenants called emergency and Richie disappeared again. It took weeks to find out where he'd gone. Jeff, who's been on the block longer than almost anyone, hung a sign in his storefront window and many along the street, on telephone poles. WHERE'S RICHIE? The signs lined the block. We all missed him. Maybe Jeff's lover Juan didn't, but I never talk to him, he's very unfriendly.

Richie usually stands in front of the door where he sleeps. The rock group gives him a bed and food. He stays outside during the day, rain or shine. When Richie's in one of his moods, having a psychotic episode, he walks back and forth and shouts: "Where's the sixties?" "Where's Central Park?" "Who killed Kennedy?" Sometimes he just howls like a wolf. When he comes out of it, he washes and combs his hair, cleans himself up, smiles at you, and says, "Hi, how are you." Makes small talk. If you can make small talk, that means you're well. One time I dreamed he was my boyfriend. Maybe because he's so steady in his own particular way.

It takes time to discern behavior different from your own. When I first moved in, I called the police because there were strange and loud noises on the street. I thought someone needed help. A cop said: "You'll learn to tell when they're funnin' and when they're serious." I think the neighbors below me used to beat each other up. A tall, thin Black woman, a tough blond white woman, and the Black woman's adolescent daughter. Sometimes I'd run out my door and stand in front of theirs, ready to knock loud. But I never did. Two years later I saw the blonde go into an Alcoholics Anonymous meeting on Saint Marks Place. There's always a big mob of people outside just before and after the meetings. "A good place to meet men," I heard one woman say to another as I strolled past. The fights downstairs have stopped. We've exchanged names—Mary, Jari, and Patricia—and now we complain together about the landlord and the super. I like the women, there are always wonderful cooking smells coming from their apartment. Their daughter seems okay, but it's hard to tell how kids will turn out. Maybe in the midst of those fights, the little girl cowered in her room, on her bed, or was protected by an imaginary friend. Rescued by someone like Sigourney Weaver, in *Aliens*, who kind of looks like her mother.

Not so long ago, Telly Savalas was filming here. The dealers down the end of the street yelled to him, "Hey, Kojak, how's it going, man?" Savalas gives the high-five sign, and the guys are content, even proud to be, if only for a second, part of the big picture. We're accustomed to our block being used as background, local color, for TV movies or features, even commercials. Cops and robbers. Drug busts. Hip and trendy scenes, the location for galleries, weird boutiques, that kind of thing.

If I were to make a movie of the block, one version could be based on *Blue Velvet*, titled something like *Under Tenth Street* and starring Roberta as the Isabella Rossellini character, one of the rock-and-roll guys as the boyish voyeur, and Richie as Dennis Hopper. It might open with a shot of a large rat on a roof, blinking its eyes at the camera, and some country-and-western music playing on the soundtrack. The big-city romance of the small town set in a big city.

Sandra might be from a small town in Utah. I see her about once a week. She could be the daughter of a farmer and his hardworking wife, long dead, American Gothic types carrying pitchforks. I figure Sandra escaped to the big city years and years ago. She's down on her luck, without a home and with a drinking problem.

Sandra's emaciated. Walking along the block, she's carrying two tote bags and clutching a cardboard box to her thin chest. She heads for Susy, a punked-out seventeen-year-old, and says, "I'm sixty-seven, can you give me a dollar?" Susy gives her a dollar, then counts her money to make sure she's got enough. As she counts her money, someone moves up on her. Susy shoves the money in her pocket and jumps in the other direction. The guy behind her, one of the rock-and-roll guys, is rushing and he shakes his head but doesn't look at Susy. He looks at Sandra. When Sandra notices him, she asks for another dollar.

What I think happens to Sandra as she walks off the block, or set, is that she goes to the B&H for a bowl of soup. It costs $1.35 and comes with two slices of bread. Afterward she'll reluctantly spend the night in a shelter where she'll have to hide her money because somebody might steal it. It's safer on the streets than in the shelter, but at her age it's too cold and she might freeze to death in her sleep. I don't know why, but Sandra has an inordinate fear of being buried alive. She keeps a notebook—she used to be an editor for a Condé Nast publication before she started hitting the bottle—that details her life on the street and her fears. After she dies of hypothermia or malnutrition, the notebook might be found and published in *The Sunday Times Magazine*.

Susy's about fifty years younger than Sandra. To me she looks a little like Rosanna Arquette in *Desperately Seeking Susan*, when the Arquette character dressed up to look like Madonna. After Susy pushes the wallet into her pocket, she looks again in the rock-and-roll guy's direction, needing a bed, or a fuck, a little love. Maybe she's a teenage runaway.

Susy enters a door near where the dealers hang out and where they, in gestures and movements as choreographed as any ballet, walk past each other or a client and exchange small plastic envelopes for money. Susy disappears behind a dark-gray steel door. Behind this gray door the girl might be shooting up, doing her nails, abusing her child, or talking to her mother on the phone. On the other hand she could be a lab technician. (From across the street I follow her disappearance, the door an obstacle to my camera, not, of course, to my fantasy.)

I think: Susy's in her room, or someone else's room, or in a hallway on the third floor. I try to picture her. I ask myself, What's she doing? If I could I'd follow Susy inside, and stand invisibly next to her, then maybe I'd rob her story, steal it away to look at and consider.

Recently I watched a TV program about a woman robber who did her breaking and entering in Hollywood in broad daylight. (She said steel doors were practically impossible to get past, but she could open anything else. She loved the thrill of being inside somebody else's house, knowing that at any moment the owner might walk in and that she might get caught.) A variation on the primal scene, I suppose. Part of her punishment, in addition to going to jail, was to be videotaped teaching cops how to catch a smart thief like herself. She enjoyed telling what she knew to people she outsmarted more than four hundred times. She enjoyed being on camera, caught by it, performing for the cops, her captors. But like Susy's story, the robber's story, even though documented, is hidden from view, blighted by incoherence and the impoverishment of explanation. Still, I can see her on the job. Maybe I'm another kind of thief with desires just as strong as those that compelled the Hollywood woman to break and enter in broad daylight and to want to get caught. I don't want to get caught.

Suppose Susy's caught up with a crowd, as in *River's Edge*, a crowd so alienated and detached they don't report the murder of a friend by a friend. Every day they go and look at her body decaying. They watch her skin turn yellow and green, her lips dark purplish black. Perhaps Susy's the one who wants the movie's good guy to tell the police. Perhaps she's as fascinated with the rotting body as I am with her story. Or maybe she's more like the dance instructor in *Dirty Dancing* who needs to get an abortion because one of the young, rich patrons at the hotel where she works got her pregnant but he won't help her out. Now Susy's on Tenth Street, a runaway carrying a baby she doesn't want.

Watching her with me, I'm sure of this, is a man in a wheelchair who lives on the ground floor behind a plate glass window. He has as unrestricted a view of the street as you can get. We never speak, nor do we say hello. I don't know his name, but I think of him as Jimmy Stewart in *Rear Window*. Except for some reason he's the predator, not the victim. It may be that he's collecting their stories, too, and we're natural competitors. He lives next door to the man with seven dogs and ten cats. I know Jimmy Stewart watches Susy because his wheelchair moves ever so slightly when she walks down the block and he bends from the waist to see her better. He seems sinister to me, his fascination a little like mine. When I look in his plate glass window, I see him and a reflection of myself, in fact I'm just to the left of myself.

Suppose Jimmy Stewart leads a secret life, is not actually handicapped, is in fact a murderer, and has his eye on Susy. Or on one of the rock-and-roll guys, or on Roberta. Funny Roberta. She passes a lot of time in front of Jimmy's window. Many of her parking spots land up right in front of it. Or maybe Jimmy's a Vietnam veteran who got shot in the legs. Most likely he was at My Lai, that's where I see him. His actions during that massacre live with him daily, and he will never, never forget or get over them. Like the machine he was supposed to become in training, like the boys who become men in *Full Metal Jacket* by learning to kill and then doing it to rock-and-roll songs on the soundtrack of the movie, Jimmy Stewart was transformed at My Lai into a human monster more terrible than he could ever have dreamed or than could ever be shown in horror movies. What was inside him was as destructive and grotesque as what was around him. His thoughts then. His thoughts now. Maybe he sees nothing when he looks out his window. Maybe it's all just a big blank. On the other hand, he reads *The New York Times* every day.

I pass by his window. He's gripping his head in his hands. Roberta's on the sidewalk, struggling with her mutt and trying to clean up the shit from her two poodles. Richie's in a doorway three buildings from this scene, and he's humming a tune, which sounds like Sinatra's version of "My Way." Usually he sings Motown classics. This could turn into a musical comedy, with Richie, all cleaned up, a Marlon Brando–type hood in *Guys and Dolls*, or maybe Richie'd get the Sinatra role, Nathan Detroit, since he's singing one of his songs already. Roberta could be the heroine and work for the Salvation Army. Jimmy Stewart could be one of the guys, a third-rate mobster looking for a crap game. Better yet, it's *The Buddy Holly Story,* and instead of Gary Busey as Buddy Holly, he's played by one of the rock-and-roll guys, with Richie, the acoustic bass player for the Crickets, and Jimmy Stewart as a record executive who wouldn't, of course, do any singing.

Actually, I don't think the man in the wheelchair would ever get cast for a part in a musical, rock or otherwise, not even *Pennies from Heaven.* He's a Bruce Dern type, a bitter man with a dark past. Or, as he's already in a wheelchair, he could be Raymond Burr in *Ironside.* Nothing like a courtroom and a trial for that intense excitement, drama, and awe once found in the church or theater.

When the sun goes down, people either stay in and watch TV or go out. As I said, Sandra disappears. Richie stands in the doorway till pretty late in the evening, then wanders. The neighbors below me cook and listen to music. Larry and Martin, a couple who run the thrift shop on First Avenue, usually pick up Harvey, who has a bad heart, and take him to one of two hangouts, B and Seventh or Bar Beirut. Every neighborhood needs a couple of bars, every neighborhood movie or TV series needs a meeting place, where the richness and complexity of human life unfolds in a series of interlocking vignettes. The bar on Avenue B and Seventh is my choice since it's already been used for numerous Miller beer ads as well as for Paul Newman in *The Verdict.*

Imagine the place. A corner building. Red-and-green glass windows on two walls of the bar, so that the light filters through in color and it's always dark, even in the afternoon. Pinball machines. A locked toilet that costs twenty-five cents to use, to keep the junkies out. A TV above the door. A horseshoe-shaped bar. The jukebox is good and loud, draft beers still cost a dollar. It's *Cheers* or *Archie Bunker's Place* except the ethnic groups are different. For the regulars, it's a home away from home.

Tonight at one end of the old horseshoe-shaped bar sits Harvey, unemployed salesman, a *Death of a Salesman* type, except I don't imagine he's had children. Just out of the hospital—another heart attack—Harvey hasn't stopped smoking or drinking. He's with Larry and Martin, and they're not fighting with him about it. Since AIDS hit the block—two young men died recently—and the city, so many people are sick, I don't see them arguing as much. Larry's got his arm around Martin's back. To me Larry looks like James Woods, especially in *Salvador*. Martin doesn't look like anybody. He waves to Susy when she walks in. No one waves to Roberta but me. Her cars must all be parked and the dogs walked. Now she can relax, drink a whiskey sour, and shoot the breeze, if anyone will talk to her. Richie never comes in. He sometimes stands outside, like a watchdog, acting protective.

I take my place at the other end of the bar from Harvey and watch him flirt with Kay, a relative newcomer to the neighborhood. Larry and Martin are talking animatedly to Susy. She certainly doesn't look pregnant. I've heard that Kay's boyfriend took a walk, a permanent one. Tonight she'll even put up with sad, chubby Harvey.

Kay's wearing a cut-up T-shirt with a Bruce Springsteen logo on the back. She reminds me of Sally Field. Her small breasts are encased in a push-up bra. She likes wearing a push-up bra to get a little cleavage. I watch Kay look at her breasts resting in their cups of cotton, silk, and lace, then she looks at Harvey. Tomorrow she's going to have a mammogram because she's over thirty-five. One out of ten American women, she tells him, gets breast cancer. Then she drinks a shot of vodka and rolls her blue eyes at him, as if she were Demi Moore in *St. Elmo's Fire*. They talk about disease. His heart. Her breasts. AIDS. Kay's good friend Richard died two months ago, and she still can't believe it. Life, she tells Harvey, wasn't supposed to be like this. Kay slides off the barstool, goes to the jukebox, and plays "Born in the U.S.A." and "Girls Just Want to Have Fun."

Joe the bartender is nothing like Archie or Ted Danson, the guy from *Cheers*. He's a tall Black guy, sort of like the lead in *The Brother from Another Planet*. Joe lived in Harlem before moving down here. He's friendly but cool, suggesting that when he works, he works. He keeps his eyes on the couples and singles around him. Sometimes I watch the scene through his seasoned, professional eyes as they pan the bar, scanning the crowd for trouble and requests for more drinks. He doesn't betray much. He tells Larry and Martin the rumor is that Edouardo, who lives two houses from Susy, got caught dealing heroin, and he and his older cousin are in jail, probably at Rikers.

Edouardo's about eighteen, Hispanic, the oldest of seven children. Seven children from the same mother—she moved to New Jersey about when I moved in—and three different fathers. Their grandmother, who always looks tired and usually carries an open can of beer in a paper bag, lives with them and takes care of them. In their crowded apartment Edouardo—or Eddy—screams at his brothers and sisters, controls the TV set, and leaves the lights on all night so that the youngest ones find it hard to sleep. On the block he plays the big man and struts his stuff, even holds doors for the "ladies." Then he laughs behind their backs. I wondered why I hadn't seen him around lately.

Standing outside the bar is his sixteen-year-old sister, Maria. Months ago Maria and I were in the corner bodega, the one run by three Syrian brothers. A man walked in and in front of everybody started shouting at her: "I'm your father. I don't want you on the streets. Comprende? I'm your father." As if we were watching television, a soap like *Dynasty* or a docudrama about a family in trouble, the Syrian grocer and I pretended not to hear, pretended to go about our business. When Maria left with the man who claimed to be her father, she didn't look at us, stood up tall, stretching her small frame, and projected a sullen dignity that I respect. Ahmed says to me, *Family Court.*

I'm pretty sure Maria is working the street. Tonight she could be dealing herself or dope. This is a crack-and-cocaine area, unlike Tenth Street, which is primarily weed. Anyway, she never comes into the bar, maybe because it's mostly white, then Black, hardly ever Hispanic, or maybe it's because she respects certain traditions, like a girl doesn't go into bars alone. Maybe it's just that they won't let her in, she looks her age, or they know she's a hooker. I'm not sure. Edouardo used to come in sometimes. Both of them frequent Bar Beirut on First Avenue, where the motorcycle crowd hangs out when they're in town.

Joe hands me a draft beer and says, conspiratorially, "I couldn't see you living in the country. You're a real urban woman." He's never said anything like that to me before, and since I'm there invisibly, a kind of Hitchcock walk-on, I'm reluctant to become part of the action. Kay, who's never really talked to me before, overhears Joe's remark and, for reasons I'm not sure of, doesn't go back to her seat next to Harvey but sits down close to me. She does most of the talking and I realize she's flirting with Joe. They talk about real estate—what landlord has bought which building, which ones are being warehoused—and about the squatters on Ninth and C, the closest Manhattan comes to having a tent city for the homeless. It looks something like England's Greenham Common.

Kay orders a martini and Joe, to lighten the mood, says he's just heard on the news that martinis are the favorite drink of 11 percent of Americans. Kay says martinis make her think of thirties movies, a different time. What about *Moonlighting?* Joe asks. Roberta takes a stool next to Kay and talks about a story she heard on the news. A pet psychologist refused to divulge the name of the golden retriever she was working with "because of the confidentiality of the doctor-patient relationship." Then Harvey, still chasing Kay, wanders over and pretends to be talking only to Joe about the porn he's been renting from the video store, the one that's also a dry cleaner's, owned by Kim, the Korean who's got a lot of good selling ideas. That's the way Harvey puts it.

Highlights from the Iran-Contra hearings play on the TV above the door and everyone but Joe turns to watch, listen, and laugh. One old guy screams support for Ollie North. He's drunk, says Martin. But he's not alone, says Larry. Roberta switches from pets to vets and tells the story of her window washer, a Vietnam vet who said he wouldn't ever fight again unless they were landing on Coney Island. If I were really part of this movie, I'd ask, Who are "they"? But I don't and instead think about the man in the wheelchair who never comes in here but has been known to go to the pasta restaurant on Avenue A and sit in the window glowering.

Kay remarks that Freud once said Coney Island was the only place in the US that interested him. This gives Harvey a chance to talk to Kay again, and he says, "You one of those Freudians?" She throws him a disgusted look. Now he realizes she'll never sleep with him. Martin and Larry probably are aware that Harvey, who gets very aggressive when he drinks, is about to lose it, having lost an opportunity with Kay, and they take Harv by the arm and lead him out the bar.

It's not such a hot night at Seventh and B. Kay says Bar Beirut is better on weekdays. She says she's just gotten a part in an independent film being shot in the neighborhood. The mood changes when Susy strolls by, her arm around another young woman. Joe, in an uncharacteristic gesture, takes out a teddy bear from behind the bar and hands it to her. Susy's friend looks angry, as does Kay. It's all in close-up: their anguished faces, Joe's mischievous grin, Susy's sense of her own power, her hands on her slim hips. Sets of eyes dart back and forth. It turns into a rock video, something like Michael Jackson's "Beat It," and I see them all moving around the bar, snapping their fingers, taking positions and pulling knives out of their pockets. What's going to happen? I ask myself, wandering home. How's it going to end? Will Susy sleep with Joe and desert her girlfriend? Or will Kay outstay Susy and land him, if she really wants him?

I've often wondered what it would be like to shoot a bar scene using as extras all those actors who work as famous look-alikes. These characters could wander back to the block, each to her or his own particular place on it, with their own thoughts about the night they've just had. If Susy were the dance instructor in *Dirty Dancing*, and Joe turned into Patrick Swayze, and Kay into Jennifer Grey, they'd dance out the bar and into the street, exploding in an ecstasy of pelvic thrusts and utopian feeling. The extras, of course, would all join in. Or, as in *Hill Street Blues*, it could end in a freeze-frame with Susy opening her steel door, while Kay and Joe kiss in the foreground.

I don't like endings. Besides, though the night has drawn to a close, and is a natural ending, the next day Tenth Street bustles again. Roberta's revving her engine. Richie's upset and is shouting about Bush and the CIA. The thrift shop has opened a little late, because Martin's hungover. Jimmy Stewart's in the window, staring. And Kay and Susy pass each other on the street, but don't say hello. I decide that Susy did sleep with Joe. When an ambulance pulls up next door, its siren blasting, I run to the window, wondering whose life might be in danger. Last week an apartment house went up in flames, the fire engulfing and destroying three floors within minutes. Everyone watched. Disasters bring people together. I hope they're not taking Richie away again.

Absence Makes the Heart

The woman said don't leave me, then walked into a ballroom, the kind that is easily imagined. He saw her, she who had been left, in a purple gown. Her dress froze in the space she inhabited, and it seemed to him it was by this lack of movement that she projected a singular state. The wine, musicians, perfume, dancing men and women, and the breath of lovers coming in quick, hot, uneven spurts was a tableau of such familiarity, unoriginality, she did not need to look. Separate from the others, she seemed to him a duchy, defined by borders both real and imaginary. No doubt those borders were in dispute, and she chose to stand alone. He did not think of her as stateless, bodiless, unincorporated. Such metaphors might occur with the absence of others. There was such plenitude, so much given to the imagination.

Her hand touched a mouth whose very construction seemed to spell pleasure. What a mouth, he thought, a mouth to create hunger rather than satisfy it. His eyes lingered on the lips as if they, too, were eyes that could swallow his by their very reception. Her breasts rose and fell, and that she breathed, was alive, was to him a miracle. Such beauty could not be real. Her round breasts must be the mountains and valleys of that unimaginable state. Hadn't he once admitted that one could not imagine a mountainless valley, a linguistic impossibility. But she was flesh, and he was careful to conceive of her—her breasts, for instance—as possible. He thought, Unimaginable is not the state, not-yet-realized is better. He was drawn to her, as if drawn by her, her creation. She was a painting, a study in purple, she was a dangerous flower, she was a fountain bringing youth to those who drank her. He felt stupid, like a story that doesn't work.

It was a battle for her to think. It was pointless. She spoke to herself. I am the one who waits. I am the one who will be waited upon. I have the kiss that can change men's lives. I can awaken the dead. I can never die. I am empty. I am perfect. I am full. I am all things to all men. She shook her head violently. He watched everything. The shake of the head, a sign to him. A fire lit. Something was burning. He felt ill, he felt wonderful. She was sublime, and he wondered how words like that existed before her.

His approach across the floor was a dare, a move, as if the floor were a chessboard and he had made his opening. He approached and avoided, missing the hem of her dress by inches, causing her to move slightly, but just enough to let him know she could be moved. Her movement irritated him. When he looked back, he saw that she had resumed her previous position. His irritation fled and fell into an unwanted past. Her position was irresistible and unknowable. He thought, If she turns out to be like pudding, sweet but thick, it will be easier to leave her.

Just then, as he was toying with flight, a woman hurried to her side. The woman cupped her hands to her mouth to speak words meant just for her. He imagined that someone had been slighted, her indifference to someone had been noted, or perhaps it was a practical matter. She had to leave in order to be ready for an early-morning rendezvous. With a married man. An important figure in the government. The woman took her arm and the two walked out of the room, their shadows larger than life. Were her eyes full of tears? Was she that delicate, so easily hurt or affected, such an angel to feel for others. The crowded room emptied with her departure, and love that is despair led him to follow her, to find her.

Her father lay in state on a hospital bed. Nothing was attached to him anymore. His head was turned from her and frozen. Couldn't she give him life, she who loved him more than any man. His hand was ice. His ankles were swollen and purple like her dress. His eyes were fixed and dilated. He did not know she was there. This must be death. And as nothing is attached to you anymore, no tubes dripping colorless liquids, I must also become detached from your body. Now, what man will love me, and who will I be able to love.

He did not expect to arrive at this place, a hospital. He covered his mouth with a handkerchief, telling himself it was merely a precaution. Her purple dress disappeared down uninteresting white halls. The sterility hurt his eyes, yet he knew she would see his compassion, especially in this setting, and think well of a stranger so much in love with her as to appear in her hour of need. He would rescue her from grief, whatever it was, and she would be his.

Her face was ugly with crying, red eyes covered by eyelids that were swollen. The corners of her mouth turned down, her beautiful mouth framed by sad parentheses. The color had run from her cheeks and in its place was none. She had aged, suddenly. If she had seen herself in a mirror, she might have imagined it was because she was unattached. She startled him. He was the mirror she could not look into to see herself.

Her transformation was temporary, he reminded himself. He told her he had come, even though she didn't know him, because he loved her. Would love her forever. He recognized, he said, the absurdity of his approach, but having seen her and felt what he did, could the ridiculousness of feelings be a reason not to act on them. Weren't they all we had, inadequate as they were. He told her that he knew one day she would love him, too. He told her he could soothe her pain.

I cannot compare death to words. Death is too great a contrast to life. And love is an invention, but death is not. I was not able to give my father life, though I am unchanging and eternal. And you, too, will die and blame me. Blame me for having been born. Or you will leave me before you die, saying I have hurt you, shortened your life. Taken your best years. I do not want to take your breath away.

With these words he determined to have her. It was true, her voice was not as mellifluous as he might have wished. But what man could believe her words, words meant, he was sure, only to test him. He had waited forever to meet a woman who might challenge him to appreciate the brevity of life. Her reluctance must be read as mystery, a deception from one whose own creation was exampled in the stories he loved.

She turned from him, racing down the hall, her dress swinging around her legs, jumping at her ankles. Don't leave me, he called. Don't leave me. She stopped abruptly and spoke to him from such a distance that he could not really see her face. And he could not hear what she said, her words strangled in a cry that seemed closer to a laugh. Don't leave me, I, too, said, then walked into the ballroom.

Hold Me

(9 Stories)

She liked her body when she was a child. Naked, she would look at it in the tall mirror in her parents' bedroom. Then the house was quiet, and she was unique, alone. The house to her was like her body, but it was big and magnanimous and accepted her into it, always. Like a lover, it jealously guarded her from outsiders and kept her to itself.

On those days of solitude, she lay on its cool, naked floor, pressed her face to its wide chest. She pretended her lover was under her, stroking her, caressing her small body, even tracing a path along her spine, fusing top to bottom in sensation. She lay still, quiet as the house, and, full of unrecognizable feeling, she waited.

When the girl heard familiar voices outside, she raced upstairs to her room, whose arms embraced her and made her feel safe. She would, she thought, as she put on her gloves years later, never feel so safe again.

The pensive young woman lifted the scissors from the table and grabbed a bunch of her thick hair. With one motion, she sliced the bunch off. She chopped at the rest, her hair collecting on the floor like discarded thoughts. Rubbing the short, severe hairs on her head, she studied the phone as if it might tell her how she looked. Then she picked up the receiver and punched in a number.

She said: Hi. Listen. Don't say anything, okay? I have to say this. I want quiet the way you do, sure, comfort, but I want things amped, big, things I don't know, I want to go where I've never been. I don't really care about a nice home, I'm not nice. I want privacy. I like being alone. I don't want falling in love, I don't want it. If it runs me, it runs everything. I don't love you. I don't want to love you.

She hung up and cradled the stupid telephone against her chest.

The dental hygienist held the man's jaw and pulled his lip farther from his gum.

"When I was a kid," she said, "every night, I sat at dinner with my parents, and both of them had false teeth, complete sets, and they were only thirty, and the sound of their teeth when they chewed, I hated that sound, you ever hear it?"

He hadn't but he nodded. Her face was too close, intimate as a lover's. Her makeup was thick over tiny pimples and large pores.

"So I knew what the future was going to bring," she said.

The hygienist poked a sensitive area. "That's your bad pocket," she reminded him. He winced. The hygienist patted his cheek as an afterthought.

"I knew I'd have to marry a dentist or go into the field."

To friends, he'd described her as the Nazi hygienist, because she loved her work too much.

She persisted at the bad pocket, ripping anxiously at his rotten flesh. Then she paused, to wipe blood from the corners of his mouth, and somehow he started crying. The hygienist nodded, with compassion, he decided, chose a different sharp instrument, and went back to work.

Even last night's dirty dishes looked like rebukes.

The fragile wineglass slipped from her grip and shattered to pieces. Last night's grease had congealed on everything, the plates, cups, fat had separated into ugly units. The tiny glass splinters presented more domestic dangers. She scrubbed the pots, urged the fat off forks and knives, and scoured the sink. No justice, no peace, she thought, restively, and read the label on the dishwashing liquid. So many little words. Her sister's anger left her none.

She picked up a disgustingly clean plate. Maybe she'd smash it against an innocent wall. She raised her arm and held the pose too long.

Instead, she went to bed and, like a child, pulled the covers over her head. She smashed wordless ghosts of things in her dreams.

He took a determined breath in the cold room and, naked, pressed his body against a large picture window. The brilliant fall forest declared itself vital, impressive, and indifferent. He thought he should shave. He traced the contours of his face.

Grieving was the most private act a human being could do, next to shitting, he figured. You could have sex in public more easily than you could shit in public. Grief is shit.

No one had cried, no one in his family broke down, they held on to what they felt, it might expose more than sadness, they kept it in themselves. He listened to his own intake of breath, he watched his mother furtively wipe her eyes, he saw his brother's brow furl like an insignificant ripple in an otherwise placid lake, he watched his father grimace and his arm jerk involuntarily at his side. The gestures commenced a sort of mourning show. He'd never seen their faces like this, stunned silly by life's ultimate weapon.

His grief had no public now. It was when he jerked off and tried to feel good that he let go.

Earlier, what he had said was, You have to take loss, handle it, grab it, just take it. It's your life, you make it what it is. In him, like a drumroll, his words repeated, and as he worked in the garden, digging holes and planting seeds, he felt the world enclose him like an oversize coat. There was no use, no protection, she had answered, and pulled her hat on. She disappeared a little then, tugging at the shapeless hat, tucking unruly hair inside, touching the stiff collar on her coat—and this would not protect her, either. He swallowed, the heat of the day hit him, and then he wiped his brow. His body was mimicking itself, no, other bodies, he decided, and nothing was natural really.

The green ocean spewed dirty foam, the roiling mess spit its way to the shore. The man tensed against the wet, cold air and dropped his shoulders. Then he clenched them and wrapped his black scarf carefully around his neck and under his blue summer jacket. He moved one leg farther from the other and stood with them spread wide apart. He thought, idiotically, I'm facing the ocean. He stuck his chin forward and wondered if he might appear heroic to someone. He looked at the horizon. He smiled at himself, chin jutting into the wind, arms hanging loosely by his sides, a man of a certain age alone on the beach at winter. Noli Me Tangere, he thought. Then he looked around, saw no one, and slapped himself in the face.

Love stories are remarkably the same, she said to the guy she secretly loved. He lit her cigarette, nimbly. Then, and she knew
he would, because he always did, he tossed his head to the left
and glanced at her. He was whimsical today, playful. She noticed,
the way she always noticed, how blue his veins were, how uneven the tone of his skin, how ragged his nails. His palms were
plump, like the belly of sparrows. His flesh was him, untouchable,
ungraspable.

She imagined taking a razor and drawing a line in his soft palm.
She imagined blood seeping out, wantonly exposing the stuff
inside him, the secret of him, which, like his love, she wouldn't
know.

The mother knitted, the son watched MTV, the daughter drifted away, disconsolately tugging at an earring, as if she might remind herself of something that was escaping. In a moment, the mother looked up, awake now to her intense, nuclear world, and pulled bright-red yarn from the cloth bag at her feet. How long had she had the bag? As long as they were alive.

The mother had always knit. The staccato of the knitting needles would be how the son brought his mother back, evoked her, long after she was gone—she's going now, the doctor had whispered. The daughter had despised the click clack of the needles, the mother's measured, persistent beat behind her every runaway daydream.

The daughter drifts off and tugs at an earring. Something eludes her. She strains to hear the fitful sound.

LIVING WITH CONTRADICTIONS

He didn't want to fight in any war and she didn't want to have a child. They had been living together for three years and still didn't have a way to refer to each other that didn't sound stupid, false, or antiquated. Language follows change and there wasn't any language to use.

Partners in a pair-bonded situation; that sounded neutral. Of course living with someone isn't a neutral situation. Julie and Joe aren't cave dwellers. They don't live together as lovers or as husband and wife.

How long would this century be called modern or, even, postmodern? Perhaps relationships between people in the fourteenth century were more equitable, less fantastic. Not that Julie would've wanted to have been the miller's wife, or Joe, the miller. In other centuries, different relationships. Less presumption, less intimacy? Before capitalism, early capitalism, no capitalism, feudalism. Feudal relationships. I want one of those, Julie thought, something feudal. What would it be like not to have a contemporary mind?

Intimacy is something people used to talk about before commercials. Now there's nothing to say.

People are intimate with their analysts, if they're lucky. What could be more intimate than an advertisement for Ivory soap? It's impossible not to be affected.

The manufacture of desire and the evidence of real desire. But "real" desire is for what—for what is real or manufactured.

Other people's passions always leave you cold. There is nothing like really being held. They didn't expect to be everything to each other.

The first year they lived together was a battle to be together and to be separate. A silent battle, because you can't fight and fight together, it defeats the purpose of the battle.

You can't talk about relationships, at least they didn't; they talked about things that happened and things that didn't. Daily life is very daily.

The great adventure, the pioneering thing, is to live together and not be a couple. The expectation is indefatigable and exhausting. Julie bought an Italian postcard, circa 1953, showing an ardent man and woman, locked in embrace. And looking at each other. Except that one of her eyes was roving out, the other in, and his eyes, looking at her, were crossed.

Like star-crossed lovers' eyes should be, she thought. She drew a triangle around their eyes, which made them still more distorted. People would ask "Where's Joe?" as if there was something supposed to be attached to her. The attachment, my dear, isn't tangible, she wanted to say, but it is also physical.

New cars, new lovers. Sometimes she felt like Ma Kettle in a situation comedy, looked on from outside. You're either on the inside looking out or the outside looking in. (Then there's the inside looking in, the outside looking out.)

Joe: We're old love.

Julie: We're familiar with each other.

Julie didn't mind except that she didn't have anyone new to talk about, the way her friends did. Consumerism in love. One friend told her that talking about the person you lived with was like airing your clean laundry in public.

Familiarity was, for her, better than romance. She'd been in love enough. Being in love is a fiction that lasts an hour and a half, feature length, and then you're hungry again. Unromantic old love comforted her, like a room to read in.

Joe: You hooked up with me at the end of your hard-guy period.

Julie: How do you know?

Joe: I know.

So Julie and Joe were just part of the great heterosexual, capitalist family thrall, possessing each other.

Contradictions make life finer. Ambivalence is just another word for love, becoming romantic about the unconscious.

Where does one find comfort, even constancy. To find it in an idea or in the flesh. We do incorporate ideas, after all.

You can accept the irrational over and again, you can renounce your feelings every day, but you're still a baby. An infant outside of reason, speaking reasonably about the unreasonable.

Calling love desire doesn't change the need. Julie couldn't abandon her desire for love. It was a pleasurable contradiction and it was against all reason.

THAT'S HOW WRONG MY LOVE IS

A while back, I watched a pair of mourning doves in their nest every day, watched as one then the other sat on an egg; saw their baby emerge from the egg, watched its being carried food and fed, saw them all fly away one late summer morning, never to return, I thought. But there are many mourning doves around my neighborhood, and maybe those three are back.

Every morning, right to the window; every afternoon, come home, open the door, right to the window—I witnessed the entire cycle of a nesting mother and father, a chick's beak cracking through the eggshell, the baby's care, its parents' nurturing it, the baby's first flight.

The mother and father took turns sitting on the egg, and I was informed by a genuine birder, a nature writer, that this behavior was unexpected and unusual. One bird sits, the other flies away and returns with food, the sitter flies off, then the food gatherer guards the egg, mother and father switching roles to protect the egg, that was unusual I was told.

The nest rested in an empty planter on a windowsill on another building directly across from my window; I strained to see it, a city backyard away. I thought about getting a telescope, but in the city—remember *Rear Window*—that can be dangerous or at least provocative. I would have to train my sights carefully and somehow declare my looking benign, when most looking is not. As far as I know there is no gesture, like waving a white flag, to signify a lack of aggression in looking. As for the people whose window it was, and whose planter it was, I never met them, or saw them at the small window, and I often wondered how they felt about the avian family on their ledge. After the birds left, the planter was quickly filled with flowers, so I understood that they disliked the birds' nesting at their window. I disliked them for that, since mourning doves are supposed to return to their nests, and now they couldn't. This might sound strange to non–New Yorkers, but many backyards of smaller apartment buildings are quiet, untrafficked, almost bucolic settings. It's quiet and calm behind many buildings, which are not in midtown, and perfect for birds.

I read about mourning doves' habits and that the males have red streaks on their necks, while the females don't; still, I couldn't tell one sex from the other. Rising in the morning and rushing to the window, cup of tea in hand, I'd make sounds I hoped they'd associate with me, friendly noises, but I was never certain that they were, or if they might be inimical in their language. I was sure, though, they noticed when I whistled or cooed.

Mourning doves have a distinctive call, a melancholy coo, melodic and even hypnotic. Curiously, the voice doesn't seem to come from them, their beaks don't look open. But if you get close enough to them, you'll notice that the feathers on the necks fluff out, and their little chests puff out and vibrate. A dove's coo is in the lower range, there are usually four or five calls in a row, sweetly mournful, though what they are mourning can only be supposed. I like their sound, though if they carried on day and night, I'd go crazy.

The reason I imagine they looked at me or in my direction, though what image they saw is a mystery, was confirmed on a special, sad morning. As usual, I made myself a cup of tea, and, cup in hand, went to the window to see the birds and the nest. They weren't there. The nest was empty. It was terrible. I gave my cry and whistled, and immediately I heard a rustling noise. I looked to my left, and there were the three birds, sitting on the bough of a big New York weed tree.

This is what happened: I whistled again, the three gazed at me, now closer in proximity than they'd ever been, the baby half the size of its parents, so slim and sleek, and with their heads turned in my direction, there was a long moment during which we continued to look at each other. Then, suddenly, but in unison, they flew away. They'd waited for me to come to the window, they'd wanted me to know they were abandoning their nest. And me, perhaps.

I realize this sounds corny, ridiculous, or just another piece of anthropomorphism, or vanity, if feeling appreciated or recognized by birds is vanity. Yet I believe it was their intention, though I have since learned that mourning doves lack cunning and are not bright.

Not long ago, I saw a documentary about many varieties of migratory birds—*Migration*—who fly thousands of miles twice a year for food and a safe place to nest, raise their chicks, and return when the elements change; their lives are full of duress and hard work. They have little rest. While the airplane with the cinematographers flew beside the flock, the birds ignored it and single-mindedly moved forward, their wings beating rhythmically and constantly, though occasionally they glided, and they might have been exhausted; yet they kept going, determined to eat, to nest, to procreate. While the film's angles were gorgeous, and I did feel as if I were in the sky beside the birds, I had the beginnings of vertigo and was disturbed almost all the way through. I thought their travails necessitated small, light brains; otherwise, with heavier, big brains, how could they manage flight and why would they go on living like that? If they could think, they might think, as many humans do, Life is meaningless if all I do is fly back and forth.

The next spring, with the planter full of flowers, no birds nested across the backyard. But one day, I don't remember when, a mourning dove appeared on the fire escape at the front of our apartment, four stories up. I wondered if it were one of the three. I bought birdseed and began putting it out on the window ledge. I made the whistling and cooing sounds I did for the first family, and that bird or another and others began showing up. I also hung a birdseed feeder for finches, and they came within a week, but with five or six on the feeder, the feeder shook so much, the seed landed on the sidewalk, and hundreds of pigeons took up residence and shitted all over it. I love finches, their brilliant and subtle coloring, their tiny rounded chests, but I had to remove the feeder, or become another character on the block who caused a nuisance.

In my building there is a young woman who cannot throw out anything; she appears normal, whatever that is, but if you went into her apartment, which I was forced to do one day, to search for my absent-minded, runaway cat, Louis, the madness of her place—moth-eaten, worm-ridden, filthy rugs piled high upon a moldy couch, nearly to the ceiling; a sole, scraggly path through the

apartment, between boxes and mounds of junk, probably teeming
with vermin; shelves and lamps leaning against other furniture, so
if one object was moved, everything would fall down—this chaos
describes a very different person from the bubbly young woman
who zips happily around the neighborhood. Inside her apartment
that one time, I recognized some of the pieces I had thrown out
years ago. She's a hoarder, a photographer, who shoots me when
I don't know she's there, gleefully catching me unaware, and also
a fire hazard, possibly a schizophrenic, a psychoanalyst told me,
but none of us tenants would dare tell her to examine or change
her ways. Occasionally I see her daintily dropping a tiny bundle
of trash into the building's garbage can.

I've been leaving seed on the ledge for about five years, and there
are mourning doves who appear every day at the same time,
morning and late afternoon, but I've given up trying to distinguish one from the other. Sometimes I think I can recognize them
by their intelligence, but I can't really. I signal, and one, two, or
three might fly to the fire escape and watch as I shovel out the
seed. Some are not afraid anymore; I think they're the smart ones,
they move closer to the ledge, to the seed. Some show fear and
fly off; the dumb ones, even if they stay, never touch the food,
even when they see it, and then many pigeons—mourning doves
are in their family, but pigeons are ugly and twice their size—
congregate and greedily consume all the seed.

There is nothing I can do, I have tried various methods. The smarter
mourning doves recognize that, when I open the window and wave
my hand in the air to shoo the pigeons, I am not shooing them away,
because they remain on the fire escape and wait to eat. Yet, even
after having waited, they might not go to the birdseed—again, a

mystifying mix of smart and stupid. Some always do, the ones I think are smart, and then they get it before the pigeons swarm.

The mourning doves have become habituated to being fed at my window, and I have made feeding them a habit. They are dependent on me, to some extent. I should put seed out every day, because they expect it. If I forget, they boldly approach the window and push their heads through the window gates; when the window is open, or if the window is closed, they stare into the apartment, patiently, or tap their beaks on the glass and look inside. It's odd, but they know where I live. Sometimes I leave town, and, if I remember that I'm not doing my duty to them, I feel a little guilty. Then I tell myself there is food everywhere on the streets of New York, there's a park down the block . . . When I return, I continue the habit.

By now the mourning doves may have learned that I am erratic or inconsistent, and maybe they don't wholly depend on me, but think of my window as a candy store, where they get treats, not real meals. But I do feel burdened with a responsibility I didn't predict when hoping to see them again.

Still, there are daily and surprising pleasures. I have seen them have sex. Mourning doves mate for life, I've been told, and they're tender with each other before and after sex. The seduction begins when the female grooms or teases the male—I can tell male from female only then, because side by side the female is much smaller. The female pokes and ruffles the feathers of her mate, and, after a while, they face each other and kiss. They kiss a few times, open beaked, then the male mounts the female, there's a brief spasm or shudder, and the male alights, he again sits next to the female, they nuzzle and face each other, and then kiss a few more times.

This behavior is not an anomaly, all the mourning doves who have had sex on my fire escape follow the same ritual.

I love animals, I am an animal, I'm a mammal, a human being, I like most people, love many, despise one person, though I don't want to hate anyone. I am also selfish and want what I want. My greatest and most enduring problems in life are ethical, but living ethically is necessarily a conscious endeavor, the unconscious is not ethical, and questions and riddles about correct behavior are endless in variation, new issues coming along all the time— stalking on the internet, for example. Not feeding the mourning doves regularly is wrong, but I generally give myself a pass. My not feeding the pigeons because I find them big and ugly is unethical. A self-named animal lover should feed all creatures alike. Worse, I am not a vegetarian. I love animals but discriminate among them and eat some. I eat less meat than I once did. I like steak, but usually resist it—for my health more than for the cow's; I rarely resist roast chicken. I don't eat bacon, I eat fish, crustaceans, but I would never eat horse, cat, or dog.

If I were starving, caught in a war, desperate to survive, like the Donner Party, who ate their dead colleagues, like most people I would ultimately succumb, with remorse and disgust.

I hope to do no harm, yet I cause harm, about which I may have no knowledge, which is a dilemma I don't expect will change or that I can entirely overcome: the predicament between principle and desire. There are things I like to do, and I do them, and, as much as I can, I don't do what I don't want to do.

Dead Talk

I am Marilyn Monroe and I'm speaking from the dead. Actually I left a story behind. I used to be jealous of people who could write stories, and maybe that's why I fell in love with a writer, but that doesn't explain Joe. Joe had other talents. I didn't even know how famous he was when we met. Maybe I was the only person in America who didn't. I was glad he was famous, it made it easier for a while, and then it didn't matter, even though we fit together that way. The way men and women sometimes fit together. It doesn't last. I got tired of watching television. Sex is important, but like anything that's important, it dies or causes trouble. Arthur didn't watch television, he watched me. People thought of us like a punch line to a dirty joke. Or maybe we had no punch line, I don't know. Anything I did was a double entendre. It was different at the beginning, beginnings are always different.

Before I was Marilyn Monroe, I felt something shaking inside me, Norma Jean. I guess I knew something was going to happen, that I was going to be discovered. I was all fluttery inside, soft. I was working in a factory when the first photographs were taken. It was during the war and my husband was away fighting. I was alone for the first time in my life. But it was a good alone, not a bad alone. Not like it got later. I was about to start my life, like pressing my foot on the gas pedal and just saying GO. And the photographs, the first photographs, showed I could get that soft look on my face. That softness was right inside me and I could call it up. Everything in me went up to the surface, to my skin, and the glow that the camera loved, that was me. I was burning up inside.

Marilyn Monroe put her diary on the night table and knocked over many bottles of pills. Some were empty, so that when they hit the white carpeted floor, they didn't make a sound. Marilyn made a sound for them, something like whoosh or oops, and as she bent over, she pulled her red silk bathrobe around her, covering her breasts incompletely so that she could look down at them with a mixture of concern and fascination. Her body was a source of drama to her, almost like a play, with its lines and shapes and meanings that it gave off. And this was something, she liked to tell her psychiatrist, that just happened, over which she had no control. After three cups of coffee the heaviness left her body. The day was bright and cloudless and nearly over. She thought about how the sky looked in New York City, filled with buildings, and how that was less lonely to look at.

Marilyn just wanted to be loved. To be married forever and to have babies like every other woman. Her body, in its dramatic way, had other ideas. Her vagina was too soft, a gynecologist once told her, and Marilyn imagined that was a compliment, as if she were a good woman because her vaginal walls hadn't gotten hard. Hard and mean. But maybe that's why she couldn't keep a baby, her uterus just wouldn't hold one, wouldn't be the strong walls the baby needed. Marilyn's coffee cup was next to her hand mirror and she was lying on her white bed, looking up at the mirrored ceiling. She was naked now, which was the way she liked to be all the time. When she was a child, the legend goes, she wanted to take off all her clothes in church, because she wanted to be naked in front of God. She wanted him to adore her by her adoring him through her nakedness. To Marilyn love and adoration were the same.

Marilyn took the hand mirror and opened her legs. Her pubic hair was light brown and matted, a real contrast to the almost white hair on her head, which had been done the day before. It was as if they were parts of two different bodies, one public, one private. My pubic hair is Norma Jean, how I was born, she once wrote in her diary. It was hot and the air conditioner was broken. She could smell her own smell, which gave atmosphere to the drama. Her legs were open as wide as they could go and Marilyn placed the mirror at her cunt and studied it, the opening into her. Sometimes she thought of it as her ugly face, sometimes as a funny face. She made it move by flexing the muscles in her vagina.

He said he'd marry me but now I know he was lying. He said I should understand his position and have some patience. After all, he has children and a wife. I told him I could wait forever if he just gave me some hope.

Marilyn took the hand mirror and held it in front of her face. She was thinner than she'd been in years. Her face was more angular, even pinched, and she looked, finally, like a woman in her thirties, her late thirties. She looked like other women. The peachiness, the ripeness that had been hers, was passing out of existence, dying right in front of her eyes. And she couldn't stop it from happening. Even though she knew it was something that happened to everyone, it was an irreparable wound. Her face, which was her book, or at least her story, did not respond to her makeup tricks. In fact, it betrayed her.

Marilyn needed to have a child, a son, and she wanted him with the urgency of a fire out of control. Her psychiatrist used to say that it was all a question of whether she controlled Marilyn or Marilyn controlled her. Marilyn always fantasized that her son would be perfect and would love her completely, the way no one else ever had.

Sometimes I meet my son at the lake. One time he was running very fast and seemed like he didn't see me. I yelled out Johnny, but at first he didn't hear. Or maybe he didn't recognize me because I was incognito. He was so beautiful, he looked like a girl, and I worried that he'd have to become a fag. Johnny said he was running away from a girl at school who was driving him crazy because she was so much in love with him and he didn't care about her at all. I asked him if she was beautiful and he said he really hadn't noticed. Johnny told me every time he opened his mouth to say something, she'd repeat it. Just staring at him. As his mother I felt I had to be careful, because I wanted him to like women, even though I didn't trust them, either.

Marilyn had asked her housekeeper to bring in a bottle of champagne at five every afternoon, to wash down her pills. And because champagne could make her feel happy. Mrs. Murray knocked very hard on the door. Marilyn was so involved in what she was thinking about, she didn't hear. Marilyn was envisioning her funeral, and her beautiful son had just begun crying. There were faces around her coffin. But his was the most beautiful. No, Mrs. Murray said, he hadn't telephoned.

I told Johnny that more than anything I had wanted a father, a real father. I felt so much love for this boy. I put my arm around him and pulled him close. I would let him have me, my breasts, anything. He looked repulsed, as if he didn't understand me. He had never done this before. He had always adored me. Johnny wandered over to the edge of the lake and was looking down intently. I followed him and stared in. He hardly noticed me, and once I saw again how beautiful I was, I felt satisfied. Maybe he was too old to suck at my breasts. But I wanted, even with my last breath, to satisfy his every desire. As if Johnny had heard my thoughts, he said that he was very happy just as he was. He always lost interest anyway when someone loved him.

The champagne disappointed her, along with her fantasy. Deep down Marilyn worried that they had all lied to her. They didn't love her. Would they have loved her if her outsides had been different. No one loved Norma Jean. She could hear her mother's voice telling her, Don't make so much noise, Norma Jean, I'm trying to sleep. But it was Marilyn now who was trying to sleep, and it was her mother's voice that disturbed the profound deadness of the sleep she craved. If she couldn't stand her face in the mirror, she'd die. If they stopped looking at her, she'd die. She'd have to die because that was life. And they were killing her because she needed them to adore her, and now they wouldn't.

I hear my mother's voice and my grandmother's voice, both mad, and they're yelling, Save yourself, Norma Jean. I don't want to be mad. I want to say goodbye. You've got my pictures. I'll always be yours. And now you won't have to take care of me. I know I've been a nuisance and sometimes you hate me. In case you don't know, sometimes I hate you, too. But no one can hate me as much as I do, and there's nothing you can do about it, ever.

Her suicide note was never found. Twenty years after Marilyn Monroe's death, Joe DiMaggio stopped sending a dozen roses to her grave, every week, as he'd done faithfully. Someone else is doing it now. Marilyn is buried in a wall, not far from Natalie Wood's grave. The cemetery is behind a movie theater in Brentwood.

THIS IS NOT IT

If I were only somewhere else than in this lousy world!
—LUDWIG WITTGENSTEIN

Whenever I arrive, it's the wrong time. No one has to tell me.
The right time is a few minutes earlier or later. Invariably I arrive
at the wrong time in the wrong place. Wherever I am, it is the
wrong place. It's not where I should be. No one says a word when
I arrive. I am always unexpected.

Because it's the wrong place, I want to be someplace else. I always want to be in the place where I should have been. The place
where I should have been is paradise on earth. It is inaccessible to
me, because I cannot arrive on time at the right place.

(I try to be still.)

Because wherever I am is not where I should be, I am always
ill at ease. I'm in an uncomfortable position. I have conversations
with the wrong people. I should not be speaking to them. They
know this, but everyone is polite since each of them may be sim-
ilarly indisposed. They never remark that my presence is a problem to them. They put up with me; I put up with them. I always
wonder when I can leave gracefully. I'm never graceful, because I
don't fit in wherever I am.

(I try to control myself.)

In the wrong place at the wrong time, the wrong people and I
are obviously in a drama, a tragedy or comedy. Whatever tragedy
I am in, unwittingly and involuntarily, it's not the right one for
me. It's either too grand or pathetic, an exaggeration, considering
my position or station, which is an impossible one. A neighbor-
ing tragedy, the one next door, would be better for me. But it is
unavailable to me. It is doubtless the tragedy I was born to. But
my tragedy would not be invigorated by comparison. Just the opposite. The emptiness at its center, with me as the wrong hero,
makes it funny. People laugh at my dilemma. In someone else's
tragedy, my dilemma would be acknowledged appropriately.

(I try to be unobtrusive.)

Whatever comedy I am in, whenever I inadvertently partic-
ipate, it is being played by overly tragic people. It's the wrong
comedy. I am unsuitably sad. I forget the punch lines and tell
jokes badly, with the wrong timing. People cry at my ill-timed
jokes. I cry when I should laugh. When I am mistakenly in the
audience, at someone else's tragedy or comedy, my reactions are
consistently wrong.

(I try to leave.)

Whenever I attempt to go, I ask a friend which is the right way.
But whoever is my friend is the wrong friend. This is not the person who should be my friend. Even if this person is a friend, he or
she may provide the wrong advice. Or this friend may tell me to
find the information I need in a book.

(I try to be sensible.)

Whatever book I find is the wrong book. The right book is on the shelf, in the bookstore or library, next to the wrong one I discover. Once I have it and begin to read it, I know it's the wrong book. No wrong book will tell me what I need to know, but I keep buying and reading books. I buy the same books again and again. Because I put them away in the wrong place, I forget I already have them.

(I try to find myself.)

Whenever I flee to a place I think I've never been, I discover that I've been there before. I hated the place on my first visit, but I've repressed the memory of it. I return to hated places often. I have seen many movies again, too. I go twice to places and to see people and movies I should never have visited or seen in the first place.

(I try to abstain.)

Whenever I see myself in a mirror, I don't believe the person is me. I believe I'm seeing the wrong person. This person masquerades as me. This person apes me. I try to catch this person unaware by sneaking up to surprise the mirror image. I am always disappointed when the wrong person shows up. The wrong person consistently makes the wrong appearance.

(I try not to trust appearances.)

Since I am in the wrong place, it must be the wrong mirror. The wrong mirror must not mirror the right image. It can't be me.

But I am disappointed never to see myself. I keep looking. I may simply be the wrong person.

(I try not to want to escape. I try not to cry or laugh. I try to remember. I try to act differently.)

If I am the wrong person, this must be why, whatever world I am in, there is a better one elsewhere. Whatever money I have, more money is waiting somewhere else. This is why I do not like what I see. It is why I don't want what I have and why I want what is nearby.

Whatever I have is not what I should have. Whatever makes me happy ultimately makes me sad. I am the wrong person living my life. Someone somewhere else must be better off.

(I try to fool myself.)

Whoever I am, I am wrong. I try not to expect anything. It's impossible not to expect the wrong things in life. But I can't expect nothing. Nothing's certain. This may be wrong.

(I try not to jump to conclusions.)

Madame Realism's Torch Song

The other night, as he sat near the fire in Madame Realism's study, in the place where chance had made them neighbors for a period of time, Wiley said: "Things go on we don't know about. They happen in the dark, metaphorically sometimes, but maybe you don't want to talk about dark stuff now."

"Marilyn Manson," Madame Realism said, "told someone on MTV that Lionel Richie was the heart of darkness."

"There's the light side. But it has a shorter life." Wiley struck a match.

"It sparks, flares, burns, burns out."

He turned from the fireplace, where he was watching the fire, to her. Wiley looked grave or intent. Madame Realism felt strange, the way she often did. She hadn't known him very long, and, for a moment, he spooked her. Then he returned his attention to the hearth.

"Fire's positive, negative, amoral, not capable of reason, which reminds me of something . . ."

"Are you going to tell me a ghost story?" Madame Realism asked.

Wiley's large, almost childlike eyes were a silvery gray, like his hair, but his irises were flecked with brown and yellow, and especially when the fire caught them, they luminesced like a cat's. He stoked the fire, and it leaped higher into the air.

"Do you believe in ghosts?" he asked.

Tonight Wiley's manner or words or tone or bearing bordered on the dramatic. Did she believe in ghosts? She felt ghosted. Ghosts had a place in her vocabulary. Did it matter if they existed? She expected to be haunted by her past, and bodies kept turning up. Wiley might be someone who knew her differently from the way she knew herself, or he might be someone she once knew, disguised. His voice soothed and disquieted her. It was oddly familiar, but then lately everyone seemed familiar, which was a benign kind of horror.

"You and I are sitting together, talking. We came here to get away, and far off, in a place you've never been, or at home, something is happening that could undermine your plans, a lover is slipping out of love, or someone is scheming against you."

Madame Realism noted to herself that she'd found a dire soulmate, another paranoid. Wiley nodded circumspectly or as if he'd heard her thoughts.

"We have very little control, all our small plans can be overturned in . . ."

He snapped his fingers. It was an old-fashioned gesture. His fingers tapered elegantly at the ends. In another life, he might have been a Flamenco dancer.

"In politics, nothing is really hidden. In your life, if someone moves faster, or decides to play hardball, or has a scheme and you have a small role, or you're a bystander, or an obstacle, your life changes. We're ants, or tigers, or rats, and we run from one place to another, avoiding or ignoring what's probably inevitable. Something, an enemy, could just . . ."

Wiley tended to finish his sentences with his hands, and this time he moved his left hand in the air, drawing a line through the space in front of him.

Madame Realism focused on the fire, because his eyes were becoming impenetrable, like colored contact lenses. She stared into it, seeing and not seeing, hypnotized or lulled. His words and pauses were the soundtrack to its chemistry.

"But it's important to let things develop, even in the dark, because surprise is like fire—positive and negative. So I like found poems and objects, and this may be crazy, but I make things disappear, just to find them. I study ordinary actions and reactions and all kinds of innocent signs. The collision of uneven things provokes a third element."

Wiley clapped his hands together.

The flames burned indifferently in the fireplace, and Madame Realism thought of alchemy, which usually never came to mind. There was a time, she supposed, when art and science were indivisible and the place where they fused might have been alchemical.

"Do you love fire?" he asked.

"I don't know if I'd call it love."

To herself she proposed: Imagine life without fire. But she couldn't. The world was raw, endless and empty. She got no further.

"I've considered pyromania," she went on, "but I don't know what it'd be in place of, unless there's an infinite parade and you could love millions of different things. Would pyromania substitute for heterosexuality? I could be attracted to men and want to start fires and see them burn, while watching handsome men put them out."

Wiley stared at her now, with open affection. She thought about the true marriage of opposites, attraction wedding repulsion, and a headline: Pyromaniac Is a Firefighter.

Earlier she had started the fire that glowed now by twisting single pages of old newspaper into rodlike forms and placing kindling on top of them, arranging the thin sticks of dry wood into a configuration she'd never tried before, but which Wiley had employed, effectively, when Madame Realism first visited him. He was, in his words, "originally a country person, adept at fire building." His wife had disappeared two months or years ago, Madame Realism couldn't remember now, and he didn't say more about it or her. He went about building the fire, patiently teaching her his surefire method, which she hadn't yet perfected.

"What matters to me," Wiley said, "is the subtle experiment. It appears insignificant but breeds results no one would expect. Unexpected results from ordinary things are wonderful."

Not unwanted pregnancies, she thought, and poked the fire, which was alive and raised its red-hot head quickly. She always wondered what ordinary was. She always thought she would remember which was the best technique to start a fire, but she didn't. She didn't write anything down; she relied on memory. She didn't like tending a fire; she was easily distracted. She didn't like having to watch it to make sure it kept burning.

"I don't want my illusions to protect me," Wiley said, warming to his subject. "I need to protect them. I have to distinguish between fantasy and evidence, the world outside me. I want to produce fantastic things and control the things I make and do, but I also don't. I'm caught in that drama, a two-hander, but they're my hands, so I'm playing with myself."

The double entendre dropped plumply at her feet. Wiley didn't seem to notice; he was inside his own theater. Madame Realism hesitated.

"I don't want to be manipulated," she said.

It was an ugly word, but she pronounced all its syllables distinctly. Then she added: "But sometimes manipulation is fun. So maybe that's not true."

Tonight the fire caught easily, but she didn't know why. Yesterday she had placed the kindling in approximately the same way, and it hadn't. There was a blazing fire now when yesterday the fire had died out, because of the wetness of the wood or a slight difference in the configuration of the kindling and small logs with which Madame Realism always began or because she had become absorbed in other matters. Maybe she'd forgotten she'd started a fire.

"That's the battle," Wiley said, seemingly out of nowhere or out of no place she was. Was he thinking about manipulation? Or fire?

"What I love most I can't control," Madame Realism said.

Like conversation, the immediacy of it, and how she never knew why it had started, what its necessity was, where it was going to end up, or what its lasting effects might be, if any. Conversation was ordinary, but it was also an unforeseeable element that allowed for eruptions in the everyday. Madame Realism saw herself vacillating inside the grid, with other creatures, temporary set pieces on a chessboard. She often wanted to leap into the corny unknown. Something about Wiley and his wondrous eyes—Renaissance orbs—encouraged that longing. But escape, she'd been told a million times, was impossible. It also had predictable forms and outcomes.

"In ordinary encounters," he went on, "we expect people to hold up their end of the bargain. If you or I did something strange at dinner, didn't pass the salt, or if you didn't answer a friend's 'How are you?'—something as nothing as that—the whole situation would become tense, people would get angry, and all you'd done was not respond."

Madame Realism considered responses, his and hers, and the fire's. A fire dies out, when it's not tended, not responded to, but it could do the opposite; it could spread rapaciously, but if she were in the room, she'd notice it, because the heat would become overpowering. I'd sense it, she thought, though sometimes when Madame Realism was working or on the telephone, she did not notice something that could, if not checked in time, hurt her. A fire might spread quickly and overcome her. If she didn't escape fast enough, she could be badly burned, maybe suffer grotesque disfiguration, requiring costly surgery to return her face to relative normality—normality is always relative—though not ever again to be pretty or even attractive. Or she might die.

Madame Realism didn't know how much time had passed. A minute. Maybe more. Wiley waited quietly for her to return. His having come from the country implied reserves of patience, to her. But Madame Realism hadn't asked which country. Still, farmers everywhere wait for eggs to hatch, crops to ripen. Wiley seemed an unlikely farmer. She knew little about him; he could be anything. She wondered why his wife had left him, or if she even existed; she wondered if he missed her and still wanted her, if he would forever, no matter what her response to him was now.

When Madame Realism was no longer in love, her lover's eyes, which in the middle of an exacting passion she could not leave, whose every glance she scrutinized to discern greater meaning and which she thought unforgettable, when she was so far from any feelings of love or lust as to make recollection or meaning impossible, she lost interest in her lover's eyes and every other aspect of him lost interest, as if he and they had never been capable of exerting it. Bliss metamorphosed into disgust. In that sense, love was an experiment with unexpected results. Relationships were unpredictable. She had been told, by men, that men were more generous or more practical than women and could easily have sex again with anyone they once loved. She didn't feel she could ask Wiley about that, yet.

He bunched up a sheet of newspaper and placed it nonchalantly near the flames; it might catch if the fire moved its way. Then he dropped a chocolate-covered cherry into his mouth and straightened its crinkly gold wrapper on the slate floor as if he were ironing it. She liked the smell of clothes being ironed but wasn't sure if she liked that gesture and questioned how much meaning to give it.

"A fire changes all the time," he said, in an ordinary way. Madame Realism now watched it like a movie, whose characters she invented. She sat closer to it, wanting everything in close-up. She tried to feel what she believed she was supposed to feel near a fire, heated by its quixotic flames.

The fire changed, but it also stayed the same, a blur of blue purple yellow orange red. Ephemeral, shifting, restless. With just a sheet of newspaper tossed casually onto it, it roared approval and grew bigger. She liked watching it, but it could also become boring, tiresome, the way anything could, especially when you were older and more in need of novelty. Sometimes she found herself feeding it like a child, until she lost interest, which she shouldn't if it were.

Wiley stood up, brushing off his black jeans.

"Do you think about beauty?" he asked.

"Sometimes, but I'm not sure how," she said, feeling a little melancholy, the way she did on her birthday. Beauty was the point, and it was pointless, too.

"Is your ghost story about beauty?" Madame Realism asked.

"Beauty's a ghost that haunts us," Wiley said, comically. Then he hunched his back and extended his arms, spreading them wide like the wings of a bat or an angel.

A figure of loss, she thought.

Together and apart, they looked inward, or at the hearth, and wandered silently into the past. The greedy fire, meanwhile, consumed everything.

"What ghost are you?" Wiley asked, finally.

"Everyone dead I've ever loved."

"Beautiful."

After the fire died, what remained were traces of its former glory, ashes and bits of coal-like wood. Wiley and Madame Realism walked outside, into the cold night. They went in search of shooting stars and other necessary irrelevancies.

A Greek Story

A friend announced that what she was going to tell me was the best thing she'd ever done. It was her best story.

She and her friend were about to start traveling in Greece. On the first day they were in Athens, where my friend lives, she stepped on her very nearsighted friend's glasses. The nearsighted friend insisted anyway on being the driver of the car they rented. The nearsighted one pasted a piece of paper over the shattered lens and off they drove. The nearsighted friend drove everywhere. But they contacted another friend in the States, to send a new pair of glasses as soon as possible.

Everywhere they went the nearsighted friend saw out of one eye only. Maybe this is why, when they arrived at Mesolongi, where Lord Byron witnessed the massive battle against the Turks, she especially found the local population menacing.

Then finally it was time for the nearsighted friend to go home, to the States. By now, at some poste restante in Greece, they discovered that a FedEx package was waiting, with the nearsighted friend's new glasses. A note told them that the package was being held in the customs building at the international airport, from which the nearsighted one would fly home.

On the day she was to leave, they went to that building. It was very hard to find the door to enter it, it was a very large, impersonal, and opaque-looking building, and for a long time they couldn't find its entrance. When they did, finally, my friend, who speaks Greek, asked an official the whereabouts of her friend's package. They were directed to a series of rooms, and, in each room, hundreds of packages, some marked URGENT, were strewn on many tables. Many of the cartons and large envelopes were broken or torn. In about half an hour, though, my friend miraculously spied the FedEx envelope with the glasses. But at the door was a customs official who informed them, in Greek, that there was duty to pay on the contents. A lot of duty.

At first calm, my friend explained that her nearsighted friend was leaving for the States that very day and wouldn't even be bringing the new glasses into Greece. The customs official said that it didn't matter and repeated that there was duty to pay and she had to pay it. My friend became agitated and also repeated the same thing: the contents were her friend's personal property, which she wasn't even bringing into Greece, and she was leaving that day. Nothing had any effect on the customs official. He continued to say money was owed, and it had to be paid. Then, my friend told me, she launched into Greek anger, that's how she explained it, which naturally made me think about Greek tragedy.

My friend began cursing and shouting in Greek, a torrent of words. All the while the nearsighted friend listened but didn't understand. My friend shouted and shouted and then, as she shouted, she surreptitiously opened the FedEx envelope, removed the eyeglass case, and took the glasses from it. Then still shouting vehemently in Greek, she returned the case to the envelope, closed it, threw the envelope on the table in front of the customs official, took her nearsighted friend by the hand, and stormed out. When the two had gone through the door, my friend took the glasses from her pocket, gave them to her friend, explained what she'd done, and said, *Run*.

After my friend told me the story, I reminded her how she began it, by saying it was the best thing she had ever done. Oh, she said, that's awful if it's true.

MADAME REALISM'S CONSCIENCE

Whatever it is, I'm against it.

—GROUCHO MARX, *HORSE FEATHERS*

Way past adolescence, Madame Realism's teenaged fantasies survived, thought bubbles in which she talked with Hadrian about the construction of his miraculous wall or Mary, Queen of Scots, right before the Catholic queen was beheaded. Madame Realism occasionally fronted a band or conversed with a president, for instance, Bill Clinton, who appeared to deny no one an audience. Could she have influenced him to change his course of action or point of view? Even in fantasy, that rarely happened. She persevered, though. At a state dinner thought bubble, Madame Realism whispered to Laura Bush, "Tell him not to be stubborn. Pride goeth before a fall." Laura looked into the distance and nodded absent-mindedly.

Over the years, Madame Realism had heard many presidential rumors, some of which were confirmed by historians: Eisenhower had a mistress; Mamie was a drunk; Lincoln suffered from melancholia; Mary Lincoln attended séances; Roosevelt's mistress, not Eleanor, was by his side when he died; Eleanor was a lesbian; Kennedy, a satyr; Jimmy Carter, arrogant; Nancy Reagan made sure that Ronnie, after being shot, took daily naps. When Betty Ford went public with her addictions and breast cancer, she became a hero, but Gerald Ford will be remembered primarily for what he didn't do or say. He didn't put Nixon on trial; and he denied even a whiff of pressure on him to pardon the disgraced president. Ford's secrets have died with him, but maybe Betty knows.

> The pope, President Clinton, Henry Kissinger, and an Eagle Scout were on a plane, and it was losing altitude, about to crash. But there were only three parachutes. President Clinton said, "I'm the most powerful leader in the free world. I have to live," and he took a parachute and jumped out. Henry Kissinger said, "I'm the smartest man in the world. I have to live," and he jumped out. The pope said, "Dear boy, please take the last parachute, I'm an old man." The Eagle Scout said, "Don't worry, there are two left. The smartest man in the world jumped out with my backpack."

Whatever power was, it steamrolled behind the scenes and kept to its own rarefied company, since overexposure vitiated its effects. So, when a president came to town, on a precious visit, people wanted to hear and see him, but they also wanted to be near him. They stretched out their arms and thrust their bodies forward, elbowing their way through the crush for a nod or smile; they waved books in front of him for his autograph, dangled their babies for a kiss, and longed for a pat on the back or a handshake. Madame Realism had listened to people say they'd remember this moment for the rest of their days, the commander in chief, so charismatic and handsome. And, as fast as he had arrived, the president vanished, whisked away by the Secret Service, who surrounded him, until at the door of Air Force One, he turned, smiled, and waved to them one last time.

Without access to power's hidden manifestations, visibility is tantamount to reality, a possible explanation for the authority of images. Everyone comprised a kind of display case or cabinet of curiosities and became an independent, unbidden picture. Madame Realism dreaded this particular involuntarism; but interiority and subjectivity were invisible, they were not statements. Your carriage, clothes, weight, height, hairstyle, and expression told their story, and what you appeared to be was as much someone else's creation as yours.

> You never get a second chance to make a first impression.

If the president of the United States—POTUS, to any *West Wing* devotee—dropped his guard, power itself shed a layer of skin. Ever cognizant of that, one of the great politicians of the twentieth century, Lyndon Baines Johnson, called out to visitors while he was on the toilet. Suddenly Madame Realism took shape nearby, and seeing a visitor's embarrassment, she shouted to the president, "Hey, what's up with that?" LBJ laughed mischievously.

It gave her an idea: maybe he had consciously made himself the butt of the joke, before others could. A Beltway joke writer had once said that self-deprecating humor was essential for presidents, though Johnson's comic spin was extreme and made him into a bathroom joke. Presidential slips of the tongue, accidents, and mishaps supposedly humanized the anointed, but the unwitting clowns still wielded power. Laughter was aimed at the mighty to level the playing field, but who chose the field? To her, the jokes also zeroed in on powerlessness; and Madame Realism trusted in their uneven and topsy-turvy honesty. To defame, derogate, offend, satirize, parody, or exaggerate was not to lie, because in humor's province, other truths govern.

> Any American who is prepared to run for president should automatically, by definition, be disqualified from ever doing so.
>
> —GORE VIDAL

She herself followed, whenever possible, G. K. Chesterton's adage: "For views I look out of the window, my opinions I keep to myself." But presidents were nothing if not opinions, and, at any moment, they had to give one. Maybe since they were kids, they had wished and vied for importance, to pronounce and pontificate, and they had to be right or they'd die. The public hoped for a strong, honest leader, but more and more it grew skeptical of buzz and hype, of obfuscation passing as answer, of politicians' lies. Yet who one called a liar conformed to party of choice.

> Some people are talking, and one of them says, "All Republicans are assholes."
> Another says, "Hey, I resent that!"
> First person says, "Why, are you a Republican?"
> Second person answers, "No, I'm an asshole!"

Some jokes were all-purpose, for any climate. Madame Realism first heard the asshole joke about lawyers, but most proper nouns would fit, from Democrats to plumbers, teachers to artists. Jokes could be indiscriminate about their subjects, since the only necessity was a good punch line that confronted expectation with surprise, puncturing belief, supposition, or image.

> Mr. Bush's popularity has taken some serious hits in recent months, but the new survey marks the first time that over fifty percent of respondents indicated that they wished the president was a figment of their imagination.
>
> —ANDY BOROWITZ,
> *THE BOROWITZ REPORT*

Her fantasies often skewered Madame Realism, threw her for a loop, but at times they fashioned her as the host of a late-night talk show, when, like Jon Stewart and Stephen Colbert, she held the best hand. Madame Realism imagined questioning presidential also-rans who had sacrificed themselves on the altar of glory and ambition—Al Gore, John Kerry, the ghost of Adlai Stevenson. Suddenly Adlai stated, out of nowhere, "JFK never forgave me, you know, for not supporting him at the Democratic convention." Then a familiar, haunted look darkened his brown eyes, and pathos quickly soured their banter. Pathos didn't fly on late-night TV.

Anyone but an action hero understood that even a rational decision or intelligent tactic might awaken unforeseen forces equipped with their own anarchic armies, and some presidents agonized under mighty power's heft. In portraits of him, Abraham Lincoln morphed from eager young Abe, saucy, wry candidate for Congress from Illinois, to a father overwhelmed with sadness at his young son's death, to a gravely depressed man, the president who took the nation to its only civil war.

Madame Realism treasured soulful Abraham Lincoln, because he appeared available to her contemporary comprehension, a candidate ripe for psychoanalysis. She pictured speaking kindly to him, late at night, after Mary had gone to sleep, the White House dead and dark, when words streamed from him, and, as he talked about his early days, his ravaged face lit up, remembering life's promise.

What do you call Ann Coulter and Jerry Falwell in the front seat of a car? Two airbags.

In the nineteenth century, even Thomas Carlyle believed "all that a man does is physiognomical of him." A face revealed a person's character and disposition, and, if skilled in reading it, like physiognomists who were its natural science proponents, why human beings acted the way they did could be discerned. Also, their future behavior might be predicted. Criminals and the insane, especially, were analyzed, because the aberrant worried the normal, and, consequently, deranged minds had to be isolated from so-called sane ones. The sane felt crazy around the insane.

Though face-reading as a science had gone the way of believing the world was flat—poor Galileo!—facial expressions dominated human beings' reactions; each instinctively examined the other for evidence of treachery, doubt, love, fear, and anger. Defeat and success etched an ever-changing portrait of the aging face that, unlike Dorian Gray's, mutated in plain sight. Animals relied on their senses for survival, but beauty made all fools, democratically. And though it is constantly asserted that character is revealed by facial structure and skin, plastic surgery's triumphal march through society must designate new standards.

For instance, Madame Realism asked herself, How do you immediately judge, on what basis, a person's character after five facelifts?

> Images are the brood of desire.
>
> —GEORGE ELIOT, *MIDDLEMARCH*

Before appearing on TV, politicians were commanded: Don't move around too much in your chair, don't be too animated, you'll look crazy, don't touch your face or hair, don't flail your arms, don't point your finger. Their handlers advised them: Keep to your agenda, make your point, not theirs. The talking heads tried to maintain their pose and composure, but these anointed figures faltered in public, and, with the ubiquity of cameras, their every wink, smirk, awkwardness, or mistake was recorded and broadcast on the internet, the worse the better.

At a political leadership forum led by his son, Jeb Bush, former president Bush wept when he spoke about Jeb losing the 1994 governorship of Florida. Madame Realism took a seat next to him after he returned to the table, still choked up. "Did you cry," she asked, "because you wish Jeb were president, not your namesake?" President Bush ignored her for the rest of the evening.

> Why are presidents so short?
> So senators can remember them.

A happy few were born to be poker-faced. A rare minority suffered from a disease called prosopagnosia, or face blindness; the Greek *prosopon* means face, and *agnosia* is the medical term for the loss of recognition. An impairment destroys the brain's ability to recognize faces, which usually happens after a trauma to it; but if the disease is developmental or genetic, and occurs before a person develops an awareness that faces can be differentiated, sufferers never know that it is ordinary to distinguish them. They see no noses, eyes, lips, but a blur, a cloudy, murky space above the neck. What is their life like? Their world? How do they manage? But she couldn't embody their experience, not even in fantasy.

> He wants power
> He has power
> He wants more
> And his country will break in his hands,
> Is breaking now.
>
> —ALKAIOS, CA. 600 BC,
> FROM *PURE PAGAN*,
> TRANSLATED BY BURTON RAFFEL

Those who ran for president, presumably, hungered for power, to rule over others, like others might want sex, a Jaguar, or a baby. Winning drives winners, and maybe losers, too, Madame Realism considered. Power, that's what it's all about, everyone always remarked. But why did some want to lead armies and others want to lead a Girl Scout troop, or nothing much at all? With power, you get your way all the time.

She wanted her way, she knew she couldn't get it all the time, but how far would Madame Realism go to achieve her ends. She wasn't sure. And, why were her ends modest, compared, say, with Hadrian's. Like other children, she'd been trained not to be a sore loser, to share, not to hit, but probably Hadrian hadn't. And, what a joke, she laughed to herself, the power of toilet training.

> Things are more like they are now than they ever
> were before.
>
> —DWIGHT D. EISENHOWER

Thought bubbles gathered over her head, and she attempted, as if in a battle, to thrust out of those airy-fairy daydreams the fates she didn't crave, like serving as a counselor in a drug clinic or checking microchips for flaws. In fantasy only, Madame Realism ruled her realm, and she could go anywhere, anytime. She would be lavished with awards for peace and physics and keep hundreds of thousands of stray animals on her vast properties. Fearlessly and boldly, she would poke holes in others' arguments, and sometimes she did influence a president. She did not imagine having coffee with the owner of the local laundromat, she didn't make beds or sweep floors. Though she believed she didn't care about having great power, her wishes, like jokes, claimed their own special truths.

> The King of Kings is also the Chief of Thieves. To
> whom may I complain?
>
> —THE BAULS

There was a story stand-up comic Mort Sahl told about JFK and him. Mort Sahl was flying on Air Force One with Kennedy, when they hit a patch of rough turbulence. JFK said to Sahl, "If this plane crashed, we would probably all be killed, wouldn't we?" Sahl answered, "Yes, Mr. President." Then JFK said, "And it occurs to me that your name would be in very small print." The comic was put in his place, power did that. Madame Realism wondered how wanting power or wanting to be near it was different, if it was. Maybe, she told herself, she would give up some of her fantasies and replace them with others. But could she.

HELLO AND GOODBYE

Friends are exasperated. I don't do long goodbyes, I say goodbye, turn around, and walk toward the door. Goodbye, goodbye, I say twice, turn and head for the door, ready to leave, hand on door. My friend, or friends, whoever I am with, isn't ready. They say they haven't said goodbye to everyone they should, and I think, Why didn't you, you've been milling around, you didn't say it, and, then they tell me, actually they haven't even said hello to many people, so they must do both, hello and goodbye, which takes more time, or they just want to say more goodbyes, which is irrational. How many goodbyes can there be unless it's saying goodbye to the dead in a coffin. Those goodbyes never end. You can't say goodbye when the other can't respond, it's not reciprocal. Someday friends will be saying goodbye to me, a dead person, and I will be silent.

I attend events or parties alone so I can leave whenever I want. I do it quickly. Goodbye, I say, so good to see you, great to talk, let's get together, I say, and find the door. It's called a French goodbye, but my French is very poor.

Friends are exasperated. The bill comes, and someone generously pays it, or we all dutifully hand our cards to the server and ask, Divide it, please, then the server, if we are more than four, might display some displeasure. The fancier the joint, the less likely the server will show displeasure, because, in a fancy joint, you are paying to be served like kings and queens by pleasant, even unctuous, people. People with money want to be treated better than other people, and pay for it. They themselves may be unpleasant people but never mind.

We have paid the bill, my friends or associates, or whatever they are in the moment, which might change, and continue to talk. I have already slipped on my jacket or coat, which is on the back of my chair, and I am standing up. We have paid the check, dinner is over, it's time to vacate the table, and I want to leave. My friends or associates linger, something else needs to be said. No one else has put on their coat or is standing next to their chair, the way I am. They ignore me, but sometimes I have already left the table and am standing near the door, and then they notice I am not at the table. My name is called, I have to return, coat on, and will be forced to sit down, and what is the point, dinner is over.

I am not a patient person, and it's a good thing I am child-free, because I don't want to wait. A friend who takes her time walking, saying goodbye, leaving a restaurant, is in no hurry, and she wants to know what's my hurry, why do I put on my coat so fast, why am I out the door, she asks, before anyone is even standing up after paying the bill.

Well, I say, that's a long story, and it goes back many years to when I was a baby. I was the last child, everyone was much older, my sisters and, naturally, my parents, I say, and when you're the baby of the family, no one waits for you. My mother had no patience for a third child. My sisters didn't want to wait for me, to take me to the movies or watch me in my carriage, and I understand that, though I didn't then and didn't recognize the burden I was to them, especially to my mother, who had waited six years after her last girl, whose birth tore up her insides, for a boy. My parents had waited for a boy, and I wasn't one, but my father didn't mind, even if he had wanted a boy, because I was the last, athletic, and watched baseball and track with him.

I say to my friend I don't like long goodbyes or lingering at the table after paying, most likely because of my toilet training, which I don't remember, though I have a vague somewhat ugly image of me or another child squatting on a potty. When you are the last child, the smallest and weakest, you must accomplish everything fast, otherwise you're a great burden to everyone, and also your toilet training will be rushed. You can discern from disapproving glances or seeing your siblings waiting at the bathroom door that you should do it and get out. In all my years, it never occurred to me not to get in, do it, and get out.

I could take my time, I know that now. I could also linger in a bathroom in a bathtub, I could soak for an hour, it's good for whatever ails you, I'm told, but after I fill a tub and get into it, in a few minutes, I wonder why I'm there, and what's so great about lying in a lot of hot water, that I have wasted water, a scant resource all over the world, and I have thrown in bath salts, Epsom salts, and moisturizing oil, and know it's a waste, it won't help me at all.

I'm told some people go to the toilet, take a long time, even thirty minutes, read the newspaper, savor their bowel movement, and feel some kind of satisfaction from doing it, a kind of accomplishment. I find this strange. I'm told people take their time, believe the bathroom is a refuge, a place to be alone, a place where no one can intrude. But people don't have to be present to intrude, I live with that knowledge. With no one around I have been intruded upon.

Some people must have learned they could take their time because they were toilet trained calmly. My training would have happened during my family's general and usual melee, frenzied shouting, parents angry with each other or my sisters, my mother distracted, and there was no time.

Defecating and urinating are instinctual, natural, biological urges, but these can be interfered with by anxious, neurotic parents who want their babies to achieve, and pressure them. Some babies won't defecate and hold it in, which is the beginning of an anal personality. That was never true of me, I didn't want to hold it in, while my mother impatiently waited for it. I wanted it out, to get it over as fast as I could. Consequently, I did everything fast, because I needed to catch up, needed not to be a burden, and to be ready. My mother called me Kid Speed, because I ran when I could have walked.

I tell my friend whose eyes have widened so I can see thin red veins in the whites that, over the years, my impatience and need to leave when I want have only increased, I have to leave when I want to, regardless of friends, and have come to wish I had fewer friends who kept me waiting, because I feel I am trapped and will never be free. Trapped, I say again. My friend is exasperated, sitting at the table, looking at me standing up at my chair, trying not to put on my coat.

Boots and Remorse

This story has a beginning. I have a friend named Amy who, years ago, had seven cats. Not only did she have seven cats, but at the time she also fed strays. I remember her telling me about one cat who lived behind a wall. She would leave food for it in front of a slit in the wall, a hole, and somehow, in the miraculous way cats have, the cat would squeeze through the hole and eat the cat food. Every night Amy made her rounds with cans of cat food, a can opener, and water, too, and she would deposit everything at the appropriate though improbable homes and imperceptible feeding holes.

Our family had a cat. Her name was Griselda, and she was a brilliant calico. I didn't know, for example, that you weren't supposed to train cats to sit up and beg, or crawl, but because I was only five and Griselda was compassionate, she let me teach her. She also used to imitate my mother and wear her lipstick, rubbing her thin cat lips on an uncovered lipstick tube, or, uncatlike, she'd give birth only if my mother was in attendance, assisting. When my mother visited friends, Griselda would wait outside their houses, ready to walk her home. The Griselda tale had a sad end, one that still infuriates everyone in my family; I don't want to write it.

I loved cats, but I didn't have one. Amy wanted me to adopt one of the strays she fed. I was resistant, undecided, and guilty, since every night she'd go out and care for animals I supposedly loved but did not provide a home for. With a lot of excitement Amy announced that she had a cat for me, one she'd been feeding since he was born. She said he was the perfect cat for me and she continued: He is the most handsome cat I have ever seen. And the smartest. I told Amy I'd consider him. I was tempted by her high praise, which I never considered might be hyperbolic. It came from someone who'd seen many cats and had many of her own. The smartest. The most handsome.

One night I returned home to find a message from Amy on my answering machine: I've trapped your cat with turkey. I lured him into the cat carrying case and he's in my hallway, I can't bring him into my loft because of the other cats. Call me as soon as you get home, no matter what time it is.

I called her and went right over. In the hall Amy opened a large cat carrying case—she had several that were big enough to take two or more cats in case of fire. A skinny black-and-white cat with a pink nose and long face emerged. He was terrified, dirty, and scrawny, and he was ugly. Anyway I thought he was ugly, and I don't like cats with pink noses, but there Amy was, standing next to me, and she thought he was handsome. I couldn't say anything. We were in a sense both trapped in a sort of arranged marriage. I told Amy I liked him. He became my cat. I named him Boots because of his best feature, his white paws.

Amy says that it didn't happen this way. She says, first, she brought me to the car under which Boots lived, to view him, and then, when he came out, terrified, scrawny, and dirty, and in my eyes ugly, I was unenthusiastic. But this, Amy explains now, did not deter her; that is, she knew I didn't want Boots, but she trapped him anyway.

•

Boots and I reached my loft, or office. I was living on the six-teenth floor of an office building on John Street. We residentials were illegal tenants, sharing the building strangely with jewelers and other businesses forced to tolerate us. As soon as I opened the cat carrying case, Boots jumped out and ran crazily around the room until he found a hiding place. He disappeared for at least a week. I put food out and left the room, and when I returned, it would have been eaten, but I never saw him. It was as if he weren't there. I hated him but he was my cat.

It was the end of summer. I was working at a job that I also hated. As I was addressing envelopes for a bulk mailing, I realized with a tremendous shock that I had left my windows open, wide open, and that Boots, the cat I hated and had never even petted, that Boots might leap out and fall sixteen stories and land splat on the street, and die. And it would be my fault. Melancholic, I began to think about Boots, what a nice cat he was, how scared he was and what a terrible person I was, so unfeeling, ruled by an aesthetic that excluded pink noses and so on. I thought I would die until I returned home. Finally, breathlessly, I did. I looked out the windows and down and I looked all around the room and even behind the refrigerator. There he was. My Boots, alive. How I loved him. He didn't become a lap cat or even an affectionate an-imal, but he started to come around, and when David, a musician, moved in with me, Boots took to him.

David says that I did not find Boots immediately. He says that I arrived home in a panic, and when I couldn't find Boots any-where, I telephoned Amy. She advised me to move the refrigera-tor. And there he was.

•

Boots liked David, who was and is much more patient than I. David taught him how to play, for instance. Life went on, and Boots began to sleep under the covers next to David, which for a cat shows trust. Boots loved David; I don't think he ever forgave me for my initial lack of interest.

There were many reasons he might have had for not forgiving me. One night I came home drunk. I don't actually remember doing it, but I found another black-and-white cat on the street, picked him up, carried him home, and he terrorized Boots. By the time David returned—which was and is usually late, musician time—I was asleep, dead to everything. The cats were engaged in territorial combat, and they kept David up all night. It must have been pretty strange for David, two black-and-white cats where there had been just one, mirror images screaming and racing around the apartment. We gave the cat away the next day and I don't remember exactly how or to whom.

David says that he did not stay up all night. He says he woke me right away and forced me to take the other cat downstairs, to the street, where I'd found it.

Sheila lived on the sixteenth floor, too—she had a cat named Ocean—and we were making a film together. After five years, we were finally editing the film. By then Sheila had moved away and David and I had also moved, with Boots, to East Tenth Street. The first night in our new apartment Boots was so terrified that he didn't come out from under the blankets. He also didn't move for the next day or two. He stayed absolutely still while the neighbors downstairs yelled murderously at each other.

Boots adjusted gradually to his new home. The more I think

about him, the more I realize how insecure and disturbed he was. Which makes the story I'm telling even more heartbreaking and me even more horrible. But I'll go on.

Sheila and I were editing our movie in an office on John Street, where we'd once lived, and one day, before starting to work, we went to Chinatown for dim sum. Leaving the restaurant, we encountered a black-and-white cat who came out from under a parked car and followed us. He was so short and stocky, he looked no more than ten months old, a kitten, I thought. Sheila said we had to rescue him. She grabbed the cat, which was easy—he didn't resist, he wanted to go with us—and carried him wrapped in her jacket all the way back to the editing room. Once we were there and settled into our editing positions, Sheila at the controls, me behind her in another chair, the cat settled into his position on my lap. He was more than a lap cat, he was a rug, since he didn't so much sit on my lap as cling to it.

I knew I had to have him and so I went home that night and began telling David about the new cat and how adorable he was and how we had to have him and how Boots would one day adapt to him and how he would like a friend and how we couldn't put him back on the street, how cruel that was, and how I loved him. David was adamant. No, never, one cat, that's all, not another cat, you can't do this to Boots. I already knew Boots didn't want a companion since he didn't like company, and scarcely wanted to be with us—or with me, anyway.

I had to have the new cat. Every night, after working in the editing room where the little stocky fellow was alternately loving and angry, but always clinging and needy, I pleaded with David. I did this for a month until David, enervated and exhausted with saying no, reluctantly agreed. He resigned himself to it, but he was, and remained, against the idea. It was greater than stubbornness. David identified with Boots. It was as if I were bringing a new man, a lover, into our home. This made David and Boots even closer.

David says he never agreed. He says that his music workshop teacher died around this time and he was depressed, in mourning. He says I took advantage of his weakness.

I brought the new cat home and named him Tuba after the latest instrument David was playing. I suppose I was hoping to inveigle the cat Tuba into David's musician heart just through its name, a cheap shot that did not melt David. He viewed Tuba as an interloper and a threat, to Boots and to himself. I was the engineer, the agent, of this destruction; I was breaking up our home and staying in it. If she could do this, I felt David felt, she could do anything. David paid even more attention to Boots to compensate for my sin. He hardly even looked at Tuba and almost never petted him.

The most important thing, though, was how Boots reacted to and treated Tuba, how they got along. They fought, of course, all cats fight with each other initially. And although Boots was furious, attacking, and ferocious, Tuba, from the very beginning, was imperturbable, indifferent, and fearless. Tuba's ears were notched, marked by many battles; he had a hairless scar on his thigh from a car accident or a devastating and calamitous catfight. He was, let's say, streetwise and cocky. Tuba did not seem to have any worries about Boots, the older, much bigger cat whose territory he was invading. This must have further disheartened Boots, who was, as I've already described, insecure, paranoid, and long-suffering.

On Tuba's first night with us, Boots slept, as usual, under the covers next to David. I awoke to discover Tuba sleeping snuggled into the crook of my arm, with his head on my shoulder. From the start, Tuba wasn't afraid to be on the bed even though it was Boots's place. In cat parlance, I believe we humans were to Boots the dominant cats, especially since we provided food for him, but Tuba was neither wary of us nor concerned about Boots. He assumed his place immediately. After a while, Tuba liked to sleep on top of Boots as he lay under the covers. What Boots made of that I don't know. He may have been indignant.

Tuba annoyed Boots. The younger cat wanted to play with him and liked to tease him. No matter how many times Boots let Tuba know he wasn't interested, that he didn't like him or want to play, Tuba insisted. He was unstoppable. Jauntily, insouciantly, Tuba always came back for more. Unlike Boots, Tuba is sure of himself. Overall, Boots was, I think, immune to Tuba's charm.

Four years passed. Boots was becoming stranger and stranger; I now know this in retrospect. It's that imperceptible thing, like the slits in walls cats can squeeze through, how you can live with someone, a friend, a lover, a cat, and not recognize, because they're so close, or that's what one tells oneself, because one has a stake in not knowing, most likely, not recognize what's happening to that cat, that lover, that friend.

More and more, strange noises disturbed Boots. Increasingly, strangers coming into the house angered him. Everything upset him. I didn't put it all, pull it all, together. There were incidents that seemed isolated, at first. My friend Diane came over to give me a shiatsu massage; Boots went for her legs. She was shaken. I played it down. Boots even went for David's legs once, but not badly. I became wary about having friends over because I didn't know what Boots would do. (It's a strange worry: Should I ask so-and-so over; what if Boots attacks?) Incidents were building one on top of the other, but then Boots would be fine for days on end. So I'd push away the bad event, already a memory, and decide it was an anomaly after all. Then, suddenly, he'd get weird or crazy again. It was like having a mad dog in the house except it was a cat. *Chat lunatique.* Boots was changing for the worse, and life with him was extreme and unpleasant in the extreme, at least for me—he and David had a good relationship still, which was not easy to bear. I didn't know what was happening to Boots, what to name it, or what to do about him, and because I didn't, I tried not to think about it. Boots had his good days.

David reminds me that when his friend Wayne, another musician, visited, Boots jumped up into the cupboard and, from all the many jars and cans, threw down a can of his cat food. Wayne thought Boots was a genius. David led Wayne to believe he did, too.

One Sunday the doorbell rang. It was the upstairs neighbor. She needed something. I walked away to get it but when I walked back, to give it to her, Boots leaped out and dug all his claws into my left calf. He hung on to and clung to my bare leg, with his claws, with an insane ferocity. The neighbor stood and stared as I tore him off me. I watched tissue oozing from the bloody holes dug deep in my leg. All the fur on Boots's body stood out. He seemed double his size. I poured hydrogen peroxide on my calf and found Band-Aids. I had been intending to meet my friend Craig for dinner. I wanted to cancel but Craig wasn't well, had AIDS, and I didn't think I could cancel because of my cat's attacking me. It sounded an unlikely, insignificant, and bizarre excuse.

At the restaurant my calf started to swell and since I tend to imagine the worst, not unlike Boots, I suppose, I was distracted and worried, and also feeling immensely stupid, almost feebleminded. Luckily a doctor Craig knew was in the restaurant and I asked him if I had to get a shot, and he said I didn't, unless it looked very bad the next day. I now can't remember if I went for a shot. I still have small depressions in my calf where Boots's claws dug in, though.

Before Craig died in 1990, he had a cat for about a year. Craig discovered the cat on a rainy, miserable day, lying in a box in a garbage can in front of the brownstone where he lived. Craig wasn't sure if she was dead or not, and he asked me to go downstairs and see if she was still lying there. I carried her from the garbage pail up five flights of stairs to his apartment. She moved, was alive, so I brought her to a vet near Craig, for a checkup and shots. Craig named her Miss Kitty after the woman in *Gunsmoke*.

In the beginning Craig was anxious about whether Miss Kitty was happy or not. I think she was. She rewarded Craig with affection and devotion, spending most of her time lying next to him on his bed. Craig was less lonely because of her. Toward the end he couldn't care for her anymore, and I helped find her a home. That was a sad story, too. Craig never knew it didn't work out exactly as planned, but Miss Kitty at least did find a home, even if it wasn't the intended one.

Now that Boots had attacked me, badly, something had to be done. It was obvious. Boots was watching my every move. The farther from the bed I walked, the more alarmed Boots became. He would follow me, stalk me, his fur sticking out from his body. He'd walk very close to my legs. I was afraid, and to be afraid of a domestic animal is disorienting. First of all, you feel insane being terrified of your pet, and everyone else finds it funny. Even I thought it was funny in a way. Tuba noticed nothing, I think.

I telephoned the vet I trusted—she had discovered what four others had not: Tuba had an obstruction that was causing his constipation, which meant he had to eat baby food mixed with fiber softener for the rest of his life. I described Boots's behavior. She said that some people had had success with a pet therapist, whose number she gave me. I assumed a pet therapist was an animal trainer, a behavior-modification trainer. I made an appointment. Boots behaved himself for days before the appointment and I began to think it was unnecessary. But the doorbell rang at 10:00 a.m. as planned. I went downstairs to let the pet therapist in. She was wearing a yellow slicker and hat, had come on a bike, and was very short, like an elf.

She and I walked the four flights to my door, and when I opened it, Boots assumed an attack position not ten feet from us. He wasn't going to let her in. It was uncanny. He'd never done this before; I'm sure he knew why she was there. For about ten minutes she stood in the doorway, making cutchy-cutchy-coo noises to Bootsy-wootsy. Boots, his fur all fluffed out, was unmoved. She said again and again, He wants to attack. Yes, I said.

David was in the shower; he was leaving for a tour of Germany later that day. Our apartment is a large railroad, and the only room with a door is the bathroom. When the shower water stopped running, the pet therapist said: Get David to distract Boots, to call him, and then have David put him in the bathroom and shut the door. David distracted Boots, put him in the bathroom, shut the door, and she was able to enter our apartment. We sat down at the kitchen table while Boots meowed in the bathroom. David packed.

First the pet therapist instructed me to record on audiotape what was spoken in the session. In addition she asked me to play a tape of Keith Jarrett–like music that she had brought, so that the music would also be recorded as background to her voice. All of this I did.

Then she opened her writing pad and inquired about Boots's history. I was in analysis at the time and not unfamiliar with the kinds of questions she was asking, although, with the putative patient locked in the bathroom, this was irregular. I was impatient but trying hard to take her and the process seriously since this might be Boots's only chance.

I narrated the sad story of Boots's life, where he was born, how Amy fed and then trapped him, that he was paranoid, that I was the one who brought Tuba in, that Boots loved David more than me, and on and on. I kept expecting that soon she would open the bathroom door and do something with Boots, begin to retrain him or talk to him at least. The more I related to her—Boots didn't trust me, I had betrayed him—the more I felt I had destroyed Boots, just as David told me I would. I spoke for about twenty minutes, answering all her questions to the best of my ability. Then she said that she was going to write up her assessment and, while she did, I could read an article about her. It was in *The New Yorker*, a Talk of the Town column. Apparently she'd had some success with a large, unhappy gray cat and appeared to have been taken seriously by several of her clients. By the time I finished reading the favorable, only mildly ironic story, the pet therapist had finished her analysis of Boots.

She looked penetratingly, steadily, into my eyes. Gravely she explained that Boots was suffering from "kitten deprivation syndrome." Then she gave me instructions. I was to play the tape of her voice for Boots three times a day, to calm him. Since Boots loved David, she asked if David would say something to Boots on the tape, a message Boots could listen to so that he would know David was coming back. David was still packing, dressed in his terry cloth robe; I brought him to his studio area, where she asked him to record his personal message to Boots. I believe he said, with an aggrieved smile: Hey, Boots, I'll see you later, man. She wanted me to call her in a few days. Then she left. But before she left I paid her. Eighty dollars. Everyone always wants to know that. To me that was insignificant, the least of it. I telephoned the vet and complained. I never thought that when the vet said "pet therapist," she meant that. The vet suggested Valium and having Boots's front claws removed. I agreed. The alternative was worse.

Sometime after that, Boots went for my legs again and even without his front claws, he ripped the skin. And he received a greeting card from the pet therapist, addressed to "Sir Boots Tillman." The card had a picture of a happy cat on the cover. On the inside, in a scrawl, she wrote her message: "Dear Sir Boots, Don't worry, everything's going to be all right. Signed, Sunny Blue the Wizard."

David left again for a tour of Canada, just a weekend, but I would have to be alone with Boots. Boots and Tuba. Tuba was hardly a comfort when he was one of the reasons Boots hated me.

By the way, during this period of extreme desperation, and out of curiosity as much as anything else, I did once play the pet therapist's tape for Boots, who, of course, ignored it. I also gave him Valium and took some myself.

While David was out of town, late on the Saturday night of a Fourth of July weekend filled with loud bangs and blasts, Boots jumped up onto the kitchen table. All his hair fluffed out and his head rolled from side to side on his neck. His eyes, as big and round as headlights, followed me like radar. It was something like the effect in *The Exorcist* when Linda Blair's head spun around. Boots was bigger than ever. Somehow I found the courage to grab him by the neck, throw him into the bathroom, and close the door. Boots hated the bathroom because that was his room for punishment, for isolation. But I was afraid to sleep with him near me. I thought he might go for my eyes. I'd seen that in a movie.

I awoke in the middle of the night to find Boots sleeping not on the bed beside me but on the floor next to the bed. That was startling. First of all, how had he gotten out of the bathroom?

The night before, I had taken the precaution of bringing his cat carrier down, just in case. I decided to get out of bed, to move very slowly, not to alarm Boots, and walk to it. I wanted to shove Boots into it and keep him there, locked inside, until David came home. As I walked toward the carrier, Boots began stalking me, his fur thickening and fluffing. I grabbed him by the scruff of his neck and stuffed him into the case. I did this very quickly, in one motion, as if I had trained for it. Then, terrified, I telephoned David in Canada and demanded that as soon as he returned he take Boots to the animal hospital, to have him killed. I could write, to have him put to sleep, but *killed* is right. I would keep Boots in his case until then.

The next night, Sunday, David arrived home. It was late. He put his suitcase and bass down and with barely any words between us, he lifted the cat case and left. He was gone about two hours and when he returned, without Boots, I cried. I sobbed, I think. David had held Boots while the doctor injected him. David said Boots's eyes rolled back into his head. He died instantly.

David says it didn't happen this way. He says that he came home early on Sunday morning, but I was out of town, on Long Island for the Fourth of July. He took Boots out of the case and they spent a relaxed and happy day together. When I arrived home late, and saw Boots out of his carrying case, I insisted that David take him, right then and there, to be killed. Murderer, David says now, half-seriously.

Craig died early on the morning of a Fourth of July two years later. My mother wanted me to incorporate all her Griselda stories into my Boots story. I told her I might.

In case I ever forget, there are photographs of Boots and Tuba sitting next to each other. The sun is shining brightly on them, their bodies casting long shadows on the floor. Both cats are looking at the camera, serenely, as if posing for a formal portrait. They seem peaceful, even content. They were known to groom each other on occasion and even to nap next to each other, but they always fought. Boots may have been going senile. He may have had a brain tumor. There are explanations, one can look for and find explanations, but I don't know. I can't explain what happened.

ON THE SMALL ACT OF LEAVING THE HOUSE

I am myself, because I do the same things every day. I do them now, make the bed, a pot of tea. There are things I don't do, never do, things other people do, cook fish, for example. I don't need to know why I don't do them, but often I do know, and this is what makes me.

In a room, I think about what I will do, myself, about others. I remember others, memory includes others, friends lovers sisters father mother ex-friends. Figures in mind, like Kafka, who abjures himself, and the dead, they live with me now.

In a room, I am reading, glancing out of the window, or I am looking at what I am writing. Then I stop. Discouraged, distracted, I am exhausted, lie down, sit up, touch my toes, swing my arms, make a phone call, ignore a call, hear a voice, see a message, answer it, don't, there is plenty of time, too much time. Only time.

In a room, I am restive, restless, and bore myself.

I look at my books, shelves overwhelmed, actually I watch them, I am their guardian. I read this, that, Natalia Ginzburg, Lyndall Gordon on Charlotte Brontë and Virginia Woolf, a book on spies. Books live for me to read, books are alive when they are read, but mostly I fail them, and they rebuke me.

I look for distractions. I look at my cat, my cat is not worried, and I am I.

·

Now, as I did yesterday, and the day before, I shower, dress in my oversize jeans, a loose cotton shirt, then give myself a task, to go outside, and walk. Fresh air is good. I find out the temperature. I will go to the post office.

I pull on a pair of white sticky latex gloves. I carry a bag with a small spray bottle of fluid to vanquish invisible bacteria, because the virus awaits. I walk down three flights of stairs, not holding the handrail, though I fear, and have always feared, tripping and falling down a flight of stairs, breaking my neck. I know I will die this way, if the virus doesn't kill me. Still, I don't hold the handrail.

I reach the street, I walk, watch everyone, create the mandated social distance, and weave a path on the sidewalk. I will keep six feet away, I try to, some people don't, many, children don't. I reach the near-empty post office, and wish I had packages to mail, there are no long lines, when there are always long lines, but I don't have a package, just a letter I slip into a slot in a wall, disappointingly.

I walk to the door, push the door open with my shoulder, it's heavy, when a woman suddenly is close beside me, and breathes on me. I walk away fast, then look back at her. Who is she to endanger me?

She is very old, wearing a misshapen black cloth coat.

Everyone is an enemy in a virtual war.

I look back at the very old woman. She has stopped walking, bent over, maybe catching her breath, and watching me. She is wondering why I am fleeing her. I think, You are not keeping enough distance between us. Do you want to make me sick. Will I make you sick. Are you sick. Now I feel sick, but I am not sick.

I walk home, wary, avoiding humanity, and reach the front door of my building, wipe the doorknob, and wonder if I should post a message to the other tenants: Let us know if you are sick. If you are sick, stay away.

Upstairs, I brush off the soles of my shoes on a rug, unlock the door, carefully take off the gloves, and wonder if they should be washed, can be washed, can be reused, and if I can waste a pair of gloves, or how many will I need. I wash my hands, happy birthday happy birthday, lather up, consoled by the hot water, wonder if there will continue to be running water, wash my hands, happy birthday happy birthday, singing too fast, I think, and wonder who will be saved.

THE SUBSTITUTE

She watched his heart have a small fit under his black T-shirt. Its unsteady rhythm was a bridge between them. Lost in the possibilities he offered her, she studied his thin face, aquiline nose, tobacco-yellow fingers. In the moment, which swallowed her whole, she admired his need to smoke. She wouldn't always, but not being able to stop meant something, now. Certain damage was sexy, a few sinuous scars. He'd be willing, eager maybe, to exist with her in the margins.

She'd set the terms. Ride, nurse on danger, take acceptable or necessary risks. Maybe there'd be one night at a luscious border, where they'd thrum on thrill, ecstatically unsure, or one long day into one long night, when they'd say everything and nothing and basely have their way with each other. She wasn't primitive but had an idea of it—to live for and in her senses. She'd tell him this. Then they'd vanish, disappear without regret. She was astonished at how adolescence malingered in every cell of her mature body.

Helen met Rex on the train. She taught interior design to art students in a small college in a nearby city. He taught painting. She liked it that he sometimes smelled like a painter, which was old-fashioned, though he wasn't; he told her he erased traces of the hand (she liked hands), used acrylics, didn't leave his mark and yet left it, too. Still, tobacco, chemicals, alcohol, a certain raw body odor, all the storied ingredients, reminded her of lofts and studios and herself in them twenty years before, late at night, time dissolving.

Between Rex and her, one look established furtive interest, and with a fleeting, insubstantial communication they betrayed that and themselves. They were intrigued dogs sniffing each other's tempting genitals and asses. Being an animal contented her lately, and she sometimes compared her behavior with wild and domestic ones. Reason, she told an indignant friend with relish, was too great a price to pay daily.

Her imagination was her best feature. It embellished her visible parts, and altogether they concocted longing in Rex. She could see it; she could have him. She couldn't have her analyst. She held Dr. Kaye in her mind, where she frolicked furiously in delayed gratification. But Rex, this man beside her—she could see the hairs on his arms quiver—engaged her fantastic self, an action figure.

Rex's hands fooled with his cigarette pack. Her analyst didn't smoke, at least not with her, and she didn't imagine he smoked at home, with his wife, whose office was next door, she discovered, unwittingly, not ever having considered that the woman in the adjoining office was more than a colleague. Cottage industry, she remarked in her session. Dr. Kaye seemed amused. Maybe because she hadn't been curious about the relationship or because it took her so long to catch on. That meant more than what she said, she supposed.

Rex's hands weren't well shaped, beautiful. If she concentrated on them . . . but she wondered: Would they stir me, anyway. She shut her eyes. She liked talking with her eyes shut, though she couldn't see her analyst's face. Dr. Kaye wore a long tie today. It hung down over his fly and obscured the trouser pouch for his penis.

When she first saw him, she was relieved to find him avuncular, not handsome like her father. Men grew on trees, there were so many of them, they dropped to the ground and rotted, most of them. Dr. Kaye hesitated before speaking. She imagined his face darkening when she said things like that. Whatever, she said and smiled again at the ceiling. I like men. I'm just pulling your leg. She could see the bottoms of his trousers.

When she approached him on the train, Rex had a near-smirk on his lips, just because she was near. She liked his lips, they were lopsided. If he didn't speak, she could imagine his tongue. He might push for something to happen, actually, and that was exciting. Her heart sped up as Rex glanced sideways at her, from under his . . . liquid hazel eyes. She squirmed, happily. Hovering at the edge tantalized her. The heart did race and skip; it fibrillated, her mother had died of that. What do you feel about your mother now? Dr. Kaye asked. But aren't you my mother now?

They flirted, she and Rex, the new, new man with a dog's name. Did it matter what he looked like naked? They hadn't lied to each other. Unless by omission. But then their moments were lived by omission. Looking at him staring out the window, as if he were thinking of things other than her, she started a sentence, then let the next word slide back into her mouth like a sucking candy. Rex held his breath. She blushed. This was really too precious to consummate.

Dr. Kaye seemed involved in the idea. He had shaved closely that morning, and his aftershave came to her in tart waves. She inhaled him. She—Ms. Vaughn, to him—weighed whether she would tell him anything about Rex, a little, or everything. With Rex, she wasn't under any agreement. She measured her words for herself and for him, and she told him just enough. He was the libertine lover, Dr. Kaye the demanding one. With him, she drew out her tales, like Scheherazade.

First, Dr. Kaye, she offered, her eyes on the ceiling, it was the way he looked at me, he was gobbling me up, taking me inside him. I liked that. Why did I like that? Because I hate myself, you know that. Then she laughed. Later, she went on, I pretended I didn't see him staring at me. Then I stopped pretending. In her next session, she continued: He wanted to take my hand, because his finger fluttered over my wrist, and his unwillingness, no, inability, I don't know about will, I had a boyfriend named Will, he was impotent, did I tell you? His reluctance made me . . . wet. She sat up once and stared at Dr. Kaye, daring him. But he was well trained, an obedient dog, and he listened neatly.

Rex was sloppy with heat. Their unstable hearts could be a gift to Dr. Kaye. Or a substitute, for a substitute. She trembled, bringing their story—hers—to Dr. Kaye in installments, four times a week. It was better than a good dream, whose heady vapors were similar to her ambiguous, unlived relationships. Not falling was better, she explained to Dr. Kaye; having what they wanted was ordinary and would destroy them or be nothing, not falling, not losing, not dying was better. Why do you think that? he asked. This nothing that was almost everything gave her hope. Illusion was truth in a different guise, true in another dimension. Dr. Kaye wanted to know what she felt about Rex. I don't know— we're borderline characters, she said. Liminal, like you and me.

And, she went on, her hands folded on her stomach, he and I went into the toilet . . . of the train . . . and fooled around. She laughed. I was in a train crash once . . . but the toilet smelled . . . like your aftershave, she thought, but didn't say. Say everything, say everything impossible.

Looking at Rex reading a book, his skin flushed, overheated in tiny red florets, Helen wondered when the romance would become misshapen. Her need could flaunt itself. She wanted that,

really, and trusted to her strangeness and his eccentricity for its
acceptance. Or, lust could be checked like excess baggage at the
door. They'd have a cerebral affair.

But their near-accidental meetings sweetened her days and
nights. They were sweeter even than chocolate melting in her
mouth. Dark chocolate helped her sleep. She had a strange metabolism. How could she sleep—Rex was the latest hero who had
come to save her, to fight for her. If he didn't play on her playground, with her rules, he was less safe than Dr. Kaye. But Rex
was as smart, almost, as she was; he knew how to entice her. She
might go further than she planned.

Dr. Kaye's couch was a deep red, nearly purple, she noted
more than once. Lying on it, Helen told him she liked Rex more
than him. She hoped for an unguarded response. Why is that?
he asked, somberly. Because he delivers, like the pizza man—
remember the one who got murdered, some boys did it. They
were bored, they didn't know what to do with themselves, so they
ordered a pizza and killed the guy who brought it. The poor guy.
Everyone wants to be excited. Don't you? She heard Dr. Kaye's
weight shift in his chair. So, she went on, Rex told me I'm beautiful, amazing, and I don't believe him, and it reminded me of when
Charles—that lawyer I was doing some work for—said, out of
nowhere, I was, and then that his wife and baby were going away,
and would I spend the week with him, and it would be over when
his wife came back—we were walking in Central Park—and I
said no, and I never saw him again.

One night, Rex and she took the train home together. When
they arrived at Grand Central, they decided to have a drink, for
the first time. The station, its ceiling a starry night sky, had been
restored to its former grandeur, and Helen felt that way, too. In
a commuter bar, they did MTV humpy dancing, wet-kissed, put

their hands on each other, and got thrown out. Lust was messy, gaudy. Neverneverland, never was better, if she could convince Rex. How hot is cool? they repeated to each other, after their bar imbroglio.

Helen liked waiting, wanting, and being wanted more. It's all so typical, she told Dr. Kaye, and he wanted her to go on. She felt him hanging on her words. Tell me more, he said. The bar was dark, of course, crowded, Rex's eyes were smoky, and everything in him was concentrated in them, they were like headlights, he'd been in a car accident once and showed me his scar, at his neck, and then I kissed him there, and I told him about my brother's suicide, and about you, and he was jealous, he doesn't want me to talk about him, us, he thinks it'll destroy the magic, probably . . . stupid . . . it is magic . . . and he wanted me then, and there . . . but she thought: Never with Rex, never give myself, just give this to you, my doctor. She announced, suddenly: I won't squander anything anymore.

The urge to give herself was weirdly compelling, written into her like the ridiculous, implausible vows in a marriage contract. Dr. Kaye might feel differently about marriage, or other things, but he wouldn't tell her. He contained himself astutely and grew fuller, fatter. He looked larger every week. The mystery was that he was always available for their time-bound encounters, in which thwarted love was still love. It was what you did with your limits that mattered. She imagined she interested him.

Listening to her stories, Dr. Kaye encouraged her, and she felt alive. She could do with her body what she wanted, everyone knew that; the body was just a fleshy vehicle of consequences. Her mind was virtual—free, even, to make false separations. She could lie to herself, to him; she believed in what she said, whatever it was. So did he. To Dr. Kaye, there was truth in fantasy.

Her half lies and contradictions were really inconsequential to anyone but herself. He might admit that.

But the next day, on the train, Rex pressed her silently. His thin face was as sharp as a steak knife. He wouldn't give her what she wanted: he didn't look at her with greedy passion. There was a little death around the corner, waiting for her. She had to give him something, feed his fire or lose it and him.

So she would visit his studio, see his work, she might succumb, Helen informed her analyst. She described how she'd enter his place and be overwhelmed by sensations that had nothing to do with the present. In another time, with another man, with other men, this had happened before, so her senses would awaken to colors, smells, and sounds that were familiar. Soon she would be naked with him on a rough wool blanket thrown hastily over a cot. Her skin would be irritated by the wool, and she would discover his body and find it wonderful or not. He would devour her. He would say, I've never felt this way before. Or, you make me feel insane. She wouldn't like his work and would feel herself moving away from him. Already seen, it was in a way obscene, and ordinary. She calmly explained what shouldn't be seen, and why, and, as she did, found an old cave to enter.

Dr. Kaye didn't seem to appreciate her reluctance. Or if he did, in his subtle way he appeared to want her to have the experience, anyway. She knew she would go, then, to Rex's studio, and announced on the train that she'd be there Saturday night—date night, Rex said. He looked at her again, that way. But she knew it would hasten the end, like a death sentence for promise. Recently, Helen had awaited Timothy McVeigh's execution with terror, but it had come and gone. No one mentioned him anymore. Others were being killed—just a few injections, put them to sleep, stop their breathing, and it's done, they're gone. Things die so easily, she said. Then she listened to Dr. Kaye breathe.

Saturday night Helen rang the bell on Rex's Williamsburg studio. All around her, singles and couples wandered on a mission to have fun. Soon they'd go home, and the streets would be empty. Rex greeted her with a drink—a mojito—that he knew she loved. His studio was bare, except for his work and books, even austere, and it was clean. The sweet, thick rum numbed her, and she prepared for the worst and the best. There was no in-between.

His paintings were, in a way, pictures of pictures. Unexpectedly, she responded to them, because they appreciated the distance between things. Then, without much talk, they had sex. She wasn't sure why, but resisting was harder. Rex adored her, her body, he was nimble and smelled like wet sand. He came, finally, but she didn't want to or couldn't. She held something back. Rex was bothered, and her head felt as if it had split apart. But it didn't matter in some way she couldn't explain to Dr. Kaye. She heard him move in his chair. She worried that he wasn't interested. Maybe her stories exhausted him. Rex called her every day. She wondered if she should find another man, one she couldn't have.

A Simple Idea

This happened a long time ago. My best friend was in Los
Angeles, and she and I talked on the phone a lot. I urged her
to move to New York, and finally she did. She drove cross-
country, and when she arrived, she was told she didn't have to
worry about the $10,000 in California parking tickets she had
on her car. There was no reciprocity between the two states,
she was told, so there was no way her car's outlaw status would
be discovered in New York. The guy who told her said he was
a cop. They met in a bar, then they had sex. Anyway, I think
they did.

My friend started accumulating NYC tickets. Blithely, for
a while. She shoved the tickets into the glove compartment. I
suppose people kept gloves in those compartments at one time.
When there was no room left, she threw them on the floor of
her car. Then she decided she'd better find a parking lot. But she
didn't want to pay hundreds of dollars for a space.

One day she noticed a parking lot near her house barred from
entry by a heavy chain and lock. A week later she noticed a
man walking to the lot. He used a key to unlock the gate. She
got up her nerve and asked him if she could park there if she
gave him some money. Would he make her a key? He said he'd
think about it. The next day he telephoned her and said okay. So
every month my friend handed the man fifty dollars in a white

business envelope. It was illegal, but she wasn't getting tickets from the city and throwing them on the floor of her car.

She was relatively happy parking in the lot, relieved anyway, because there was one less thing to worry about. But after a while she thought some of the other drivers—men going to work in the building attached to the lot—were looking at her weirdly, staring at her and her car. Some seemed menacing, she told me. But then she was paranoid. She knew that, so she decided not to act on her suspicions.

Time passed. Time always passes.

One afternoon my friend received a call from a man who identified himself as a cop. He said, Hello, and used her first name, Sandra, and asked her sternly:

—Are you parking illegally, Sandra, because if you are, and you don't remove your car from the lot right now—I'm giving you ten minutes—I'll have to arrest you.

My friend hung up, threw on her coat, ran out the door to the lot, and drove her car far away. Then she phoned me and told me what happened. She was terrified. She thought the cop might show up and arrest her at any moment, she thought she'd be taken to jail.

—That was no cop, I said.

—How do you know? she asked.

—A cop wouldn't phone you and give you a warning, I answered. But I was worried that I might be wrong, and that she might be arrested.

—And he's not going to say he's going to give you a second chance, because you don't get second chances if you're doing something illegal and they find out, unless they're corrupt, and he wouldn't say, I'm a cop. He'd give his name and rank or something.

My friend listened, annoyed that I was calm, and she wasn't satisfied or convinced. She thought she might be under surveillance and would be busted later. She owed thousands of dollars in tickets in two states. It might be a sting operation, something convoluted. I had to convince her she was not in danger of going to jail. I told her I had an idea and hung up.

It was simple. I'd call a precinct and ask the desk cop how a cop would identify himself over the phone. I'd learn the protocol, how cops wouldn't do what that so-called cop had done, allay my friend's fears, and also show her I was taking her anxiety seriously.

I looked up precincts in the telephone book and chose one in the West Village, where I thought they'd be used to handling unusual questions.

—Tenth Precinct, Sergeant Molloy, the desk cop said.

—Hi, I have a question, I said.

—Yeah.

—How do police identify themselves over the phone?

—What do you mean? Molloy asked.

—If a cop calls you, what does he say?

—What do you mean, what does he say?

—I mean, how does he say he's a policeman? What's the official way to do it? The desk cop was silent for a few seconds.

—A cop called you. What'd he say? What'd he want?

—He didn't call me, he called a friend.

—What did he say to your friend?

I couldn't hang up, because I wouldn't get the information I wanted. If I hung up, Molloy could have the call traced. I'd be in trouble for making harassing calls to precincts, which would be extremely ironic.

—He said to her . . . he said, Hello, I'm the police.

—Yeah. Then what?

—And then, then he said . . .

I didn't want to tell him the story, give my friend's real name, tell him about her tickets in two states, and her car being parked illegally, and her bribing the guy in the corporate lot. But I had to give him some sense of the situation in order to get the information I needed.

—He said to her, Hi, Diana. Hi, I'm the police. Then he said, he said, Diana . . . Diana . . . have you done anything wrong lately?

There was a very long silence.

—Have you done anything wrong lately? Molloy repeated.

It was weird coming from a cop's mouth. He gathered his thoughts, while I remained breathlessly quiet.

—A police officer wouldn't say that, Molloy answered soberly. A police officer wouldn't say that.

—He wouldn't, I repeated, just as gravely.

The cop thought again, for a longer time.

—Listen, I want you to let me know if he ever calls your friend again. Because a cop shouldn't do that . . . He trailed off.

—That guy's impersonating an officer.

—Oh, yeah. I'm sure he won't . . . he probably won't call her again. But if he does, I'll phone you immediately, I promise.

—You do that, Molloy said.

—I will. Thanks, I said.

—Yeah, he said. Maybe Molloy didn't believe any of this, but he did the whole thing straight.

I called my friend, and we stayed on the phone for hours, laughing about how crazy I was to say "Have you done anything wrong lately?" to a cop, with all its implications, and we laughed about her racing out of her house to the corporate lot, jumping into her car, and driving off in search of a legal parking space as if she were being chased by the devil.

Maybe the devil was chasing her and me. Because we laughed off and on for about a year more, and then we had less to laugh about, and then nothing to laugh about. I don't know, we grew to distrust each other, and stopped being friends. Maybe Molloy laughed later.

TINY STRUGGLES

He managed the walk to Main Street, three blocks, two long avenues, and didn't worry about how he looked—a big whitehead poking along the sidewalk. Things were getting better, not that Tiny knew the absolute right moment to leave his house, because out the back door his garden merged with theirs, and the neighbors might be around. Summer weekends, everyone hung out.

He could leave through the front door, but that resembled a first entrance in the middle of the second act, which was why, finally, Tiny quit acting. That excruciating second, when his presence onstage was unmistakably felt, disarmed him nightly. Even appearing in the soaps got to him, but he'd made a bundle. Tiny's new existence in the country was awkward, remarkable— remarked upon by those who knew him—exciting, and maybe permanent. He'd figure it out as he went along.

—It's not really the country, the row houses on your block, they're city structures, one friend said.

—You're in the hood, another said. The ghetto.

—It's a mixed nabe, Tiny said, imitating a nightly news guy, the face of the real America.

Not much separated the houses, a few feet, low fences, honeysuckle, ugly weed trees no one bothered to dig up. To build high fences or plant overbearing trees could appear unneighborly or sinister. Inside his private domain, anything was possible, he could do anything, but he didn't, no one does, or few do, anyway. No one used all his freedom, and, wherever Tiny was, nameless others entered his mental space.

Upon awaking, Tiny pulled the curtains half-open, for some natural light and to show the neighbors he had nothing to hide. To his left, the neighbors were also city converts, professional people, architect and designer, a Black and white couple, Nicholas and Arthur, who kept to themselves and had friends over occasionally. Tiny was invited when he first arrived, but informally they agreed to preserve a sense of the city and be neighbors who borrow a figurative cup of sugar.

Most days and nights, the street was dead quiet. A few shouts and bursts of loud music, nothing much. The other night, or early morning, was anomalous, because Tiny woke up to cries and yowls that wolves make when their cubs are killed or kidnapped. An obese white woman, who sat on her ruined porch every warm day and night, was wailing to a disheveled, skinny man, You're not leaving are youYourenot leaving me are youYou're not walking out are youYou're not you can't leave me. Tiny squirmed below the window ledge. No one had ever yowled at him, he found it kind of magnificent—the passion. Nothing like that, unless he counted the stinging email rebukes from his older sister, Georgina.

Tiny, On the phone, you acted like everything was fine and dandy between us, and I'm supposed to pretend the way you do. You feel your behavior doesn't call for an apology. But when your friend's dog bit me on the calf, and their dog went RIGHT FOR ME, instead of comforting me, you said the bite was nothing, Look, you're not bleeding, you said. Nothing, no compassion. How would you like it if . . .

•

Family. Tiny couldn't escape them, even now, three hours away from them and their city. He was the baby and the tallest, perversely nicknamed Tiny. His given name was Theodore, after the fat Roosevelt, which his father thought was funny. His father had bought the farm six years ago, his mother was doing the big fade, and before he moved away, Tiny had split with his girlfriend of six years. His twin brothers were jerks, and his sister was angry at him for being born.

It was a new life he wanted.

Some stores in town were easier to enter than others. Some owners or managers welcomed him, some greasily, others held back, restraint or contempt, he couldn't judge. He was no judge, that was his father. This afternoon, the pale, lithe woman in the cheese store, her blond hair screwed into a furious top knot, seemed disagreeable. Tiny intuited that Top Knot despised selling jams and cage-free eggs from happy chickens. This is where I end up, she's thinking, slicing a chunk of aged Gouda for . . . She couldn't find words for him, Tiny decided—what and who was this tall, fortysomething, pale-skinned, dark-haired man in faded jeans and an unironed shirt, untucked. He watched her, fascinated.

It was an up-and-coming town, at least it had been up-and-coming when he bought the house; now people were saying it would come back. The town will come back, you'll see, it always comes back. The town thrived and failed, an organism dependent on visitors who savored its Victorian houses and country-style stores selling thick bars of French soap and 1920s dish towels laundered in bleach. Now Tiny was moving through a fastidious space. He picked up a bath-size fluffy white towel, which could wrap a small car, and fingered its thick pile. He hovered over an ample bunch of dried lavender, whose scent offered instant sanity.

Mostly, the native population was out of work, Blacks, whites, integrated and equally downhearted. The town-kids' future didn't seem unknowable: taxes low, public schools abysmal. More and more stray cats, who would never be neutered, screamed in Tiny's garden, because he liked cats and fed them scraps when no one was around. His sister always said, "You make your own messes." He couldn't walk on the grass without sliding in shit.

Main Street stretched on and on against real time. Tiny strolled toward an unhurried café or good bar; he wasn't hunting, exactly. The best bar in town served a mixed-up-everything clientele, and weekend nights drew a big crowd from surrounding towns smaller than his. His town. Our town. Above the bar's spotted mirror, to the left, Tiny read reassuring words on an old-fashioned blackboard: "Use PARA- word in sentence. Your sentence wins— Martini on the house!"

That Victorian she couldn't afford—paradise.

He advertised in the local paper for a paramour. His bad!

Tiny usually needed an incentive and took a seat at the long, white marble-topped bar. The only person he'd ever met, down one end, was a solitary, bookish man who dressed up as James Joyce, so Tiny forgot his name because he unfailingly thought: James Joyce.

Paradox, paralysis, paranoia, parasite, parataxis, parallel, parachute.

Near Mr. Joyce, ignoring him, an exasperated fiftyish man exclaimed to his group, "It's not the fine arts, it's the construction business." Down the other end of the long bar, a svelte woman about his age peered at him. He drank his vodka tonic. She peered again. Tiny smiled. She peered again, anxiously. He walked over to be friendly.

—Do we know each other? Tiny said.

—I'm sorry, I thought you were someone else. I'm not wearing my glasses.

—But I am someone else, Tiny said.

She looked perplexed, not amused, so he tipped an invisible hat and returned to his end of the bar. He called to the red-faced buxom bartender, "Another, please?" And to restore his cool, Tiny murmured, intimately, "No good deed goes unpunished, no bad deed goes unpublished."

This is a wit's end, he told himself.

Life's just full of niggling compromise. Tiny wouldn't sweat the small things, that was city life. Walking home along the dreamy back alley, Tiny fed his fantasies, starting one, replaying it, she's on her knees, starting another, staring at the huge blue sky, sun still a flaming red ball. The new version fails to start, he can't get it started, but how can he fail at his own fantasy? Defeated, momentarily, Tiny remembered his college friend Tom, who looked upset one morning in the cafeteria. Tom habitually dreamed he was flying. "Last night," Tom said, "I couldn't get liftoff."

His neighbors Nick and Arthur's lights were on, three more cars in their parking space meant guests, while his other next-door neighbors—renters not owners—sat at a long, wooden picnic table, eating corn and hot dogs. Barbecue smells, country life, the sweet life.

—Nice evening, folks, how're you doing?

—Just great, how're you doing? one of the men said.

Five adults and one child lived upstairs in the two-story house: two stringy white guys, one hefty Black woman, one scrawny white one, all in their thirties; a lean, light-skinned Black woman, twenty maybe, and a ten-year-old white boy. Tiny had heard the boy call both men "Daddy." He couldn't tell them apart, either. The family must view him as a weirdo, the weirdo in their midst. The scrawny white woman took her time responding, as if on delay. "We're fine, thank you . . . and how are you?" She had a singsong voice, emphasizing "and how." He dubbed her the ironic one. The lean young woman appeared to be sulking, her thin face drawn with cheekbones like flying buttresses. She didn't greet him at all, she scarcely raised her head, but he wished she had. Her name was Chelsea, her black cat, Satan. Unfixed, he was sure.

The old sun started its descent, and Tiny was aloft on his terrace, squinting at the newspaper, and watching the birds on his lawn—sparrows—peck away at masses of birdseed he'd thrown into a superlarge metal salad bowl. The birdseed company advertised its seed as irresistible to colorful birds—he'd had two blue jays, one red-breasted robin. Hundreds of sparrows arrived the same time every morning and evening, positioned on electric wires, waiting, a scene from *The Birds*, until he refilled the bowl. No one else fed the birds the way he did.

This was great, this was better than living in the country, he reckoned—it was sort of a city in the country, with benefits like gardening, feeding birds and stray cats, renewal along with the seasons, the chance to be natural and free, because things were different here.

Tiny fixed himself another vodka. Everyone spied on their neighbors, and why he cared about getting caught or being nosy, he didn't know, except it conformed with his being citified, a veneer to shed. Tonight, a large white-frosted cake appeared, ablaze with candles—the birthday of the scrawny woman, thirty-five. The neighbors to their right, who kept a beautiful garden, were barbecuing in tandem; by outward appearances, they were white, one father, one mother, two sons, the traditional family. The hulking blond boys, close in age, nineteen or twenty, stood at the fence, flirting with Chelsea. She leaned in, they leaned in, three bodies pressed against the flimsy barrier. He wondered which one she would choose. Not him, that was certain.

Tiny followed the progress of Chelsea's romance like a sitcom, a week of daytime backyard flirting and fence-leaning, the brothers in baggy shorts, she in her polka-dot bikini, then nighttime hanging out, until one evening Tiny spotted Chelsea in the other backyard, at their dinner table, while her family, eating their dinner, glanced at that other backyard, ruefully, and he thought, like a soothsayer, there's going to be trouble.

It didn't take long, Chelsea selected the bigger of the two. Tiny tried to gainsay why, because they both appeared to be good-natured hunks. Maybe one had a great personality or was a better kisser. Chelsea and the boyfriend pitched a tent for two in his family's backyard, and every night, they'd disappear, and every morning, she'd scoot back to her house, or, if she'd gone home to sleep, Tiny would awaken to the boy's calling her name, sort of mournfully, Chel-seeeee. She'd emerge from her house, sleep-deprived and sleepy-faced, and glowing. Chel-seeeee. Chelsea began saying hello to him, too. And then the boys did. She was blooming in her new world, from the looks of it a better one.

The two families didn't actually acknowledge each other. They weren't feuding but there was a gulf between them. Like families separated by the Berlin Wall, some in the East, some the West, unable to communicate, raised so differently. Satan regularly jumped over the fence into the wrong yard, and Chelsea carried him back, not saying a word, returning quickly to the other side. More and more, the scrawny woman turned her back to the girl, who was or wasn't her daughter, as Chelsea raced to that other backyard. And the scrawny woman started leaving garbage near Tiny's side of the fence, not taking it to the dump. When it started to stink real bad, he'd talk to her, gently.

The August weather lay heavily on everyone, oppressive as the country's news. Tiny couldn't eat dinner in front of the TV anymore, not at news time; and he couldn't avoid any of it, not by turning on the AC or the TV. Things seeped in. Tiny and his one-way street were at peace, nothing grievous happening, the obese woman sat on her ruined porch like a Buddha, the skinny man coming and going, kids played in the street, and the guys next door became friendlier, by attrition if nothing else.

In October, the weather changed to bright and zesty, plants dying, trees bursting with fall. Tiny's days were okay, a little boring or too good, so he knew it would change, because everything changed—better or worse, there was always change. "You can count on that," his mother used to say before her dementia set in. Tiny would need to find work soon, but maybe he wouldn't be able to. He might fall in love, even with Top Knot. He might win the lottery, but if he won millions, so much he didn't know what to do with it, that would become a burden. Most lottery winners led rotten lives ever after, hounded by relatives, and some killed themselves. He would apologize to his sister and promise her money when she needed it.

The weather turned colder, his first winter in the country.

He bundled into his old, heavy coat, swung his gray wool scarf around his neck, found a tote bag, and opened his front door to the world. He'd walk to Main Street, do his shopping, visit Top Knot, who had her moments. He didn't get far. Chelsea was standing in front of her house, her belongings on the street. Everything, all her clothes and CDs, had been flung out from the second floor. Five big, shapeless mounds. Chelsea, in only a T-shirt and jeans, was gathering up what she could, putting it in black garbage bags, and crying without making a sound. Tiny gathered stuff, too, and set it on the sidewalk. They did that together, silently, until her boyfriend showed up. He embraced Chelsea and looked at Tiny.

—They kicked her out, the boyfriend said.

—Kicked her out, Tiny said.

—Yeah, the shits kicked her out.

—Why? What happened?

—Because she doesn't have a job. None of them got a job, but they kick her out, and she's just eighteen.

—She's jealous, Chelsea said. She's jealous of me.

Tiny knew she was the scrawny blonde.

—Chelsea's got nowhere to go, the boyfriend said.

—Nowhere to go, Tiny said.

The words sounded like stones.

The three stood together, Chelsea bending in toward her boyfriend for protection against the wind. They looked at him intently.

They wanted him to offer her a place to stay for a while, he had a house all to himself. He couldn't. It would turn bad. He just couldn't.

—Jesus, Tiny said, this is really terrible.

—I don't know what I'm going to do, Chelsea said.

—She can't stay with us, me and my brother and her, and my parents, the boyfriend said. It can't happen.

The wind whipped around them, and Tiny drew his scarf up near his mouth. He could pretend to be tone-deaf or blind. He could explain that his mother was coming to live with him. But then it might happen. Stranger things than that happen.

—I'm sorry. I'm really sorry. I wish I could help you. You'll find someplace.

—Yeah, the boyfriend said, social services or something.

—Something's gotta happen, Chelsea said.

—It always does. Something happens. You can count on things to change, Tiny said.

He could see their hope collapse. The three of them stood there, then the two of them looked at each other, maybe for strength, Tiny thought later. Chelsea faced him, purposefully.

—You one of those toxic bachelors, she said.

—Me? What do you mean?

—You know, a fickle dude. A love 'em and leave 'em guy, she said.

—I'm not . . .

—You know, ambiguous, she said.

Ambivalent, she means ambivalent, but he wasn't going there.

—I just like living alone, that's all.

—Everyone has to live with themselves, the boyfriend said.

—Yeah, Chelsea said, you have to live with yourself.

She said it fiercely. Tiny could protest more that he wasn't toxic, but it might be better to let her think he was ambiguous. Toxic Bachelor must be a reality show. He pulled his scarf tighter. It was freezing. She must be freezing, he thought. But she held her head higher.

—I can take care of your cat, he said.

It was a gesture.

—Satan? Chelsea said.

—Sure, I can do that, if you want. I can take care of him for a while. If you want.

Chelsea studied him, her boyfriend studied him. They glanced at each other. It took a stupefyingly long time, and the ball was in her court. It was her call.

—No way, no fucking way, Chelsea said, fiercer now. My cat goes with me.

She and her boyfriend bent down, grabbed some clothes, and carried the stuff toward the alley.

The way Tiny told it to close friends, he'd given her room so she could reject him. He wouldn't ever know what she thought. Chelsea moved the next day. The scrawny woman's garbage stayed there, along with Chelsea's clothes, frozen for a long time. Tiny heard rumors about where Chelsea lived and with whom, but the boyfriend didn't follow after her. That surprised him.

THE UNDIAGNOSED

Boys will be boys /
play with toys /
so be strong with your beast.

      —MICK JAGGER, "Memo from Turner"

I remember that night. The party was in a ballroom, a magnificent rented room—Le Fin de Siècle—and I was supposed to wear a costume. I wore my father's clothes. He was dead, so I came as any dead man or my father's ghost. Hamlet's father's ghost manifested Hamlet's desire; but I didn't imagine my father whispered to me, I didn't imagine a murder had to be avenged.

No one at the party knew what man I was, and, like so much of life, it was only in my head. Costumed, I felt I could not be myself, which had obscure benefits.

The ballroom was decorated with streamers and flowers, tiny incandescent lights trailing the walls, larger globes attached to the high ceiling, then more tiny lights running the length of it. I hated the room's having been rented, as if grandness could be, intimating that all my pleasures were temporary and, worse, for sale.

Small lamps shaped like flames lit the requisite white cloaked tables. The flames twinkled on and off, inflecting the partygoers' faces with unintended seriousness or grotesqueness. They couldn't see themselves, how unholy shadows created other masks on their faces and marked them as tormented or angry. Visible to themselves, they might have been dismayed or thrilled. Some lust after distortion. But the unintended is frightening. It illuminates what schemes never do and becomes more indelible than anything that could have been made up or that people could have made themselves into. Accidents and mistakes, like an end game or a tragic virus, carry eternal consequences.

I am consumed by consequences, layered with them.

There was a long table heavy with food, another with wine, another hard liquor, another dark desserts. By the time I arrived— late, I hadn't wanted to show up—people were sated or acquiescent. Some were loonily high or indifferent; the drugs were available in a ridiculous bathroom. Some masqueraders were nearly rigid, or hoping to feel anything, and some were playing a game of promiscuity called choice.

A man dressed as a fool leaped in front of me and screamed, Are you happy? Another, dressed as a rose, exposed his penis to three men—his penis was a thorn in his side. Four women, parading as witches, laughed hysterically. I dislike women who dress up as witches. They are low minded and unimaginative.

I wiggled uncomfortably inside my father's suit. I didn't want to think of his body. I remembered the long, dark hairs on his forearms, the hairlessness of his upper arms and chest, his hazel, illegible eyes, his uneven, uncontrollable mouth, his penis when he urinated, and dressed as a man, I began thinking about men I'd known, and wondered casually, noticing other costumed miscreants and misfits, if I could remember every one of them who mattered to me, and even those who hadn't and didn't at the time when time was unimportant, and if I could see them in my mind's eye and reckon with their foreign, familiar bodies, their alien, similar lives. I'd been raised as a woman. I didn't feel I was one, and I didn't care that I didn't. I didn't know how men felt, what instantly occurred to them, raised as they were, with other postures imposed and other awarenesses impressed upon them. I watched movies about men, I read books. I had sex with them and hung out with them. I had men friends and enemies. I knew men as plumbers, theorists, hairdressers, scholars, bartenders, teachers, lovers, translators, butchers, artists, carpenters, musicians, landlords, actors, paupers, writers, dentists, shoemakers. (Dentists arouse my sympathy, and I particularly like shoemakers.)

I knew men who had no trouble being men, I knew men who were dubious about being men, I knew men who wanted to be women, I knew men who hated women, and those who relished them like succulent meals, I knew men who loved men, I knew men whose best friends were women, I knew men whose fear of vaginas vanquished them (they couldn't go through tunnels), and men who couldn't piss in men's rooms. I knew men who had sex in subway toilets, men who were celibate, men who hated sports, hated books, had eating problems, who hated life, and I knew men who hated how much they needed women, and others who turned their backs on them. I knew men who were depressed and men who were never unhappy (those blessed few). I knew men who were affectionate, lusty, friendly, remote, stupid, tender, courteous, shallow, sexy, cerebral, bold, cowardly, crude, pretentious, kind, and on and on.

I won't go on.

I couldn't remember them all, there were too many. And dressed as a man especially, I felt I knew nothing about them as men. Men qua men, I mused to myself, watching people dance and eat. I also knew little about women, in the same way, being a flawed one, having rejected or scorned what being a woman supposedly entailed. No child? No man? No food? Anyway, the categories were too general, sweeping in their assumptions, and I resist cultural imperatives and operate inside them.

The door opened, and Clint Eastwood entered. He cast a long, romantic shadow. He was rugged, too, as magnificent and big as the space where he was now temporarily installed like a tower. Not the Martello Tower, not Pisa, Watts, not the Texas School Book Depository in Dealey Plaza, but a tall, lean man, who seemed he would never fall, like the Twin Towers.

I wasn't surprised to see him, I'd been expecting him for years. Sometimes I conjured him after watching one of his movies, and then in dreams I knew him intimately. Dreams, the mind's gifts, can be sweeter than anything reality offers, and they satisfy me more than sex. Or, they are sex.

Usually when I think about someone, he or she eventually turns up. In a train station, in a bookstore, crossing an alley, around a corner, that face presents itself, stamped onto the present like postage. I have sometimes thought, overdue postage.

Now Clint was here. I was happy, maybe relieved.

The way I remember it, I strode, as best I could, awkward in my father's suit, across the floor toward him. I was trying to imitate a man's gait. Do they throw their shoulders forward more than putative women? Clint was engaged in a subdued kind of shoot-out. He couldn't help himself, or the other men couldn't help themselves. Their faces were shot through, anyway, irradiated with alarm and fear; maybe they were just stunned. Clint stood near, and they were dwarfed and dimmed by his cinematic luminosity. Stars do shine, and the men's faces registered that fact, also that Clint had taken the thin cigar from his mouth, after he had rolled it around his lips several times, the way he does in

Sergio Leone movies, which usually means something bad will happen or some decisive move will be made.

(I was, I discovered, in a state of amazement, so close to my hero, when I don't have a hero, almost incoherent, and my suit felt even more uncomfortable.) Clint was rock steady. I thrilled to his stillness, the way he held the world inside him. Silent, contained, he was unsettling as a nature morte. Decisiveness itself is still, like death. And he was, for me, a picture of a man. Maybe the main picture I had in mind against which what were called men were measured, in subtle and obvious ways.

Clint is not like my friend Hamlet. The dear, antagonistic hero acted unmanly, Ophelia and Gertrude growing out of him like branches from a tree. Hamlet had to punish and sever them, or betray his femininity. Their hateful womanishness, their weakness, that baleful susceptibility was only to himself and to other men. Nothing but men.

I thought, suddenly, men must really suffer an awful anxiety of influence. The father's ghost does linger and loom, it must threaten to suffocate them. I noticed some costumed men in the room jockeying for position, and I fit them into this idea.

My neurotic father's suit felt like a prison. But I didn't want to kill him, even if it's the murder I might be forced to commit, later. I could be forced to duel him, when I get around to experiencing my masculinity more fully. I took fencing in college, I remembered.

En garde, ghost.

Look at Clint, I remonstrated to myself, see how he doesn't lean or buckle. But the suit, and a duel, these entrapments didn't fit me. I felt extreme and silly. I wanted to slap my face. Electrifying music heightened all my responses. I was as reactive as a hive. My heart pumped, an ecstatic organ played by Brother Jack McDuff or Jimmy Smith. I needed the soundtrack, a background score, and whatever was playing, whoever the DJ was who moved time along, or kept events in time, I was glad of it. I had lost track.

I took a breath, to steady myself, and shut my eyes. With the beat, I opened them and studied the masqueraders coolly again, especially the men, when I could discern them. It was hard to maintain a distance. Each was dressed as someone he wanted to be or someone he didn't want to be, so he demonstrated a remarkable and aggressive display of self-love or hatred, enacting "I am this," "I am not this." A short, skinny man strutted as a wrestler, a tall, fat one flailed his apron—a rude housewife.

I became a restive, captive character to their ambivalence. I understood it and abhorred it, also, since unrelenting duality infuses everything I do. Every act, too, is against my limits. The body, the first limit. I try to control it, tame it, inflict pain on it, pamper it, release it, wrest it from its history or its shape. I have attempted to abandon it, gorge it, starve it, scar it, mask it, disgrace it, take pride in it, humiliate it, and disown it. But I awoke in it each morning. Still, I didn't envy those who surgically tailored themselves into different bodies. I wouldn't even pierce an ear.

I bet Clint likes his body, I thought, I bet he likes his sharp features, the cool set of his face, I bet he was often embarrassed by how handsome he was. Aging now, he had bravely exposed his flaccid chest, and even so I couldn't forget him as a young man.

The man with no name.

I wasn't his type, not the kind he married or mated with, who looked like the same woman each time, which has a certain economy—men don't have to abandon their mothers, really. But as a man, I thought, maybe he'd like me. I puzzled over this funny notion and wandered away from him.

I like to sit alone, I always have, at parties. I took a seat on a long, crimson, silk couch. Silk doesn't wear well, and it was another sign that the night, and other things, would not last. Dressed as a man, I might incite the notice of disguised strangers who would tell me things I'd never heard and hadn't bargained for. Maybe Clint would come over, if I didn't bother him.

He was glorious across the magnificent, rented ballroom, spotlighted and standing beside a woman dressed up as Andy Warhol—fright wig, shock-white powdered face. Late Warhol. Clint was showing her his boots, and others were clustered around him, hopefully. Now he looked up, with a wry, exultant expression, and in that instant, I caught his eye. Maybe I looked like someone he once knew. He bent down again, showing the group the special stitching and tooling, and then nodded, waved or motioned to me. I returned his nod. I distinctly recall the vertebrae of my neck clicking in anticipation.

Clint strode across the shiny black floor, the way I wished I could have.

Once he was beside me, I didn't know what to say. He was silent, too, but that was characteristic of him.

Finally I told him I was wearing my father's clothes.

You're imposturing your father? he asked.

Sort of.

Sort of? he asked.

My father was a difficult man to know. I'm not sure if men are different from women in any interesting way.

Men want sex, settle for money, comfort, mostly everyone settles. What do you want to know?

Whatever you can tell me, I answered.

Clint told me about his father, his father had once dug a hole in the ground, a large hole, no, a pit, and lived in it, as a protest, for a week. He pissed and shit there—he ate ants. Right in the backyard. His father was an ordinary man, a businessman in a small town. But his life, Clint said, depended on his proving he could do this. It was about his manlihood.

Had it been challenged? I wondered.

Had he been in a war?

Did he want his mother?

Is anyone ordinary?

To Clint, I asked, How did his living in a hole affect you?

Well, he said, I've never really thought about it.

Two Apache dancers—male and female—raced across the floor. The male lifted the female and sent her crashing to the ground. Then the female lifted the male and did the same.

Equal opportunity, Clint remarked.

Both of us stared, and I thought of animals, horses especially, being broken.

Three people of indeterminate sex strolled across the floor, wearing sandwich boards: He-Male, She-Male, E-Male.

It's not a good time to be a man, Clint said, looking at my suit. He turned the collar up and then turned it down.

Being a woman doesn't appeal much, either. Both positions defy me, in any case, I explained.

Clint said he was uncomfortable with prearranged affiliations, and I said, I didn't feel patriotic to a sex. I appreciated the animal in me, I said, but felt I had no nature, certainly no great love of it, so any nature in me was second nature. In all things I just wanted to do what I wanted, without resistance from others, without unnecessary conflict. Life's object was to get as much pleasure as possible or to avoid pain. I took that to heart and let the notion guide me.

We were silent for a bit then, in our own kind of Western, I realized, at least philosophically, and while I pondered my own speech, or outburst, he seemed to chew it over, too.

He told me he hated violence but was also drawn to it.

I told him I loved *Unforgiven.*

He became embarrassed. I wanted to touch his face as if it were a computer screen.

I must be drawn to violence, too, since I enjoy your movies, I went on.

What about *Tightrope?* he asked. The later ones—not the spaghettis . . .

You're not renouncing those, are you?

I don't turn my back on the past, he said.

Only the women? I asked.

Clint looked a little angry then. I worried I'd alienated him. But he just stretched and squinted, his eyes disappearing into thin folds of tanned flesh.

I had to ask him.

Are you afraid to die? I said.

Nope, he said. When your time comes, it comes.

Do you really feel that?

Yes.

Because Westerns are all about death, that's why I asked.

Oh, well, he said, if you put it like that . . . but I'm not.

Unforgiven is about that.

It's about killing, he said.

Death, I said.

We can stop killing, we can't stop death.

Clint astonished me.

In that instant, I felt I was married to him. And that night, while I watched men and women cavort and sulk, flirt and look dejected, though I felt like an observer, the way I usually do, I felt I was looking for something, too, not just at something. With Clint next to me—we sat this way for the rest of the evening, talking and not talking—and in my father's suit, sometimes forgetting I was wearing it, I thought, I don't look like my father, I'm looking for my father. (I didn't say this to Clint.) And when I find him, I'm going to have to slay him, as in days of yore.

I couldn't believe I thought that. Maybe I didn't. I know I'll never find him.

Later, when Clint left me, to return to the adoration of others, or to being himself, whoever that was, if he could ever be himself, what I wanted to do was go to the movies. I wanted to watch his movies, the early ones. I wanted him like that, then and always.

Playing Hurt

Abigail planned on retiring at forty and kidded around with her friends about how she'd better lay her golden eggs fast. But all bearers of wishes and jokes are also serious. In the future, she would be her own benevolent despot, spend what she had accumulated, and indulge herself. Maybe study Chinese or Arabic, certainly Latin, shave her head, if she wanted, because, literally, she would have earned it.

From her desk, Abigail reveled in the Chrysler Building's beautiful austerity, the sun dropping away in its own time. She admired nature's independence. Her Harvard Law School friends wondered why she worked in an investment bank, no adventure, no social meaning, they teased her, but she believed everyone had a right to happiness, and that took money. Mostly her friends came from privileged families and didn't have her special fervor, so, in a crucial way, they didn't get her. But as a scholarship student, Abigail grew up observing them and learned to recognize the secret operations of class and power.

Nathaniel Murphy walked past her glassed-in office. He still had most of his hair, his good looks, he was almost too handsome, though his nose had thickened since she'd first seen his picture when he was twenty-eight. The internet golden boy had grown fleshier, even as his world had shrunk, but there he was in his Armani suit. She could smell his aftershave lotion, vervain probably.

The numbers on the accounts blurred, Abigail pushed her glasses to the bridge of her nose, thrust her face closer to the papers, and self-consciously tugged on her short skirt. He was headed to the vault, distracted or worried, she thought, and he should be. He would soon open a security box, which probably held birth certificates, his parents' wills, some gold, jewelry, certificates. Abigail had helped the elder Mr. Murphy draw up his will; he had left most of his fortune to charitable foundations, but his son's fortune had vanished, along with other dot-commers'.

Nathaniel Murphy stayed in her imagination. His fall had been dramatic, public, and she wondered at his profligacy and hubris. While the sun sank at its own speed, Abigail imagined the younger Murphy's hand hitting the sides of the metal security box. He was in a dark hole, yet everything surrounding him gleamed. He was like a character from a Patricia Highsmith novel, not Ripley, but others whose guilt registered on a human stock market. Abigail felt she had suffered too much to be guilty about anything, but Nathaniel had cost people millions, he'd wasted everything he had from birth and more. Being poor again terrified her, the thought made her sick, but he had no idea what it was like, and, rather than provoking resentment, it added allure to his mystery, even innocence.

The elder Mr. Murphy once revealed that Nate's wife had asked for a divorce right after the crash. He couldn't help him, Nate made terrible choices; he gambled, not invested; he's a playboy, his father confided, with time to kill. He's drinking too much, and the girls sail in and out of his life. She liked Mr. Murphy, who was a gentleman, but she would have protected his son better, guided him. Abigail kept close watch on her own money, talked to her broker daily, and flushed with warmth when, each month, she saw her accounts swell.

A guard closed the vault's massive doors behind Nate. He turned a corner and walked down a hall, where Abigail encountered him. Abigail hadn't planned it, she'd gone to the women's room, and their paths crossed. They had several times before, when they would nod indifferently, but Abigail was never indifferent, she'd admit later. This time she stopped, and he did also.

—I'm sorry about your father, I liked him, Abigail said.

—Thank you, he said. He liked you, too.

She had never noticed how green his brown eyes were, almost olive, then she realized they were just standing, not talking, and she must have been staring into his eyes. She tugged at her short skirt, meaning to return to her office, when he smiled familiarly at her.

—You like it here?

—Sure, I'm here, yes, I do.

—They let you wear short skirts.

—I wear what I want.

Five weeks later, the younger Mr. Murphy moved in.

That first night in a corner of the bar at the Hotel Pierre, Nathaniel kissed her with restrained ardor, and Abigail knew much more inhabited him. He told her about his insecurity because of his father's reputation, she told him her mother cleaned houses, her father couldn't keep a job. But what mattered was being close to him. The next night, he whispered words that infuriated her, yet her breath stopped anyway. He'd been in love with her since he first saw her, his father told him she was the one, and with him her life would be happy—I am happy, she said—he could make her happier, babies, if she wanted, millions of orgasms. I've heard that in hundreds of movies, Abigail said, maybe not the bit about orgasms. After he kissed her without restraint, Abigail lost the sense of where she was. I'm not a movie, Nathaniel muttered into her ear, I'm just a soft touch for you. Curiously, she saw old Mr. Murphy in him.

You're the soft touch, her friends insisted, you're nuts, he'll screw you. They'd never seen Abigail like this, she had never felt like this. You'll wash his socks at night, her best friend quipped, but nothing swayed Abigail. Against her exasperated friends' advice, Nate moved in.

They were happy. What her friends hadn't realized was that Nate was crazy about Abigail, devoted. He lived up to his promises, she told them, he quit drinking completely, and every week he took meetings with smart entrepreneurs like himself. She knew both his desire and his drive, they both loved the game of business, and she adored him, he made her swoon. With her, she knew he'd succeed, and Nate told her he'd thrown away his little black book. But Nate had seen that in too many corny movies, so actually it went into the security box, a document of his bachelorhood, Abigail wouldn't mind.

They married in a mauve room in the Hotel Pierre, where her friends and his celebrated, his dotty mother in attendance, Abigail's family discreetly absent. A few days before, almost as a joke, they had signed a prenuptial agreement. It didn't mean anything; she was a lawyer, that was all. The newlyweds were delirious. She felt sexy and content with him, he felt like a man again.

Abigail's clients loved her, she helped them, a few lost big, there was some ruin, some bankruptcies, but, bottom line, she made money for the firm. A partnership came next. There was hardly time for sex, though Nate persisted in wanting to add to Abigail's orgasm account, as they called it. She turned him away once, saying, I'd prefer you made money, like, Make money not love. He was shocked and angry, and she took it back, but he was hurt, even wounded. You're soft, his father used to say, toughen up. Abigail tried to soothe him, but really she wanted him working, back on his feet, emotional support was one thing, financial another. She saw him retreat a little, but he'd come back, he'd understand. She didn't notice his drinking, he hid it, doing it only when she was at work or asleep. Now, less and less, he wanted to have sex, and she was too tired anyway.

Nate's best friend at Princeton called with a brilliant idea, and since Nate owned the sharpest biz head he knew, he wanted him as a partner, if Nate liked what he heard, and he did—an environmentally important and scientifically significant venture to develop microbes that absorb waste in the ocean. Nate needed a couple of million to invest, not much really, but he didn't have it. He would borrow it from Abigail, he told his friend, he'd pay her back when the business saw its first profits. She trusts me, Nate told him.

Later, Abigail unlocked the door to Nate's embrace. He repeated the conversation, every word, with embellishment more bubbly than the champagne he'd opened. She looked into his olive eyes, at his too-handsome face, and her friends' and his father's admonitions returned, as if written upon that face. He would use her, leave her, he'd take her money, he was a playboy. She fought her fear, an instinct maybe, after all she must love Nate, her husband, she should help him to succeed. Even so, she told him she needed time to think, because that kind of money was serious. Nate was stunned. Abigail saw disbelief in his eyes or weakness, like in her father's eyes, a beaten dog's eyes, in bed, far from Nate, Abigail dreamed someone was trying to kill her. Nate couldn't sleep.

Some days later, Nate said there's gold in the security box, grandmother's jewelry, take it as collateral. She hated his pleading, his putting her in an impossible position, he knew she had to protect her future. What if, she thought, what if . . . and she wasn't being selfish, life was unpredictable. She wondered why she'd ever fallen in love with him, he didn't know her at all. A hardness insinuated itself inside her, and a space opened between them that was palpable to Nate. He appeared to wither before her eyes, too insecure, she realized, he's nothing like his father. She couldn't name what he was doing to her, but it was wrong, everything about him and her felt wrong. Meanwhile, Nate's potential partner waited, an intrepid humiliation returned, and Nate even drank in front of Abigail.

Still, Abigail suppressed her nameless protests and went with him to open the security box. It was strange walking down the hall where they'd first talked and fallen in love, but more terrible she felt it was her death march. The guard opened the door, and Nate and she entered the vault, where two straight-backed chairs were brought to them and then the gray steel box. There was some jewelry, she could have it appraised, some certificates, gold, and bonds. Nate lifted one up to show her, and beneath it lay his little black book. When Abigail reached for it, Nate put his hand on her arm.

—It doesn't mean anything, I kept it like a scrapbook.

She shook his hand off.

—You lied to me.

She rose, his address book in her hand, evidence of everything she'd been thinking, no one could blame her, she wasn't responsible, leaving him wasn't selfish. But it meant nothing, he repeated the next day. It means everything, she repeated, she could never trust him again. He claimed she already didn't, she wouldn't lend him money, she insisted that he wouldn't have asked for it if he really loved her. She wanted a divorce.

—You never loved me, he said.

—That isn't true, I can't ever trust you again.

To Nate, her abandonment confirmed his father's bad opinion of him, and also that his past had caught up to him, it always would. Abigail had to protect herself, no matter what, he didn't understand.

Their prenuptial agreement made divorce relatively easy, and she was so calm, her friends believed she was in shock, but his betrayal had been awful, they all agreed. When Abigail heard he'd returned to all his old ways, proving her right, that he would've just dragged her down, she felt sad but also secure in herself. And she was herself again, her friends thought, especially because Abigail volunteered at an animal shelter on weekends and fed strays on the street as she had during law school. When people at the office asked why, she'd explain she trusted cats and dogs, humans domesticated them, so they're defenseless without us. But people, she occasionally added, people usually deserve what they get.

DIARY OF A MASOCHIST

Remember when you pissed on me in San Francisco? You waited at the bottom of the stairs; it was dark. I came down the stairs and you crouched there, leaped on me, hit me, tried to stick it in me. C was upstairs. You pissed on me, I turned over and tried to absorb the piss. C had been scared you'd destroy her work, ruin her films. Don't worry, I said, defending you, he wouldn't do that.

In Phoenix you said I was Kissinger because I couldn't explain a line in H's story. "I was eight when I had my first affair." You told me you tried to put your hand on your aunt's cunt when you were five. I didn't call you Tricky Dick for that. Kept me up all night long in a Phoenix motel room, calling me Nixon, all night long, TV on, your eyes holes in your head. I made phone calls my invisible thread for sanity.

Back at the beginning—but there's no way to compare beginnings and middles and ends—in Amsterdam you put your cock in my hand and said, My cock is yours. You had been my friend for three years. You held me all the way to NYC and, our first night fucking, worried that my sister would hear us. I thought that was strange but already I was gone and thought if you were concerned, probably you were just more sensitive.

In Buffalo you get the flu. Your hands turn red, you cry and want to go back to Holland. I nurse you; in the morning you tell me my breath stinks—I am eating less and less.

I dream two men are watching us as we lie in bed. I go up to them (they are very tall, I am barefoot) and demand that they stop. I tell you my dream and you say they were in the room and you saw them, too.

You warn me against S in Pittsburgh. I dream about your wife and how I'll be isolated again in Amsterdam. I run the bath in the dream and it overflows. I swim in its pool to turn off the faucets and my mother is angry with me for making love with a "married man."

We are not making love. That's what you decreed in West Lafayette, Indiana. There we are at Purdue University, showing films to cheerleaders, and in the Purdue Guest House you tell me you don't want to make love with me, because it deteriorates our relationship. We show the films, eat Chinese food, you can't understand why I'm upset.

I sleep alone, but every night you get into bed with me, then leave again. In the morning you beckon me to you and kiss me. The phone rings. You say I'm glad because we were being drawn in again. I want to go, you can do the trip alone, I say. You say you'd blame me and so would everyone else. Next day you act okay, the day after, it's murder again.

We get to Minneapolis. A Hyatt hotel. I write in my diary that I can't resist my desire for your tongue on my cunt. As I undress in the hotel, thinking about you and sex, I look out the window and notice a man on the sidewalk, beating off, watching me.

We change hotels. You say you've been keeping yourself from me frantically. You don't want to come, don't know what to do with the feeling. You want me to come—you start me, you stop me. You piss on the floor in your sleep. I tell you in the morning and say I'm not angry. My wife would've been, you say.

You wake me in the middle of the night and stand at the foot of the bed and say I feel I am eating myself up.

You are eating me and biting me so hard my skin turns blue and red. You bite me on the cunt and I ask you to stop. You say it hurts you more than it does me. I look at my shoulders after one of our sessions and think, The stain of you lasts so long.

The bus ride to Omaha with young Chicago guys, Black and white. One calls himself a professional fucker and puts his hand on my thigh. We change buses in Omaha, get a bus all to ourselves. I'm ready to fuck you in the toilet, going Greyhound. You say your wife would be shocked. We don't.

Get to Cheyenne. I buy boys' cowboy boots. We play pool and some man promises me a silver dollar. A whore tells me there are two ladies' rooms, a nice one and a nasty one. She asks, "Which do you want?" We both laugh, we're in the shit together.

You say you don't like my body, but you like making love with me because I'm more skilled, more exciting than your wife. I dream a man who is crippled tries to lure me to his floor, #9, and I want to get out at #4. Somehow I'm forced to glide past him.

In Boulder we meet B, the filmmaker. You tell him he's afraid to die. B says he made his wife choose making art or marrying him. B kisses me on the forehead. Feels like the seal of approval and the kiss of death. I dream four babies are placed in a plastic box as a work of art.

In Boulder we come and fight. Our host hates me, thinks I persecute you, until the last night when he sees. He apologizes to me and I defend you. I understand you, I say to our host.

On our way to San Francisco. Fifteen hours to Salt Lake City, where we register as man and wife. You tell me again never to have any expectations, any needs. We're in the Palace Motel.

On to Reno. I read, "But also all journeys have secret destinations of which the traveler is unaware." You write a letter to your wife. I ask why you're so much clearer now about the situation with your wife. You say because you are with me now. You say you're not turned on by me.

San Francisco. C's house. I dream about prostitutes and in the dream you say it's better to be a prostitute and not married. C and I are not married. You hate C and try to turn me against her. You tell me she's in love with me and can't love me. C tries to put up with you. You go mad; she screams at you, but you're too gone and I'm scared, everything's collapsing. We see W's films and you tell him one side of the screen is brighter than the other. It's such a crazy thing to say, I wonder if you're right. This is the night you pissed on me. In the morning you tell me you knew what you were doing. C tries to help me and says you're going crazy. I can't admit it to myself. She takes us to the bus and we go to Portland.

We make love in Portland. Over Chinese food you talk about your wife, your kids. We are interviewed about film for a radio program. You tell me you were C's victim. The next morning I tell you how my father hurt me and you say you'll never betray me. There's money just for one of us to do the show in NYC, to fly there and back, and besides, you're scared to death of flying. The morning I'm to go, I awaken in your arms and we begin to make love. Your cock was hard on my ass. You enter me from the back, the front, then pull out. Let's have some tea instead, you say. I cry and you accuse me of trying to make you feel guilty.

I do the show like a champ. Two days in NYC alone. Am down fifteen pounds and I can't sleep or stop talking. I show G and S 8 mm films of our trip. The hotels, the bathwater, you lying asleep in bed, views out windows to streets, an American flag, endless miles of America from a bus window, C, desert, mountains, bathrooms, lamps, snow, room after room.

Your wife phones me from Holland. I fly to Vancouver; you meet me and do not look at me. I ask you to return to your wife. I try to ignore you. We argue in front of our host again. Our host asks us to stop. We stop and you ask me what I want to drink. "Surprise me," I suggest, smiling. You say you don't think you can.

There is a party. Everyone seems so normal. I cower and when I dance see you watching me. You say only your wife can dance well. You say I should seduce my partner. You watch everything.

We leave the party and in a French restaurant become friends again, get high together, go back to the party and fall asleep in the midst of it. Your cock is again hard at my back and I don't move. I feel nothing. You ask if I'm comfortable and I lie, "Yes—and you?" You say it's none of my business.

The Dutch are supposed to be good at business. You put my hand on your hard cock and thank me for the birthday present I gave you, a fish, a jade fish. It is the end of March. We're tourists in Vancouver and taken places. Sadomasochism feels out of place in this young dusty town, only seventy-five years old. Drunk Indians fall out saloon doors into our path as we walk at night. Our hostess is pregnant.

I write to J, who should have been on this trip—"Each day a dream flies out the window." You read the card and question me three times. I refuse to explain. I know you will take your revenge when I'm weaker.

On the bus again, going to Los Angeles, where I've never wanted to go, you start the day by asking me, Why are you more hysterical? You're afraid I'm cracking up because I use my hands and gesture more. I ask that you leave me alone. You imitate my movements.

Medford, Oregon, another fight. This time you say I'm claiming you by writing in my diary. The letters I once wrote you are fraying in your pocket as we eat dinner and you insist I stop writing. I keep notes of our film shows. You tell me you don't need notes, that you'll remember. After dinner I vomit; an enormous shrimp salad, the portions are so big in America.

A friendly waitress with a ribbon in her hair served us drinks while we fought.

Before we board the bus to LA, you say, Let's be friends. You throw your arm around me and I think about Amsterdam, before all of this, and can't believe that fucking can breed such bad results.

C meets me at the San Francisco station on our rest stop. I am still defending you. C is still my friend. F comes with her to say good-bye. This time, as I board the bus for LA, I feel I am voluntarily committing myself to a concentration camp.

The first night in LA at the Cecil Hotel, a death camp for the poor who live in the strip outside the wealthy. We get a room with a bath and no stopper. A room with numbers marked in black ink along the edge of the doorframe. Cigarette holes in the carpet and a TV chained to the ceiling. Here you try to fuck me again and can't. It hurts you. You say we don't fit. I never know if you mean physically or not and you won't tell me. We fall asleep watching TV: a live wedding, a prayer drama with Raymond Burr and a policeman telling us about the latest criminals.

The next day we are picked up and taken away to the hills, to E's house, to art, to lizards in the backyard. I feel privileged, just out of the death camp, then adjust quickly. The governor lives down the road from E's house and two Secret Service men are always there. We sleep together in her house; I always try to sleep alone, you always follow me. Sunday night your cock is all bloody. You refuse to see a doctor. I phone B and S in Amsterdam and see blood on the phone booth wall. An uncircumcised cock sometimes has that problem, which is nameless in our litany. I have no one to get information from and am shy about asking W, a Dutchman in LA, to explain why your cock is bloody. I taste blood in my mouth.

More arguments with filmmakers about film. The East Coast vs. the West Coast. We play chess, you make me play. I write long letters that I can't send; you send yours to your wife. I wonder what E thinks, we're up all night. I try to stop you from biting me on the cunt. Neither of us wants to have orgasms now; and even with a bloody cock, you still try to fuck me. You tell me over and over how much you love me. You tell me you hate me because I lack passion. You tell me my pain hurts you more.

Finally we leave LA and are heading toward Texas to stay with my other sister, the one I haven't seen in years. I am nearly able to consider leaving you in Phoenix, the morning after you called me Nixon and Kissinger. Instead, I try to exact promises of good behavior. The motel we're in is on Van Buren Drive. I take a Valium and sleep on the floor. You put your hand on my cunt and I push it away. You tell me you love me, that I'm a fascist and you hate me.

Get to El Paso, midway to my sister's place; we stay at the Hotel McCoy. I fall asleep but you keep waking me during the night. The next day, passing Fort Stockton, a notice at a gas station reads, "Dean and the Fat Boys—Dance Tonight." I write it down to enjoy later.

My sister and her boyfriend meet us at the bus station. They've come from a party and are in a good mood. We have a beer with them and are taken to her home. You and I sleep together again.

Back with a family, my niece and nephew, my sister, a cat and a dog. I sleep in my niece's room. You get the guest room with the TV, so that you can smoke and drink all night. The third night you drink a quart of vodka and tell my sister you're not attracted to me. You tell her she's your type. My sister walks out. Your wife and her sisters had the same lovers, at the same time. I talk to you some more, then give up. Wake my sister and cry. She thinks I'm crazy and you're drunk and mean.

I sleepwalk through the next day. You ask me if I want to talk about last night and I say no. I mean it. I have no choice. I have nothing to say. Later that night you talk to me about your wife, the film co-op. I listen and say things, then go to sleep in my niece's room. I avoid you.

The dog gets hit by a car. I see her go under the wheels. It's a disaster the whole family can share. The dog survives.

I don't want to leave my sister's house. Back on the bus with you, I know I don't stand a chance. Fifty-six hours to NYC. We're almost broke. Just one motel more. We stop in Atlanta. Pizza in the Underground. I push you away two times when you get into my bed drunk. The third time I let you enter me. The last time.

We get to NYC and stay at N's. I sleep near the door, on the floor. You get the couch. We have dinner at my sister's, where we began our trip, and you pick a fight with us about Joan Little's defense. You talk about it for two days. N gets upset watching us. One morning I phone KLM and make a reservation for you that night. You agree to go and we buy gifts for your family. I phone your wife and let her know you're coming. N takes us to the airport and after you're out of sight, I start laughing with her. Louder and louder. Can't cry. Now that you're out of my life, there's a weird hole as big as the La Brea Tar Pits we saw together. I feel like one of those animals stuck there.

Days pass and I fly to Florida to see my parents. There's a message waiting from you: it says you've arrived safely. I get a bad sunburn and my parents buy me clothes. I fly back to NY with my mother's favorite cousin, L, who says my mother was always too much in love with my father. I have to go back to Holland and I'm scared to death. I imagine you apologizing to me and things going back to normal. I see a therapist who says I don't have to let you know when I'm arriving.

I land in Amsterdam and J meets me. The first time I see you we meet with M. You're cruel and M is shocked. He says he thought you'd never treat me like that. You phone me and call me Toots, say you don't understand what's wrong.

The last time I set eyes on you we do some film business together. I'm trying to get out clean. You drive me to S and B's and tell me you love me and that I don't understand. I look at you and ring my friends' doorbell and go inside.

One year later, I'm in NYC and you write me that you nearly killed yourself in a car crash and now you're even more beautiful. I don't believe you.

ANGELA AND SAL

Angela ran a stall at Kensington Market and sold antique and handmade clothes for infants and young children. I worked for her a few days a week, and some days there were no customers. About four stalls down, Freddy and Roger sold women's high-heeled, calf-length leather boots in many colors. Pretty, waiflike Maggie hung out there, a kind of lost soul wandering the aisles. Freddy and Roger explained to me, at the pub, that some years before, Paul had summarily dropped Maggie for Linda; and Maggie found out on the day Paul married Linda. It was Kensington Market lore. Then Freddy and Roger became Queen.

Charming Angela looked like an antique doll—alabaster skin, big blue eyes, mile-wide cheekbones. She was tall and too thin, getting over the breakup of a ten-year relationship. Fragile, her friends said. They were all de facto members of the London branch of the Australian—or Strine—mafia, including Michael and Jenny. I'd met them in Crete, and back in London they introduced me to Angela.

Life was confusing. I was confused, more than now, though now with Angela's name come others, usually an inaccessible index set in chronological, not alphabetical, order. If I were writing a novel, it's unlikely I'd present so many characters all at once. If life differs from novels, it's mostly in the management of time and incident. Einstein wrote that "the only reason for time is so that everything doesn't happen at once." During that time I was moving around fast and couldn't stop moving. When I did, it wasn't for long. Everything was temporary, even when I didn't realize it. The dollar was strong but getting weaker; I was in my twenties and getting by, shifting between Amsterdam and London. I felt I led a separate though not inviolate existence in each city.

Angela invited me to rent a room in an enormous flat where she lived, not far from where William Burroughs once stayed, in the home of English filmmaker Antony Balch. In the 1960s, Balch directed *Towers Open Fire*, whose title now seems prophetic.

Several other Australians rented rooms. Scotty raced yachts professionally; he was tan, blond, and never appeared to be depressed. Danne had traveled around Europe with the Living Theater and had a two-year-old son with her husband, a critic who mostly lived and worked in Australia.

The enormous flat had a long central hallway, like a hotel, and all the bedrooms off it were spacious, some more than others. We shared the kitchen and three bathrooms. A lovely dark-haired woman I remember as brooding, clever, and writing a book, worked as an escort. She bought an expensive designer dress for her dates. The dress had lots of material, because she gained weight when she was miserable, especially after fighting with her married lover. The flowing dress cloaked her changing figure.

Something was always going on, a party, a band playing at a club, there was always someone to hang out with. The Strines I met were fierce about having a good time, and did, except when, like anyone else, they didn't. They taught me a few of their home truths: The English had contempt for their former colonies and colonists; they considered Australians just a cut above the Irish.

Angela asked me to go with her to the Hard Rock Cafe, which had opened on Old Park Lane. At dinner, at a long table, I sat next to the lead singer of Grand Funk Railroad. I talked with him, concentrating on a conversation I can't remember. My glass kept being refilled, but I didn't notice. I hardly ever drank. The band had done a gig at the Concertgebouw in Amsterdam and was going to play, or had played, Hyde Park.

When, from somewhere, I heard Angela's voice.

—We're leaving.

—How much do I owe? I asked.

—The check's been taken care of.

—It has?

—Sal Mineo's paying.

A moment of stunned silence.

—SAL MINEO. I spoke the name aloud, with astonishment. Where's Sal Mineo?

—Here, another voice said.

I stood up. There he was, across the table—Sal Mineo. He looked at me, smiling, bemused; he had been seated across the table all along, all through dinner. Sal Mineo of *Rebel Without a Cause*, the teenaged misfit Natalie Wood and James Dean shielded, protected.

Sal Mineo wore an elegant suit. I can't remember its color, though I sometimes imagine it was cream or white, but it wasn't. That was another movie star's suit. Farley Granger, in the 1980s sitting on a couch in the lobby of the Algonquin Hotel. Hardly anyone mentions him now, but he was one of the stars of Hitchcock's *Strangers on a Train*.

Sal Mineo's curly black hair framed his baby face. His eyes were large and black, gentle. The singer from Grand Funk asked me to join him and the band "in Sal's limo." I followed him to the car and was at the limo door; Sal Mineo was already seated on the slate-gray back seat, smiling again. I was about to get in. Then Angela gripped my arm.

"You're coming with me," she said.

She strong-armed me from Sal's limo to her waiting taxi.

"You're coming home," Angela said. She was fragile and tough. In the enormous apartment, in one of its white-tiled, capacious bathrooms, I was sick for the rest of the night. One day I must have moved out of the flat, but with so little drama I don't remember it, though more of that event might spill out if I try harder. Maybe I returned to Amsterdam. About two years later, in 1976, Sal Mineo, son of Sicilian coffin-makers, once called the "Switchblade Kid" for his roles as knife-wielding juvenile delinquents, was stabbed to death. The Los Angeles police worked the homosexual angle but got nowhere. Sixteen months after the murder, Lionel Williams, a stranger to Mineo, confessed to his wife—a robbery gone bad. The wife gave her husband up; then she killed herself. Lionel Williams was sentenced to fifty-seven years but served twelve. He was released in 1990, then did another crime and was sent back.

Ironic coincidence is common as mud in actual life but appears less often in fiction because it might seem contrived.

That dinner in London was the second time I'd seen Sal Mineo. The first was during Christmas in New York, at the Mark Cross store on Fifth Avenue. I was a teenager and a reader of, among other things, movie magazines. My oldest sister and I wanted to buy a gift, a humidor, for our father. He smoked pipes and the occasional cigar.

Sal Mineo stood at the counter, arm in arm with Carol Lynley, another teen idol. My sister didn't notice, she was talking with a salesman; also she was nine years older and didn't follow teen gossip. I was rapt. According to the movie magazines, Sal and Carol were "romantically linked." They looked in love, carefree, luminous, the way stars should be.

My father never used the humidor for tobacco or cigars. He kept it on top of his mahogany tall-boy dresser and threw pipe cleaners into it. He also threw in a lot of other stuff that shouldn't have been there.

FUTURE PROSTHETIC@?

Factoid storieville or dead-time storage sways not heavy in I-o's activated-life, or such-iteration, coz me, I-o, switch off/on, extending heart-chip to fail-never. What got nomened "memory" or "history" in antiquey days not longed for. But I-o's temp-Screenie, Chrono-oldie, embedded with an ever-same implant, loads inward screens to dwell upon and splain past-eras, specially memoryland of The Other Era (TOE).

I-o ken: TOE human-sapiens marred by attitudinal distress that de-hinged being, near-deactivating future-us. TOE held to a long-log vibe of "humanity," detailed by values blah-blah—antiquey species me-ism, and how tote flowed just to human-sapiens, which did cause multi-depth mental diseases, and bound the species with body-geneticides.

In I-o's mumblie, Chrono-oldie labeled in philo-backwardness, coz h/shey entered retinal-screen, reps this temp-Screenie, in the "post-apocalyptic post-nuclear pre-tote screen age."

Pan-Eye, our Vennerable, flashed thusly of past-that, but the dates narnt confirmed, coz of casual blubber from dead-timers of TOE.

[Those simple-mindies groveled memorials and self-spinning claimers of such to splain events in their cairns. That just renegates I-o's system.]

Chrono-oldie drolls factoidally on shared-connubial tote-retinal-audio screen re antiquey storieville.

[I-o press in-pad to wide attention.]

Chrono-oldie scripts, thusly:

—There was nature-mammoth fear of extinction, nuclear threat missiles, filthy snail-mail global-microbe carriers, fevered physical-war, animal vengeance, and blame-fright speeching.

[Chrono-oldie forebear a wuzzy-neg signal.]

—Grave terroristic chants of tote annihilation sapped human-sapiens by early twenty-first or pre-then. In physical-war-period, there falls further stunting: despair of waterloss; tote-grid swine-mongers and waste-spinners; beast sun and wind-mania, and what-called patriot nations and faith-mad systems. Our far-gone ancient ancestors held to multi-forms of extinction angst that also conquered organ systems.

[I-o incred.]

—Why'd they drive that extinction-line@? I-o's active/passive program iterates aliveness, activation cum cures, plus tru-form pan-prostheses.

[I-o ken such.]

Screenie drolled of ancestors with nul signifying knowledge of such-like.

[Dumblie human-sapiens. But Screenie, a philo-antiquey s/him, adwells in momenToes of born-again entry-places and life-death syndrome. H/shey did too much droll to I-o of such, plus ever-uncertainties re bad-birth bandwidths, plus anon-blurs of sweet-tooth motherboards. Too bitty nostalgiac, for I-o.]

[I-o memories Chrono-oldie.]

—Our zero-implants crashed dark-hole humanist moodies. Me/us who do arrive, in the neo-events cyclotron, switch-out neon-ozone surrounds, duly implant retinal-screens with re-start, minus angst attachments.

[Chrono-oldie, this gene-type, favors alt. activities reveling in such-called "notlet go," the atavist-feature that weighs down heavy with remnant-chips. I-o lulls, awaiting press-back, tho blooming in else-places.]

Suddenish, temp-Screenie clamorous-luminites flare starry. H/shey palpates soft pad that bounces to sole historico-doc file I-o fewly access.

[I-o holds mini-volta for dead-time storage.]

Screenie tosses connubial eye-screen into space/time slow-mo.

[I-o trace Chrono-oldie at risk of incontinence.]

—In nomen early-twenty-first century, human-humans, neo human-sapiens, grew weary-sad and torn. Wars narnt exciting. Nam of them, tho, could stop burning, so ultimo-objects warred. Whackers, the twenty-second iteration robo-sapiens, altered screen info; thusly, wars held in safe mode. No one died warlike.

—Whoa, no eternal exits@?

—No end-death, and such deemed progress-like, coz advancing human-sapiens narnt over-killed. Humans no more hands-on battlers, just hard-pressing, round4 bottomed nerd-types, so it was said. Pre-Consternation Time arrived, with major slice of human-sapiens extended in a dumb cloud of no reproach. In their tempus fugit they did pledge and ascribe to tribes; brands; designer stores, and other spiritual cults. Human-sapiens dug terra firma and believing-systems. Whackers—robo-sapiens— performed war, and screens a-shifted in nanoseconds. Thusly, their disintegrated systems arrived. They narn ken-well one suit, store, or club from other, such was their tote-confusion. A whacker b+eared one side-camp or party-slice on-screen, another undid such, sync-like, and tote camps and slices—of which were multitudes—did and redid with neo-strategic-diabolics. Plain-out, no camp knew winning slice, old-nomen "victory," just post-jigging effects. Such also deemed advance-like by Ultraists on all screens. No winning slice! Yea! But it worsened.

[I-o flaring queries.]

—How-so, how-so@?

—Human-sapiens narnt hold one thought-bubble. Mind-bombed 42/7 on totescreens, internal/external, organ-brains got ever re-decorated in unheimlich patterns. Plain-out, not one kenned where h/she aliving. No phys-line boundaries. Winning/losing transactions through bank-screens, designer stores, national clubs: Signification burn-out. Antiquey humans aborne irrevocable-confused mind-sets. Thus said, in TOE by their species: "I can't think straight."

[I-o implanted with some-such of that info. In neo-nomen, I-o semble "thinking" but narnt xactoly. I-o morphs colors plus momentums, being-seeing, blasting this/that to temp-screenies. I-o's screen-eyes, plus 20-20, visuals totemodalities, performing Venn-like understandings, tracking Pan Vennerable.]

Chrono-oldie wanes, recharges.

—Near fin-time of TOE, human-beings turned Conster-nated. "Mind-fucked." That was The Conundrum.

—Whoa, whoa, tote tote. I-o can't sane this. Pre-tote-organ brain prostheses@?

—Human-sapiens malfunctioned pre-our-time, in POT.

[Chrono-oldie mooding, coz holding inward-like what once emoticon sad but not actual emoticon sad, a referral to sad-emoticon from that not-let-go-feature on retinal retainer.]

Suddenish, Chrono-oldie retoasts I-o with apostrophizes. H/shey drolls that it/info twill be impassable for I-o's internal activation.

—Whoa, whoa, trial on@!

—Simul, amid-descent of mental-breakdown wars, human-sapiens reveled in such-like animal-humans or domestics. Nomen dogs, cats, all four-legged fur-ridden beings. The most un-wiring to such humans arrived by such animal-humans. These domestics carried otherness, null-ing human-sapien code-scripts.

[I-o flashing darkly, neo-info ranking plus-ancient ever screen-landed.]

—Domestics external with ancient-ancients for all of TOE. Human-sapiens formed domestics of four-legged wild-beings, sand-lands, junglies, and caves, and trubly loved nomened "domestics."

[I-o narnt internal love. Narnt into funking a doodle. That troubly biz everunscrews being. Significo, I-o holds no fixities.]

—Such was human thought: Domestics loved unconditional-like, dogs specially loved. Cats forebode slavitude. There arrived dog lovers and cat lovers.

—Drolling me@?

—Narnt@! Cats did what-called meowing, dogs barking, humans delighted of such speak. But unknown, a cat's meow was ironical. Ironic-humorous vibrato. Dogs abarking, brutal-cruel talk.

—Dead-pan drolling I-o@?

—Narnt@! Cats ironical. Thusly, domestics did walk out on two-legs. It came that human-humans weight-lifted pain-angst. Organ-hearts broke down, pre-tote prosthetics. Brain-systems already in break-down of sync mind-fucking. And followed, post-domestics, laughter ended.

—Whoa, whoa@! Entry to The Serious Period@?

—In Consternated Time, no abiding laughter.

[I-o weighing heavy in neo-info mode.]

—Laughter@?

—From jokes.

[This sounds sickish to I-o.]

—Whoa@! Jokes@?

—Extincto.

—Extincto with TOE@?

Chrono-oldie flashes wooky wooks, and temp-Screenie darkening, plus fixing @ momenToe.

[I-o modes changeable-like.]

Hereby, tote-tote, I-o reviles future minting of past-dwelling, heavy remnantchip. Def, no antiquey sorties. Plus, nul backwardgazing to the microbe-driven consternated time, coz TOE extincto. Over/out.

THE ORIGINAL IMPULSE

He appeared in her sleep like a regular. Sometimes she saw the actual him on the street, then he appeared two, three nights in a row; on the street, because he remembered her vaguely or well enough, it was awkward.

Years ago they'd done a fast dance. Back then, when she studied photography, she believed artists were constitutionally honest; but his thrill had its own finish line. She missed classes, stayed out too late, ate too much, and dormant neuroses fired. She expected a man to love her the way her father did, explosively, devotedly. Months later, near where they'd first met, she ignored him; he rushed after her and apologized. Maybe he knew how bad it felt, but she never said anything. He phoned sometimes, they drove around, drank coffee, talked, not about lies, and two years passed like that, haplessly, when something obscene must have gone down, because he didn't call again. What words were there for nothing. Nothing.

Her time was full, adequate, hollow, fine, and she felt content enough with love and work, but no one lives in the present except amnesiacs. Her history was a bracelet of holes around her wrist, not a charm bracelet like her mother had worn; that was gone. Someone had stolen it as her mother slipped away. It might be on that woman's wrist now, the gold rectangular calendar hanging from it, a ruby studding her mother's birthdate, a reminder she wouldn't want. It would weigh even more with blanks filled in by anonymous dead people.

Insignificant coincidences—the actual him in a hotel lobby, a bookstore doorway, crossing a street—made loose days feel planned. She moved forward, a smartphone to her ear or its small screen to her face, and anything might happen. She read a story he'd written about an accidental meeting with a woman from his protagonist's past. First he didn't recognize her, she'd changed so much from how he remembered her; then he felt something again, maybe for the woman, mostly for himself. When he spotted her, she wondered if he felt sick alarm, too. One Saturday, she didn't notice he was walking by, watching her, and when she looked up, aware of something, she half smiled involuntarily. That could have meant anything, there was no true recognition from either of them. Without it, she couldn't perform retrospective miracles, transform traitors into saviors. When ex-friends' faces arose, stirred by the perfume of past time, they looked as they did back then. One of them, she heard, did look the same, because she'd already been lifted. But some things can't be lifted.

Abysses and miseries called down their own last judgments upon themselves. Katherine could recite many of her bad acts; it would be easy to locate her putative wounded and apologize like someone in AA, but what substance had she abused. Love, probably. Most likely they'd claim they had moved on and forgotten her. Besides, they might say, you never really meant that much to me. Or, let's be friends on Facebook. When the twentieth-year reunion committee of her high school found her, she didn't respond. Formal invitations, phone messages. They insisted her absence would destroy the entire reason for the event. The date approached. She wondered if showing up might help adjudicate the past, and curiosity arched its back. She caught a ride with a popular girl who'd gone steady with a future movie star who'd had a pathetic end. The woman wore the same makeup she'd worn then, her eyes lined slyly with black. Startling, what gets kept.

The reunion was held in the town's best country club, and in front of the table with name badges, she sank, just the way she had growing up. Someone called to her, "Kat, Kat," and another, "Kat," while another fondly blasted "Kat" into her ear, someone whose name she didn't recognize even looking at the name badge. Indignant, the girl/woman pronounced her unmarried name as if the tribe were extinct. "And I'm called Katherine now," she answered. Throughout the night, they called her Kat as if she were still one of them.

Faces had been modified, some looked aged; all the boys looked older than the girls. Provincial, well off, neither sex could believe she wasn't married, and she encouraged their bewilderment, eventually admitting she lived with someone. But no, no, she wasn't married. The girls especially looked at her pityingly, the boys lasciviously. One had been her sixth-grade boyfriend; he'd been pudgy but now his girth wasn't boyish or expectant. During cocktails, she huddled with the Black kids, the minority in town, and sat at their dinner table, still a minority. Days later, some of her former friends telephoned. One announced gravely, "I told my daughter to be like you, not me." She didn't ask why. Her pudgy sixth-grade boyfriend decided he'd ruined her life, that's why she hadn't married. He thought because she hadn't married, she must be a tormented lesbian. Katherine remembered breaking up with him for a seventh grader.

On an accidental corner, the nighttime man's spectral presence tugged at her, a leash pulling in the wrong direction. If she existed as a translation from an unforgiving past, he must, too, but translation was too dainty for what had happened to her, or him, she supposed. Words weren't patches, and the nights didn't let up, repetition after repetition, but how many ways could he appear, in how many iterations: his cheek pressed against hers, his glance, like a pardon from their past, his sexy compassion—they both had been alive then.

She heard he treated his wife badly, but they might have an open marriage, blind oxymoron. She supposed he lied to his wife, a famous rock singer past her prime, the way he was. On an impulse, he might abandon the singer, no longer the blooming girl who'd obliterated his mortality. The singer might want to divorce him but won't, because of their child, or because she doesn't care about his infidelities, since she's had her own, or none, or because she can't bear another split when suturing wouldn't hold after so much scar tissue. What had their life meant, and, anyway, he always returned remorseful or defiant, or both.

Sometimes, passing a building or café, Katherine would recollect a doorway encounter like the one on Fifth Avenue where Lily Bart was spotted by Lawrence Selden and doomed. Behind that red door, in that bodega, in that high-rise on the eightieth floor, strangers and intimates lavished attention or withdrew it, or she did. She had entertained various kinds of intercourse, and the words spoken lay redacted under thick black lines. She retrieved bits through the interstices of nodding heads.

A delicate young man trembled at the edge of recognition, but his face was now speckled like an old photograph.

She was eighteen and lay in the arms of a married man who respected, he said, her innocence, and held her close, saying he'd always remember this moment, but she wouldn't, because she didn't know how beautiful she was. There was a cool slip of a rough tongue on an inner thigh and a sensational confession. There was a southerner whose sexuality was fiercely, erotically ambiguous. He stayed in her bed too long. She roared here and soared there, dwarfed by three massive white columns as she and her best college friend mugged before a filmless camera.

People often move away from cities and towns when reminiscences create profound debt and mortgage the future. They visit occasionally and discover that the debt has multiplied. Katherine stayed where she was, in her city, along with a majority of others who resolutely called it home and became teachers, therapists, florists, criminals, food professionals, homeless, or worked with immigrants and refugees, the way she did.

Her photographs had been in two one-person shows and several group exhibitions, but Katherine stopped taking her work seriously because, primarily, she couldn't convince herself that her images were better than anyone else's. The decisive moment was an indecisive one for her. She earned a degree in social work and dallied with becoming a psychoanalyst, but decided she didn't want to work with people too much like herself. The agency where she spent five days a week, with occasional nights of overtime because of the exigencies of desperate people's lives, suited her. The agency was respected and privately funded by well-known philanthropists. Every day people entered the office with foreign-born stories of violence, terror, and humiliation; her shame was nothing compared with theirs.

Two months after the high school reunion, one of the girls telephoned to remind Katherine, agonistically, of why their friendship had ended—remember, the friend urged, senior year. The friend cited her mother's dying of cancer, her boyfriend's betrayals—she married him anyway—but all this pain had forced her to abandon their friendship. "I couldn't help you," she said, "we couldn't help each other." The friend talked and talked until her voice fell off a cliff. So that was that.

Katherine never thought about that friend or her dying mother, but now she pretended to stroll from her childhood house on Butler up Adelaide Avenue to the street—Randolph—and the door of her friend's home. The lawn was wide and green, so it must have been spring, when sad things occur ironically. She didn't open the front door, she didn't want to walk up the carpeted staircase and see her friend cradling her dying mother. The front door swung open, anyway. Her friend's father had his back to her, at the dining room table, his old head supported in her young friend's hands. Now the friend turned toward her, disrupting the image, and Katherine ran home. Did that happen?

There he was again. Katherine was sitting on a couch in a lobby, waiting for a friend. She heard his voice, he strode to the elevator, and she didn't move, her face averted. He looked her way; she didn't relax her pose. It didn't matter if the nighttime man knew her as she was now. He was a thorn pricking her side, that's all. Another of his stories appeared, and she read about the protagonist's having once received a postcard from a girl he'd been cheating with; his wife found it, and it ruined things between them for a while. He never saw the girl again. How true was he being, or could he be. He was faithless, but probably he didn't think so, not in the obvious ways. He bore an unfathomable loneliness, and he was faithful, in his way, to that.

At the agency, she listened to stories more terrible than the Greek tragedies she loved. When she learned that some friends didn't return to the books they'd cherished in school, she understood that some people lived as if the past were over. Been there, done that—she didn't know how. The Greeks would have his wife lose her voice, never to sing or even speak again. He'd suffer a downfall, realizing his hubris necessarily too late, and kill himself. The wife might kill herself, too, but not harm their beautiful daughter, who would turn vengeful, without knowing whom to blame, unalterable fate swallowing her whole.

The nighttime man played his role in her romance, reciting his few lines. She told no one, because dreams signify nothing to anyone else, and their accidental meetings were psychic jokes— those sidewalk and doorway scenes, the questions they raised, when she compared her life with his, what had occurred between then and now, all to test her self-made being. Startling, what gets kept.

On a dull February morning, a man entered the agency. Curiously, he recognized her name, because ten years back he'd seen her photographs in London, when he was covering culture for an Indian newspaper. He had a work visa—he was a journalist and visiting academic—but he wanted to bring his extended family from Bangladesh. He needed permanent residency, there were political issues, he knew important people and could get letters. He was charming, somewhat coy, especially when announcing that he suffered the curse of a minority writer. She asked what that was. She never presumed anything in the office.

"To be expected to write like a minority," he said.

"How do you mean?"

"You must write of suffering with some nobility—you people expect authenticity. I bet you first heard about Bangladesh when George Harrison organized that concert."

It wasn't a question, and he may have been right. She said she expected nothing from him. It was oddly comforting to assert that, as if he didn't exist to her the way she knew she didn't to him. He spoke about the different meanings of displacement. He refused to consider himself an exile, even if one day he would be. Outside, the bare branches of February trees looked like what he was saying, an image she might have shot once—recognizable metaphors, a formally interesting composition—but what did it really do. What was it a picture of.

That night, she told Jack about the Bangladeshi writer called Islam.

"Remember when Christian lived on the eleventh floor," Jack said.

They watched the Mets win their rubber game, a depressingly rare event, and sometimes she watched Jack and wondered if they really had a destiny with each other, and what if she left him or he left her. And what if she sent a postcard to the nighttime man, like that girl. Graciously, he didn't appear in her dream, a stranger did, Islam probably, who declared, "Ecstasy is a living language." In the morning, when she spoke his name aloud, it was too big, too much. Islam had asked why she'd stopped showing her work. She didn't know, exactly, she gave him reasons, but she thought she wasn't an artist. She wasn't committed enough, she told him, and not everyone has to be an artist. That's over, that romance about being an artist. Some things were over, she acknowledged to herself.

Walking to work, she abjured scenes that had occurred years ago at one place or another, but even when a building had been completely demolished, the blighted memory wasn't. Islam's questions bothered her, but she liked them, or appreciated them. In the past she'd documented many of these lost buildings; now, surprising new-old images were sprung free by involuntary processes. History pursues its psychic claims in disguise. She thought about photographing Islam, making a portrait of him. He had become entwined in what she'd renounced. First, Islam said he'd think about it, then he said no, and his refusal shut an unmarked door. She supposed she did have unwanted expectations. To appease her, probably, Islam invited her for a drink; Katherine said no. She wasn't sure what she wanted from him, or he from her, except the obvious. Katherine was suspicious in ways she hadn't been when she knew the nighttime man. Maybe that was a sorry thing.

Her job involved her. She watched people carefully for unusual, even unique, gestures and expressions, and listened thoughtfully. People were amazing, their stories amazed, saddened, and disgusted her. Katherine was herself or wasn't during these intake interviews. She recognized a person as a site of relationships, never just an individual, even when cut off from friends and family. But people felt miserably alone. Islam didn't—Katherine didn't think he did. He told her he was a beloved son, his mother's favorite, the youngest, adored by his father and brothers, and he said it with such vivacity and pleasure, she believed him without jealousy. In the same meeting, he chided her. "You know, Katherine, you must know, I was playing you a little. I'm not really a minority, we're not a minority, you are. You have more wealth, that's all." Then he smiled brilliantly, the adored son.

Sunday, Katherine was rambling in Central Park. The nighttime man's wife appeared in her path, and it wasn't a dream. She wore an unadorned black jacket, slim black pants, slingback shoes, understated makeup. Katherine admired how well composed her image was. The wife seemed bemused, chin held high as if loftily acknowledging something or someone in the distance. A girl walked beside her, their daughter, and when they passed by, Katherine felt a furtive intimacy with her nighttime rival, like a fragment secretly attached. The daughter was taller, longer-legged, unsmiling—what had happened—her face similar to her mother's, though much younger. Daughters manage fathers like him, and what do they tell themselves. What does he tell her. "I love your mother, this has nothing to do with you." What does the girl feel. The daughter's long, gold earrings danced at her swan-white neck.

Her mother's charm bracelet. Katherine saw it flutter, a golden relic hanging from a bare branch. That would be a strange picture, she thought, not easily dismissed, uncanny even. But how would she do it, if she did. Startling, what gets kept.

THE SHADOW OF A DOUBT

Imperfect knowledge accompanied him across the field to a big tent. It was strange, it was just like the tent Thomas dreamed about the night before, with green and white stripes and billowing white flaps spread wide like labia. Inside the tent, a three-piece band played "All of Me," a beguiling smell of gardenias insinuated itself, and five veiled women, their naked, fleshy bellies curling and uncurling—maybe the gypsy women from a small circus in southern Turkey—waved and pointed behind him, and there she was, Grace, his love, embracing him, lustily biting his lips. You're eating me up alive, he dream-talked, and everything was right in the world, until he awoke.

Déjà vu all over again, Thomas thought, entering the tent. His dream wasn't a flash of prognostication, he knew the ceremony and reception would be under a tent, so the dream made perfect sense, even if her marriage didn't. Its inevitability had plagued him for months, especially since Grace had once told him she couldn't be with him because she didn't know how to love, couldn't love, it wasn't him, she said, downcast, she was incapable. Hers was a hopeless, existential condition. My mother, she explained, made loving anyone impossible. Her mother had disappeared one day, didn't pick her up from kindergarten, and finally turned up dead, or was pronounced dead, it was murkily put, and that was all, she wouldn't say more, so he didn't prod Grace, assuming the disappearance was the result of another man, drugs, or alcohol. He doubted she'd died—her father kept the truth from her—but Thomas believed the terrifying, great loss and abandonment had diminished Grace's capacity to trust, and desperate insecurity carved out her being. Grace left it, and many other matters, open to interpretation; her vagueness shaped their relationship, until disastrously bent out of shape, it disintegrated.

Now Grace was actually marrying Billy Webster, a man— Thomas would've preferred a woman—someone she could love, presumably, unless she had other motives and reasons with which she'd tie her Gordian knot. Living gardenias cascaded down thick, moss-green plastic vines, but there were no women in veils, except for Grace, when she walked down the aisle next to her father, who looked just like the New Hampshire modern-day farmer he was. This was New Hampshire, Thomas reminded himself, glancing away from Grace's swishing peau de soie dress, whose hem touched his foot as she walked toward the other man. But how much a dream tells and doesn't, how it plays tricks, just like people. His only consolation was to attend her wedding the way he would a funeral for a colleague or a former friend, because it was required and ennobled him with easy virtue.

Thomas knew only a little about Grace's dull or bright hubby, who stood possessively by her side and appeared to sense subtle meanings in her every gesture, unctuous and fastidious in his affection, and grinned so broadly his eyes disappeared into folds of cheek, which looked to Thomas like abnormal growths. He's assertive, Thomas decided, a wimp, or a geek, and probably impotent. Grace's brand-new husband produced CD-ROMs, a movie or two, some Broadway shows, and Thomas distrusted his dilettantism, his casualness. Thomas prided himself on his vision and application of skill to one cause, graphic design, whose requirements called for a refined eye, precision, and creativity within limits. He served others rather than himself, far better than making art that encouraged self-indulgence. Billy Webster was a grandstander. Also, Billy Webster had once performed magic, which was how he got into theater, and read palms and handwriting. Grace had mentioned this, as if they were worthy pursuits.

She met Billy Webster after they'd split up, she explained to Thomas, when she also informed him, too delicately, as if his feelings were womanly, of their upcoming marriage. That's why she'd phoned him. It was chance, they were at a party, thrown by a close college friend she hadn't seen since, but the friend had converted to Scientology, which Grace didn't know until the party, when she heard a well-dressed group of men and women, all in their thirties, with too-bright eyes and eager, lubricious smiles, discuss E-meters and getting clear. She listened in, didn't say a word, fearing intimidation, and that's when she and Billy Webster found each other's eyes across the room. The antidisciples soon absconded from the religious or cultish party, to a bar. They talked all night. Until dawn, she'd said, and soon Billy Webster had discovered her and she him, they found each other.

—Were you lost? Thomas asked.

—Very cute.

—I am very cute. You're blind.

—He's psychic, he knows me better than I know myself.

—And that makes you happy, Thomas said, flatly.

—Yes, it does.

—And you can love him, Thomas said, flatlining now.

She lost color, at least she lost color, he thought later.

—Yes, I can. I do. I'm sorry, Tommy.

He hated her saying Tommy.

—What about your mother?

—Billy let her, or he let me—he expelled her.

—Like an exorcism, Thomas joked.

—Sort of, she said. Don't laugh. It can happen.

—Accidents happen, he said.

—No, she said, Billy did it.

—You fell in love with him, I'm not a moron.

She invited him to the wedding anyway.

Thomas now hated Webster with conviction, and wished he had not been decent about making an appearance at the wedding, even though he attended more as a ghost than a person, but still, he was complying with a ritual form of masochism. He thought he hated her, he hoped so, and he strode purposefully out of the tent, to cover so much ground that the tent would disappear, as if it were his bad dream, the wedding, and Grace an aerie faerie, and Billy Webster a devil with a slimy coat, sour, steamy sweat oozing, a tiny, hairy penis, or a mouse where the phallus should have been. Thomas saw him go up in a puff of smoke. All the while he felt someone was close behind him, so he strode faster, running away, exercising his legs, but he didn't look back.

The field turned into a forest, and when Thomas reached a pond, the tent gone to a recent past, he sat on a log near the water, heard birds singing inside the profound quiet, and dirtied the seat of his suit on the wet log with perverse pleasure. I can't go back now, he decided. Does she really believe that junk?

His twin sister, Antoinette—Tony—might. Her girlfriend's day job was as a lab technician, but she was also a working psychic, and while his twin sister wasn't in thrall or attuned to voices from beyond or the like, Tony sympathized with those who were. Because their mother thought it was all junk, the way Thomas did. Their mother was beautiful, still, very much in love with their father, who returned her love, and his twin had always felt left out. Her mother either didn't pay enough attention to her, or too much, of the bad kind, overly praised her, which sounded false to Tony, or belittled her, she said. His twin blamed their mother for everything that went wrong in her life, but he didn't. He loved her.

The last time the twins talked, over drinks, he had managed not to press a single incendiary button, steering their course through comfort zones, but then Tony said, her lips pressed against her teeth, "Mother didn't love me, she loved you because you were a boy. She's a bitch." She sat back in her chair, opening her legs wide like a muscleman on a subway car. Tony was more butch than he was. She liked sports and working out, she'd always been butch and, as a child, acted as if she believed if Thomas were nice, he would have changed his sex for her. Now he supposed he could cut off his penis and have the flesh made into a vagina with folds, but the thought made him sick. He just couldn't, he liked his penis, and, even if he did change his sex, Tony wouldn't be satisfied.

When Tony mentioned "our mother" again, Thomas absent-mindedly lifted a large plastic cup of water to his mouth, couldn't hold it somehow, and instead juggled it, kept juggling, until the cup flew into the air and doused his sister and him in spring water. Laughing, wiping herself off, she said, "If you'd soaked just me, bro, I'd have wondered." Later, he realized his unconscious had helped him throw cold water on the conversation, a literal-minded unconscious, and kind of great.

Tony had her revenge. He left town sometime after that, and she wanted to stay in his apartment as a break from her too-attentive lover, and he said, as he opened the door to leave, Don't break anything, okay? This stuff is precious to me. He shut the door behind him, and she marched over to the refrigerator for a beer, then to the Prouvé chair he'd paid a fortune for, plopped down on it, and it crumbled beneath her. That's what she told him when he returned.

Thomas had never liked birds much, and now they were his company. He twisted around, angled his head back, sensing something standing behind him, but there was nothing. I'm thinking it, I want someone there, I'm willing it, Grace, probably, I want her. He called her name, Grace, Grace, Grace, to an indifferent forest, which regularly responded to wild breezes, not words, and then when his echo disconcerted him, her name bouncing back emptily, he concentrated on hating her, hating what he'd loved. It was better than loving and missing her, having her in absentia only. What will come now? What will happen? The future might stroke him with good fortune or lash him with lies and broken promises, all uncontrollable, like his unconscious, which allowed him to do what he wanted but couldn't in good conscience, allowed him what he feared, and safely enabled him to engage in gory scenes, loveless sex, abusive and ugly acts with his enemies and even friends. Who was a friend, anyway. Self-interest and betrayal climaxed together, satisfied bedfellows and lovers, common as dirt. He wiped the seat of his trousers without mirth.

Another love like this could shatter him, he'd crack up, go mad, or be forever changed, and he wanted that, to be out of himself, to believe ideas he absolutely never had, suddenly, and he also wished for stability and hardly any—no—he wanted no more sad surprises. He loved Grace, what a joke. What if he always loved her, what if he couldn't stop, what if he could never have what he wanted. There was too much he couldn't control. He might as well wish on a star, have his fortune read, believe in obscure pseudoscientific lore, astrology, or handwriting analysis, roll the dice, or throw a penny into this placid pond, his own Trevi Fountain. Thomas humored himself imagining farmers at the pond, tossing in coins, dimes and quarters probably—the cost of wishes must be inflated, too—and if he peered in, he knew he'd see his reflection.

So, in the same, whimsical mood, he called up the myth of Narcissus. It seemed fitting, Narcissus's attachment to himself, to a reflection, all surface, though Echo loved him anyway. Her fate doomed her to repeat his words, which Narcissus might have ambivalently appreciated, since some men like to hear themselves talk and hear themselves in subservient women. Thomas, somewhat uncomfortably and almost against his will, he'd say later, looked down, but he didn't see his face. He saw the moss-covered still water, and soon, through the interstices of green slime, a woman's face floating a foot beneath the surface. Distorted, old, rotten. Disbelieving, even alarmed, he turned again, but again there was no creature behind him, and all the while the birds continued to vocalize their complaints and desires in a euphonious chorus, interrupted by a few squawks.

He stared at the rotten face, hoping to see something. It felt imperative now to realize something, to apprehend—"make it work" was his design credo. He felt, suddenly, less sure of himself than ever, but maybe there would come a sign to help him, though wishing for that made him feel more vulnerable. He stared, and occasionally a trace of his own reflection filtered through the muck, but only for a moment until the watery mirror exposed her face once more. The face changed, by the flow of water, he thought, its labile movements. And as he stared, meditating on her, or it, and this oddness, he noticed something, the thing behind him that wasn't there and the thing in front that was and yet wasn't. It wasn't clear, it was more a sensation than an idea or image. But then it became an idea: the face was Grace's dead mother's. She had, like Virginia Woolf, drowned herself, a suicide, that was why Grace couldn't love. And then: Grace's mother had been murdered, that's why her face looked hideous, she died in terror, thrown into a river. In either case, her mother was condemned to haunt the waterways of New Hampshire. So: Grace never stopped mourning her mother and hating her, too, her mother had left her, had not loved her, and how could un-loved Grace love—that must be it. But Billy Webster had made Grace know her mother was gone, he let her go for Grace. No, he told her that her mother had been kidnapped, that's what Web-ster insisted, and she had never wanted to leave Grace, and she believed him.

Why couldn't he have calmed her. Led her from doubt. Why couldn't he have given her what she needed. Thomas couldn't accept his fate, either, to have lost her. He wasn't her knight in shining armor.

It's not your fault, a voice whispered.

Thomas shifted around, and a form lay on the forest floor, like a woman's, a shadow, or a ghost, then of a man, a child, a woman again, but there, absolutely, it was. It appeared to be wearing a hat, with a feather, as when an Indian stood in his doorway when he was a child, and, though Thomas awoke, the Indian stayed there for several minutes, he wore an elaborate feather headdress, his bare chest smooth and brown, luminous in the dark of the bedroom.

Now she, he, or it sat up.

The indecipherable shadow muttered: Thomas, Thomas, don't be silly.

That's what it sounded like, he thought, he heard that, but do ghosts or sibyls call you silly? He was hearing things, of course, hearing what he wanted. Thomas believed the ghostlike shape was created by a weave of branches and leaves, the winds causing it to shift its shape. It was a shadow created by nature, the play of elements, and maybe of his desire, with an illusion of physicality, but even when he shut his eyes, then quickly opened them, it was there. He accepted his own explanations or interpretations and waited for more.

Someone will love you, the voice said in a deeper register.

Thomas scoffed, then he snorted, and the birds stopped singing, as if they recognized his sounds as derisive and objected with their silence. He stood up, brushed off his pants, boldly walked toward the form, and stuck his arm through the air above it. The shadow disappeared and his own shape hovered, instead. Selective hearing, selective memory, selective living. Maybe he was going mad, this was it, but he didn't feel mad. Would he ever be happy? He couldn't imagine it. A dream is a disguise, his college therapist explained, while his Spanish teacher taught Calderón's *La vida es sueño*, and if a dream is a disguise, and life is a dream, then life is a disguise, too. The tautology satisfied him since it demonstrated he was able to think, so he wasn't crazy yet, but if life were a disguise, what did it disguise. Was there a design. No, not a design, there was too much randomness, but then what does life disguise?

Thomas sat on the log again, thoroughly engaged in the question, listening to his thoughts, to the birds who sang again or argued or cried, until he fell asleep. He must have fallen asleep, because time passed and kept passing, and reality didn't feel real, he was looking at himself looking at himself. The big striped tent was back, he saw himself go through the opening, he saw her walk down the aisle, everything repeated itself, he saw himself, he saw his twin, Tony, she was a man and a woman, and she didn't hate him, his parents smiled, then looked sadly upon him. He saw life rushing by, was he dead? Life is a dream, life is a dream. Now everyone was in disguise, everyone, and he fled the tent again, horrified, because if everyone's in disguise, and a disguise is also disguise, then where does it end. IN DEATH. In death, in death. He was dead. He wasn't asleep, he was dead. Life disguises death. We only think we're alive. That was the Tibetan Book of the Dead, and, realizing that, he breathed. He wasn't dead, he was only reading a book. Nothing made sense. A dream is life, life is death, death is life, and all of it is a disguise. Everything. Lies, lies upon lies, only lies on lies only. He finished running away and again he was where he was, by the pond, and the birds were singing, and a mourning dove flew to him and alighted on his chest, so, startled, he rubbed his eyes to better see the beautiful gray bird.

The mourning dove chirped: The biggest lies are the ones you tell yourself.

Okay, that's good, Thomas said to the talking bird.

It was as if I'd seen a ghost, but I was the ghost, he explained to his friends later. He told his twin, Tony, that he knew she was a man and a woman, and he thought, in his dream, he was also. Tony liked him better then, maybe forever after. Thomas did forget Grace, he forgot Billy Webster, and one day he forgot falling asleep and dreaming at the pond, because that's what he'd told himself. It was all a dream, life is a dream, a dream is life, life disguises death, and only I can lie to myself.

WHAT SHE COULD DO

A young, straight couple, watching a play, seated in the first row, could see spittle on the actors' lips. When the actors enunciated their words vigorously, when they were close to each other, their spit landed on each other's face. They didn't wipe it off, they didn't react the way normal people would, they stayed in character, spoke their lines, went on. That's what made it theater, she thought.

The play was called, not ironically, "A Leap into the Void," and Yves Klein blue shamelessly dominated the stage—a constant background, a perpetual sky without even one cloud. The word "blue" wasn't spoken, anyway not yet.

At intermission, the young man of the couple wondered how long ago it was, how many years ago, thousands, millions, people felt a void . . . or something impossible, the young woman. It's a total concept, he said. When did the idea come about, the feeling there was nothing.

Maybe, she said, when they were hungry, and they felt empty. When she felt empty, she didn't always feed herself. But she could go to a store, and they had to hunt and kill. Or grow things, which took time and planning.

What did they think hunger was, how did they know it was for food, when did they know they needed to eat, everything had to eat, creatures have an instinct to survive.

Bad, she said, they just felt bad.

She looked at a red mark on his chin, a nick from shaving. Humans were once covered in fur, great apes toward becoming something else, Homo sapiens. And what if that were still true . . . Some men have very hairy chests, thick rugs on their chests. She pictured herself and him, furry animals having sex. Stuffed animals. Maybe that's what they were.

Their conversation came along, with pauses, with their looking at other people, with talk about whether their antidepressants were working, their wrecked brain chemistry. The human brain was big, not smart enough, because it let dark thoughts enter, like the knowledge of death. Self-consciousness, he said. We came from the sea, we came out crawling on our bellies, half-fish, half-human. She rotated her arms.

We'll go back there, when the flood hits, he said, laughing.

That's horrible, she said, everything for nothing.

He saw where this was going. Lighten up, he said. My father told me that when you go to a urologist, you're asked to void your bladder.

The bell rang, they walked to their seats, Pavlovian dogs, dawgs, he'd say.

He settled in, the way he did, shifting twice before crossing one leg over the other, recrossing, and uncrossing. It was his ritual. Maybe a habit. Habit made her disbelieve herself. During the day, when she stood at the top of the staircase, she knew it was in her, like an organ, to leap high, fly over the stairs, and land perfectly, no harm to head or limb. But where would she fly to. He used to dream he was flying, and sometimes couldn't get liftoff, he told her, so she didn't tell him.

The curtain opened, the bright-blue sky beckoned. She watched herself onstage, high up, above everyone else, floating, weightless, a bird drifting, rising and falling on the soft winds of chance. Maybe she fell asleep, because she was very startled when the blue sky, the backdrop, fell forward, and collapsed at the edge of the stage, at their feet. Florets of dust rose, and there were gasps from the audience, while the actors, attached to wires, flew up and away and disappeared into the real world. Would they come back for curtain calls, or did they want to keep to the illusion? she whispered. In the dark, people applauded, some stood in awe, and he threw his arm around her.

She thought hard, she thought if she imagined incredibly hard, if she defeated her habits, she could do it. She breathed in and out slowly, filled her lungs, and let all the air flow out. In and out. Then she held her breath, and believed there was nothing beneath her, nothing to hold her down. She was breath, not matter anymore, and lifted herself up so that only she knew.

DEAR OLLIE

Dear Ollie,

It's been a long time. I think of you sometimes, and I know you think of me. I take a perverse satisfaction in that, even in the jaded ways you disguise me in your so-called fictions. I really don't care. But I just read your "manifesto against the past." No one "votes for guilt." I also have "funny mental pictures" of that mansion we lived in on the Hudson. It wasn't "haunted," except by an unghostly Timothy Leary. Everyone said he dropped acid there. Everyone said they used to have wild parties. Even back then the term "wild parties" bothered me. No one ever gave details.

You and I were the only non–psych students living in the mansion. You and they were older, graduate students, but they were all research psychologists and thought everyone else was crazy, so they devised experiments to prove it. There was that one sullen guy who worked with rats. He had a big room near mine. I used to look in as I passed it. He kept his shoes under the chair of his desk in a certain way, everything in his room had a specific order, and if his shoes were moved even a quarter inch, he went crazy.

Remember when he drove his car into a wall? Then he disappeared. Remember it's my past, too, you want to "throw into the garbage, to be carted away by muscular men and sent floating on a barge to North Carolina."

One night, you brought a friend home from Juilliard, a fellow student. If you recall, our dining room had dark walls and no electricity. We ate by candlelight—there were many candles in different states of meltdown on the long table that night. About ten, I think.

Before dinner, one of the research psychologists suggested it'd be fun to put blue vegetable dye in the mashed potatoes. Your friend wouldn't know. We'd act as if the potatoes weren't blue, just the usual white, and even though your friend might protest and insist they were blue, we'd keep insisting they were white. We'd just pretend he was crazy for thinking they were blue. We cooked this up in the kitchen. When you came in with him, someone took you aside and told you. You went along with it. Everyone has a streak of sadism, one of the psych guys said.

I don't remember who brought in the potatoes, we all participated, though, and then we all sat down around the big wooden table. The blue mashed potatoes were served in a glass bowl. Even by candlelight, they were bright blue.

We passed the food. When the bowl of blue potatoes reached your friend, he reacted with delight. Blue mashed potatoes, he said. Someone said, They're not blue. Your friend said, They're not? They look blue. Someone else said, No, they're not. You were sitting next to him.

The potatoes kept going around. Your friend said, again, They really look blue. Everyone acted as if nothing was happening. Your friend kept looking at the bowl. He became visibly agitated. He said, They look blue. Someone said, Maybe it's the candlelight. The flames have a bluish tinge. Your friend kept looking, squinting his eyes. Then he insisted, They look blue to me. Someone said, with annoyance, Would you stop it? They're not blue. Your friend turned quiet. He kept looking, though, and we all kept eating.

The coup de grace, I guess you'd call it, was dessert. In the kitchen, someone decided to dye the milk blue. The cake, coffee, and blue milk were brought to the table. We served the blue milk in a glass pitcher. No one said much as the pitcher went around the table. Your friend watched silently. When it came to him, he stared at the pitcher and poured the blue milk into his coffee. This time, he said nothing. Nothing. At that point I ran into the kitchen. I couldn't control myself.

Later, you told him. After dinner, when you were alone with him, you told him. But I'm wondering, after all these years, did he ever forgive you? What happened to him? Does he still play the trombone?

You were good, Ollie. But somehow, in "regurgitating the past and moving on," I'm "the reckless prankster" whose "promiscuous heart" you broke. The only thing in that house you ever broke was your musician friend and crazy Roger's green plates.

Whatever,
Lynne Tillman
New York, New York

THE DEAD LIVE LONGER

My dead ex-friend had a long neck, a small head balanced on it. Her head bobbled when she danced, perched on her long neck—she might be willowy. A moon-crazed, intelligent, vain, sensitive, insecure woman, she was brought into life by a mean woman, a woman who terrified her little girl, and who became a miserly, scared widow when my dead ex-friend was seventeen, and who told her all her life: "Don't ever leave the house without your makeup, no matter what." My dead ex-friend always wore makeup to look at least presentable, even beautiful. It took her about an extra hour every day, before she could leave the house, and she was often late while perfecting her composition, a face to the world.

My friend's beauty was a question to her, and to me. I could not see her face as it was, or maybe ever see her, and then there was who she was and became. Before I met her, she told me, she had very large breasts. She told me they had bulged and hung from her chest, below her long, swanlike neck; and below her breasts she was lithe and thin. Her breasts weighed her down from her shoulders, they made her look freakish, she told me, and her mother thought so, also, I'm positive she did, because whatever her mother thought about my friend's looks, my friend believed. She hated her mother.

Before we met, her breasts had been reduced, and, during the surgery one nipple flipped, it turned in rather than out and could have been fixed. Her surgeon said he'd do it for free, but she never bothered, if it was a bother. She often mentioned it. I believe she came to admire her inverted nipple, an example of her specialness. People like to imagine their specialness.

Beneath her breasts, a wide, red-purple scar ran, a one-inch-wide scar. For a long time she didn't tell me about her surgery, even when she had told me too much. The scar's origin mystified me, and I didn't ask about it. Maybe she'd tried to kill herself or, in a mad fit, sliced off her breasts.

She made up her face religiously, religiously is correct, though she wasn't a believer; she might be considered a ritualist. She performed her ritual daily without hope, only devotion to her face's transformation, her duty or assignment to cover any errors or flaws that might detract from her plausible or implausible beauty. In the late morning, unless she were sick, she applied beauty products, sometimes taking two or more hours in the bathroom, and if the application went wrong, her hand unsteady, the mistakes took more time to remove and make right.

Correcting mistakes broadens the path to more. Removal and reapplication cause red marks, the black of an eyebrow pencil or eyeliner would have smudged the thin skin under her eyes, that delicate skin no one is supposed to rub ever, even touch. So the process toward looking beautiful, flawless, turned still more arduous and complicated, and sometimes she imagined she looked worse, and sometimes she did, all the effort showing up, when effort itself exposes what should be undetectable.

My vanity compelled me not to apply anything on my skin,

only black eyeliner to my eyes, and then only at night when I could prepare to be a mystery handsome men would hope to solve. But I was too easily disarmed.

I admired her long neck, because I read novels and watched movies whose heroines balanced pretty heads on swanlike necks, and a long neck signified gracefulness, just as thick ankles did the opposite, as though bodies determined a woman's qualities, necessitating cosmetic surgery to refute those claims. My dead ex-friend submitted to it years after I fled our curdled friendship.

My dead ex-friend spent hours putting on a face, not her face, she called it a face, and she was known by all to be late. All her life, few could see her face without makeup except close friends who might have slept the night at her house—she owned a house or rented one, when I knew her, or a large apartment, because the primary or even only way she and her mother connected, they were always entangled, was through the money her father, who had died suddenly of a heart attack when she was seventeen, left in his will.

He left it all to her mother. Her mother doled out some, she provided money for her daughter, a living wage, to rent or sometimes buy a place to live, especially if my friend had prodded her selfish mother for more, which she did regularly, and she knew how to get it. It was a struggle between them, a fight, always about money, and usually my ex-friend won, because she knew how to make her mother, who was pathetic, squirm and seethe with guilt. Her father had explained to her, not long before his sudden death from a heart attack, that her mother was crazy. She was seventeen and why, she asked me, why hadn't Daddy told her sooner, and made her life easier, but then he died and left all his money to that crazy woman, and my ex-friend never understood how he could have done that to her. He hadn't changed his will, he should have, and I said, to mollify her, he didn't know, he hadn't had time, he would have if he'd lived longer. Those thoughts occurred to her, also, but without any satisfaction, only deepening the cut, and the wound opened, and closed, and was opened, it never healed. She had realized only when she was twenty-five, she told me, that other people had feelings. Her pain made her indifferent to the suffering of others.

Her mother doled out funds according to her whims, a miser's scruples, my friend leashed to her mother's bank account, her father's money. She knew, in her yearning heart, her mother would come through, send her the money, she usually did, but her anxiety crested until it came, and, when it did, she enjoyed a victory over her mother, short-lived, getting what she wanted, and hated her mother even more for making her beg for it. It was her father's money.

This upper-middle-class servitude wasn't renounced until she was much older, had gone to graduate school, and found work at which she was surprisingly good, I heard, as a kindergarten teacher. This job came along after she'd had other positions, including work as a dominatrix or S&M prostitute, at which she was very good, I was told. She had trained for it all her life, really.

My dead ex-friend was smart, had many talents, and could be sympathetic, if it served her interests, like any seasoned narcissist, and, if you didn't know her well, and if you weren't a female like her, and if you didn't get too close so that ultimately she envied and hated you as she did her mother, with a certain emotional restraint, with distance, you could get the very best from her.

Lovers saw her naked, her face free of makeup, if they remained lovers for a while, but with a one-night stand she would rush out of bed in the morning before he awakened, so that he would not see her naked face. She wore mascara to bed and reapplied it in the morning, before he awoke. She had many lovers, one or two she stole from me, "stole" isn't the right word, but as she did with her mother, she competed with me furiously. If I liked someone and mentioned him, the way I sometimes did when I was careless, she would advance on him.

Before we stopped being friends, and we were best friends for ten years, the last two were terrible, she would say that, one day she was going to have a tattoo along the red-purple scar below her breasts, a vine of roses or another flower, a trail, she mentioned that often and never did it, to my knowledge. She liked vines, and I can barely look at a few delicate trailing plants she loved and nourished, because to me they are her, their tendrils enticing traps.

I had seen tattoos on the muscular arms of working men, but no one I knew had tattoos, not back then, she was the first person I knew to want one. She wanted to cover her scar, and she didn't. She was the first person in other ways, the first vegan I knew who wore cloth shoes that rotted in heavy rains, the first uniquely gifted, sadistic woman whose manipulations I didn't understand. So I learned from her. But I didn't know what she wanted from me.

People talk about what they may do one day, like have a nipple fixed, and never do it. It must be a compelling idea satisfied just by imagining it, knowing you can do it, or by its incompletion have a tie to future possibility. Her flaw may have satisfied her, perversely, since it couldn't be seen or known unless she was naked or pulled up her blouse, she kept a secret, and had others, one was how much she hated me.

•

She and I loved cats, there were often kittens around her house, and we played with them, laughing, and we saw movies, and both of us read a lot, she loved Blaise Cendrars—and we were always talking, about art, feminism, we had fun as long as I listened to her, and as long as I was unhappy, was depressed, and didn't have a boyfriend. If I did, she wanted him for herself. I was shocked after she told me she'd had him, then said nothing. I didn't know what to say.

She fell in love the way I did, stupidly fast, blindly, we had lots of sex with men, we compared our dates, roaring with laughter, we shared all that in our twenties, as well as long, analytical discussions about men we barely knew. Then she fell in love, really, or as close to it as she could get, with an optimistic, enthusiastic Englishman from a wealthy family whose wealth he did not want. She loved his idealism until it interfered with her desires. I don't know if she loved him, but she wanted him. He was a strapping lad, with blue-green sloe eyes, long, stringy blond hair, long, strong legs from bike-riding everywhere. He was against cars.

They married, and were married for a while, we were by then in different cities, but close, phone-talking friends, and she left him to return to the US. He was devastated and then, I heard, recovered.

After she and I hadn't spoken for as long as we'd been friends, I received a message from a mutual friend saying that her ex-husband was dead. He was in his mother's car, in the passenger seat, when she turned left onto a main road, from their hidden driveway, a car crashed into his side of the car, and he was killed instantly. By then he was married with a child, maybe two.

The mutual friend asked me to contact her and tell her, because I knew her ex-husband, and it was so intimate, and I knew her better and etc. But I wrote immediately I could not do it, I couldn't contact her after so long, especially with this tragic news. The mutual friend wrote this to her, who responded, "Oh, she hates me that much." I didn't feel hatred, I didn't think it was hatred. I felt stricken at the thought of hearing her voice, of having any contact with her. Maybe that is a hatred. She was a monster to me, maybe monsters are always hated figures.

Years after we stopped being friends, I heard she had a facelift, it was inevitable, because her mother had done it several times, and her mother had told her often she would also need it to remain beautiful. Theirs was the intense and powerful attachment only the fusion of love and hate fosters. Curiously, the only person my dead ex-friend's mother trusted to tell her when she needed another facelift was her daughter, the daughter who hated her and who didn't want to see her. Another oddity was that her mother was friendly with the woman whose capacious Upper West Side apartment I stayed in, renting the defunct maid's room, during my college years. They knew each other.

Our last phone call was flat, necessarily strangled, and I've never had another like it. She called to apologize, something she had never done before. "I was awful to you, wasn't I?" She had been mean, vicious sometimes, but I didn't want to say yes, accept her apology, or condemn her. I don't know why, not fully. Instead, I said something to lessen her anguish or pain, if she felt it or anything. "We both had terrible mothers," I told her. She said nothing, and I suppose we hung up then, awkwardly, but there must have been a silence before we did. There must have been silence, because this was it, our drama's finale. I would never see her again, I never wanted to. She would be out of my life, this dark, harsh weight, who had once been light and precious.

I sat at the kitchen table for a while, maybe absorbing the moment, the freedom I felt, and then went on with my life.

But that isn't an end.

•

My dead ex-friend had a beautiful, long neck, and was vain and insecure, could be great fun, had a good mind, but jealousy savaged her spirit. Maybe she felt unfulfilled or fulfilled, because she made a decision to die in her own time and way, and it was in character, that she decide her fate. Her death may have come at the right time for her, though she was just sixty, not old enough or young enough. She could have saved herself, but she chose not to, and I don't know what or how to think about that, and have no idea what was in her mind.

She died before her mother did, which her mother had predicted, she once told her, You will die before me. Maybe she thought so because her daughter took heavy drugs to sleep since she was a teenager. Every night she drugged herself into a stupor. I wondered what her dreams were, that she couldn't sleep without the profound oblivion drugs provided. I imagined, in her dreams, she killed her mother every night, bloody, horrifying dreams in which she vanquished her demon. The drugs might have done her organs in, aged them faster, so they and she died young.

Her mother's prophesy struck me as a terrible, sinister curse: you, daughter, will die before me. The curse of a miserable woman who should never have had a child. A daughter. A Greek curse, though I don't know of a Greek tragedy with that in its story. Here is a daughter cursed by her mother, who becomes a curse to her friends. I wasn't alone.

After she died, her close friend, a man, sent me a bracelet she had made, and I thought maybe it would be good to have, to remember the good times. The bracelet arrived, it wasn't special except that she had made it, it reminded me of Greek worry beads or a rosary, and I placed it on the mantelpiece that night, and that night or early in the morning, I awoke with a shock, unnerved, and completely awake: She had called my name in a demanding way, as if saying, Get up, recognize me. I hadn't heard her voice in thirty years, it was her voice.

I mailed the bracelet back to her friend, and explained why or gave a reason so as not to hurt his feelings, because his gesture, his offering her bracelet, was kind, recognizing our history. I knew, but didn't tell him, she was locked into my unconscious, and wouldn't leave it, and I couldn't have it, or her, around to haunt me, and, once the bracelet was out of the house, I didn't hear her voice again.

I did see her again, I'm sure I did, the scene is coming back. We didn't live in the same city, she must have been visiting, and I was at a performance of a play, where the director had hung a long and wide clear plastic sheet across the front of the stage, so we the audience were reflected in it. I was alone, watching the play, sometimes seeing my reflection, more often the other audience members', and then she appeared, a spectral figure on plastic. Her head was turned ever so slightly toward me, so I stared straight ahead, eyes on the stage, the actors. I didn't want to see even her reflection, but sometimes her face appeared on the periphery, when the plastic sheet rippled, wavered, and I believe she was crying, I'm pretty sure, but it may have been the play.

In her end, she died before her mother, and gave her mother what she wanted. I didn't know that she had died until two years after, and that also felt strange, to come upon it casually. You just never know, when a person is out of your life, if they are alive or not, though it's easier now to know.

She was out of my life for many, many years, not yet dead, but dead to me figuratively. It's very different, that kind of death. I learn that with each fresh death.

FIVE SHORT STORIES

My girlfriend is nearsighted. When she was nineteen, on a Friday night she walked into a bar to meet a guy. Have sex, maybe. She wasn't wearing her glasses. She has beautiful eyes. But really nearsighted.

The bar was long, a horseshoe bar. She stood at one end of it and ordered a beer to appear normal. After a while, she became aware of a guy looking at her. He was at the other end of the long bar. She looked at him. He was staring at her. Occasionally, she would turn away, coyly, not wanting to show too much interest. But he was staring at her, not averting his gaze. But not coming over to her. The flirting went on.

My girlfriend, she's impatient, and she became annoyed, all this eyeing back and forth, and nothing happening. She screwed up her courage, probably Dutch by then, a couple of beers in her, and decided to walk over, see what was happening.

She walked determinedly to the other end of the bar. Right up to him, when she realized there was no man there. She'd been flirting with a dark stain on the wall, and raced out of there. She wondered who saw her making eyes with a stain on the wall. That cracked her up, later.

Gene was astonished at June's quiet, her dead calm. She'd talked a lot when she was a baby, she never shut up. Their mother didn't listen, she was perpetually waiting for their father, her patriotic husband, to come home from that "crazy stupid war. Your father—don't eat with your fingers, Junie—had to do his duty." Their mother looked past them.

Her selfless husband perished in that godforsaken jungle, which sort of killed their mother, and their tiny family. Gene split, June stayed, lived at home, took weird jobs, did drugs, and their mother resented both of them. Most of all, being alive.

Then ten years later she died, and Gene came home, after many years.

"A lot gets lost in the mists of time." Gene was talking just to talk. June's silence was weird, eerie.

"Damn those mists," June said, finally. "What the hell." And she kind of snorted.

June was born with a spoon of sarcasm in her mouth. She might be pissed at him for splitting, but she didn't seem sad. Maybe relieved their mother kicked the bucket. She took care of their mother for some of the time she was sick. But he couldn't read June.

More silence. Then by way of explanation, which he thought

he owed June, Gene said, "I want you to know. I've come back to bury her."

"Not literally," she said, and snorted again.

Her former lover appeared on the street, emaciated. Cancer, liver disease, heart trouble, she didn't know. He looked terrible, dead man walking. He came up to her, she was stopped at the red light. And stood too near her. She smelled his cologne, the same one. He said hello, and she did. Then he said something, a nicety, and so she said something in return that was nothing.

He had ghosted her years back, just up and disappeared. Now, she barely looked at him, his face, his eyes were still hazel. She told him she had to split, go home, work or something, but then he started to say he was sorry. Some apologies come too late. She nodded, and didn't look back, and knew he would be.

"Wayne, you're staying here, that's fine with us. Just chill and take care of our dog. So, take it easy. I only ask . . . I want to remind you that our furniture here is, you know, worth something."

"Yeah, yeah," Wayne said, shaking his head like her big dog. He didn't need to be reminded by his perky sister.

Yeah, yeah, Wayne thought.

The dog stared at him suspiciously. Definitely.

She and her asshole husband left, walked to their Volvo, and drove away. Wayne waved from the front door, then headed to the refrigerator, grabbed a beer, and plopped down on a chair. It collapsed beneath him. The blond legs splayed under him. Pretty funny.

He laughed. The dog barked.

Wayne stared at the dog. "The dog barks, the caravan moves on."

The taxi driver was born in Georgia, and came to the US when he was ten. He told me that his English wasn't that good, and he hadn't wanted to go to college, because he didn't have to go, he was free to do what he wanted. Now, driving a cab, he had some regret, but didn't know what he would study. I asked, What interests you? He said, Philosophy, but I have the best philosophy, so why would I need to study anyone else's? I asked what his philosophy was, and he told me that things didn't name themselves, and other ideas, none of which was explained clearly. He was clearly smart, though.

He commented that we were now really talking to each other, having a conversation. I said, Yes, we are. We are trying to understand each other, I said. Yes, he said, then he said something brilliant, and I am still thinking about it: "Language is a conspiracy between two people." "Yes, that's a good definition of language."

But I was stunned, and asked, Do you know that "conspire" means to breathe together? People do that, I said. And, You believe in doubt, yes? He said, Yes, so I said, You shouldn't be sure that your philosophy is better than anyone else's. He pulled up in front of my building and took my suitcase out of the trunk. And he said it was good talking with me, I said I liked it, too, and then, as he opened the car door, he looked back. "Maybe I'll pick you up another time. It happens," he said. "Sure," I said. "It could happen."

Thrilled to Death

What makes people insecure is when they feel like they're lost in the fun house.

—PRESIDENT BILL CLINTON

Because carnivalistic life is life drawn out of its usual rut, it is to some extent "life turned inside out, . . . the reverse side of the world." In antiquity parody was inseparably linked to a carnival sense of the world. Parodying is the creation of a decrowning double; it is the same "world turned inside out." For this reason parody is ambivalent.

—MIKHAIL BAKHTIN

It is not only happiness that gives value to life.

—COLETTE

Once upon a Time

Rose Hall was riding backward on a train. She was alone. She felt as free as she would ever be. A man across the aisle had fallen asleep, and his head had dropped to the side of his body. His full lips were open and parted, like a fish mouth on a hook. She watched him, drank beer, and looked at the landscape pass by dyslexically.

Earlier she had wanted to have many lovers and a large glass of vodka. She wanted everything fast, without problems or fuss. She laughed at her fantasy of no-fuss love, and then she didn't. Even earlier she became furious at an elderly woman who barged in front of her on line. Rose Hall kept silent. She even bit her tongue. She stared out the window and nursed her wounds. It was strange how one thing didn't follow another.

Steve Whitehurst saw a man standing in front of a door. The man was holding a large pot. It appeared to have nothing in it. The street was dark and the man with the pot was in shadow. Steve crossed to the other side. He didn't want to get hit on the head. Protecting his head was weird, he thought, it probably wasn't worth it. He bought a quart of milk and returned home. He intended to take his regular route, if the freak with the pot had disappeared. But he was still standing there, holding the pot. Steve walked several blocks out of his way, past the Italian Boys Social Club. They were hopeful Mafia lieutenants. He was used to them. But the man with the pot set off an alarm. What in hell was he doing? Steve Whitehurst looked around sharply and put his key in the door.

Lily Lee Wallner kicked a stone on the sidewalk and watched it hurtle into the gutter. She had few defenses against flagrant beauty, her own impatience, and the strangeness of daily life. She was impatient with life. She succumbed to pleasure when she could. "I submitted, I gave in," she told a friend. "I was enthralled. I was on thrill." She fed her fantasies as if they were hungry. The sky was a bright plastic blue. Almost transparent. Lily Lee walked into the park, to the dog run. She stood there a long time. The dogs greeted each other or didn't, they sniffed each other or didn't. Small catlike dogs pursued unlikely big dogs. The freedom of dogs was beguiling, and Lily Lee liked to imagine an animal's liberty. She walked away, toward the playground, a fortress encircled by rough-hewn, pale-blue walls. Children slid down the slides and screamed with savage pleasure. Worried mothers frowned, and patient fathers and happy mothers smiled. Lily Lee didn't want children. She wanted a dog. Maybe that was a fantasy.

Paige Turner wrote in her notebook: "You've never been a child, or you're always a child. Or there is no childhood, or children are innocent, or they're evil, or children and adults have nothing to do with each other, or they have everything to do with each other, they are each other, or how do you stop being a child—at an event? with a recognition? and when, oh when, does childhood end? and when does being alive stop being only colors, smells, and sounds.

"You're little, you're lying in the dark, and you can barely see but you hear noises, voices. Sounds become words, you put two and two together, two words, two sentences, an explanation, everything's explained to you, you're told about the world, you overhear, you pay attention, drink in, you grow bigger, you make up your own stories, you imagine, things happen to you that you can't control, you make your way or you don't . . ."

Paige washed her hair. It was long, curly, and red. She'd heard jokes about redheads her whole life. She was sick to death of them, she hated being called "Red." Everyone said her hair was her best feature. Maybe she'd bleach it silver. I have a redhead's temper, she noted wryly to herself. Then she laughed out loud.

It was way past her bedtime. Jeff Brown read *Cinderella* to his four-year-old daughter, Kelly.

"Once upon a time, a wealthy man's wife died suddenly. The stricken man mourned her extravagantly. But luckily he had one daughter he adored. Cinderella was kind, bright, and beautiful, like his dead wife. But he was lonely, and he wanted to make a new home for them. So he remarried. Now his new wife also had children, two daughters from a marriage that ended with death. But theirs had not been a happy union, and years of strife had hardened the woman and her daughters. They were blind to anything but their own needs. One could say that she and her daughters were cut from the same loveless cloth, and loving didn't come easily to them, and they weren't easily made happy. In her way, the new wife loved her new husband. But it had been a long time since she'd been loving. She guarded her good feelings jealously, as if they could be stolen from her like her wallet. Right after the marriage, the new wife turned against her stepdaughter. Cinderella didn't like her, either. She was ordered to do menial chores and given no time to read stories, which she loved. Her stepsisters passed their days playing games, doing puzzles, studying, and trying on clothes. Cinderella didn't complain to her father, even though she wanted to. She had a lot of pride, but oddly enough, to her annoyance, her father seemed happy with his new wife . . ."

Kelly's eyes started to close. Jeff watched her face expectantly. Her eyes opened again, and she pleaded buoyantly, Daddy, read more, Daddy, read.

"So day after day, she did the dirty work, pretending it didn't bother her. Night after night, she sat by the fireplace, in a corner of the hearth, surrounded by ashes. She watched the hot fire burn orange and red, then die. She tried not to feel sorry for herself.

"Her dirty face and hands, and soiled, torn clothes, were a constant shame to her. She felt older than her years. Her stepsisters teased her and called her Cindy, because she sat by the cinders. Cinderella controlled her temper. Her face grew masklike, and she never laughed. But, however she felt about herself, she was pretty in her sisters' eyes, and they saw how their stepfather looked at her. Cinderella hadn't planned to make them suffer by comparison, but they did."

Kelly's eyelids dropped and shut tight, and Jeff, tired, jumped to the end of the tale.

"The shoe fairly flew out of the Prince's hand—or so it is said—onto her foot, making a bond with it. The sisters were astonished. So was the Prince. They were even more astonished when Cinderella pulled from her pocket the second slipper and placed it on her other foot. (She did this with a little satisfaction; she wasn't absolutely selfless or a fool.) With the second shoe on, her godmother appeared. She waved her wand over Cinderella, who was transformed again. This time, even more magnificently. Awestruck, the Prince asked her to marry him.

"Now, this is what everyone still talks about. Though she loved the Prince, and accepted his offer, what pleased Cinderella most was her sisters' change of heart. They were ashamed of their behavior and really sorry they'd been so horrible to her. And Cinderella forgave them and said she would always love them. Then she invited them to live with her in the palace. A few days later, when she and the Prince married, Cinderella introduced her sisters to two eligible bachelors. Immediately they fell in love. This made her stepmother proud, even repentant. And, though everything happened very fast, after many years, they are all still together. And so it may be said that they are living happily ever after."

By the time Jeff recited the words "happily ever after," Kelly was lost to sleep. She looked so vulnerable, he wanted to cry.

In the Brothers Grimm version, the stepsisters' eyes are plucked out by doves. "And so for their wickedness and falseness they were punished with blindness for the rest of their days." He didn't want Kelly to hear that. Jeff Brown and his white wife had recently divorced. The truth was, she left him for another man. Jeff resisted his own ugly feelings, and they parted more or less amicably. Jeff was a reasonable man. But ever since the divorce, their daughter, Kelly, had had bad dreams.

Jeff discussed the Grimm version of *Cinderella* with his law partner, Rose Hall. He told her how bloody and cruel it was. It's wild, Jeff said, no matter what version you read, *Cinderella*'s a divorce story, right from line one. Then, looking out the window, he said, I want to protect Kelly, but in this world you're a fool, living a fantasy.

Frank Green took life as it came. He prided himself on that. But he envied other people their illusions, their delusions, their dreams. He wasn't a dreamer. He wasn't like that. Plain food, plain living, he wasn't going to kid himself. He had his one chance in life, and if he blew it, that was that. He probably had blown it. But he wasn't a crybaby. He didn't care what other people thought about him.

Frank had a dream. He told his girlfriend, Lily Lee: I'm trapped in an apartment. I'm trapped in a kitchen, it's yellow. I hear a noise. Someone has gotten in. Someone wants to kill me. I see who it is. This person wants me dead, but I can't believe it. I wake up. I have to piss like a racehorse.

A yellow kitchen? Lily Lee repeated, with a wan smile. I'm the kitchen? Frank told her she was being a jerk. "I had to piss, that's all." And then he teased her the way he always did: "You're just half-Chinese."

When it was late at night or early in the morning and the city was silent—like the Tombs, Frank always put it—he opened up to Lily Lee:

"A couple of years ago I felt like, who gives a shit. I hated it, life. Hated myself. I was apathetic. I hated life. Then I wanted to get high all the time. As much of the time as I could. I wanted to feel alive all the time. I drank like a maniac, I went on benders, I caroused with the guys, got stupid, and that started to interfere with the job. I got sloppy. And then I thought about sex all the time. Sex and more sex. I wanted to feel alive. This is before I met you. But the sex was nuts-and-bolts stuff, mechanical. I made up scenes to get myself off. But I had to work at it. I couldn't get off even on my own sexual numbers. It was pathetic. I looked at nuns, I mean, I'm a Catholic, I should be able to, and even schoolgirls, in their uniforms, but it didn't work for me. I couldn't picture it. I can't get excited if I can't picture it. Then I watched porn all the time. But it made me sad. I don't get off on other people's fantasies."

Lily Lee sighed. She said, I know what you mean. Frank Green was a cop. He fascinated her. They'd met at the hospital where she worked as a nightshift nurse. To Lily Lee he was Paul Newman in *Fort Apache, the Bronx*. They turned on the TV.

Lily Lee had a dream: A man's following me. I escape wearing heels but I'm in my nurse's uniform. There's blood on it. On the road outside the house, I start walking and hitch a ride with a man on skis. I close my eyes and don't see how fast or where we're going. Then I realize I'm holding on and we're going uphill climbing the Empire State Building—no, the Eiffel Tower. Then I wake up and there's snow and ice. I hang on to his body, my arms around his waist. At first I'm afraid, then I realize I can ski.

Lily Lee put on her blades and skated around the city. She

didn't tell anyone about her nightmare. It disappeared with the day. That afternoon she met Frank, and they went to the carnival. They wanted to see "Bonnie and Clyde's Death Car," but they didn't know if it'd be there. Frank told her that when he was a kid, there were real freaks in carnivals. Now, he complained, the sideshow's on the street. Lily Lee grinned and told him to shut up.

The Omnipresent Tense

The scene overpowers Paige. She's excitable. She thinks, I'm such a cheap date, maybe I have a cheap date with fate. The carnival gates are wide open. Everyone's been invited by an imaginary host. There's no one to thank or to be grateful to. The chaotic and tacky splendor is disinterested, like a neutral party. All are welcome. Paige likes that.

The carnival seduces Paige the way it always does, ever since she was a kid. It's a phantasm, a phantasmagoric suite of sights. Anything can happen. A carnival was her first taste of sweet earthly danger. She remembers it like her first real kiss, even though the first carnival was just a bunch of tents and displays, games and food, cotton candy, nothing elaborate. But one day it appeared, out of nowhere, in a vacant parking lot, at the end of the block. Strangers lounged on the sidewalk, men with mustaches and muscles, women with red lips and muscles. The grifters seduced the suckers. The short con artists, small time and hapless, schemed and entrapped. The carney kids seemed to have possibilities she'd never know. They ran wild, her mother said. She was scared of the place and attracted to it. A dark, handsome teenager, years older than her, smiled at Paige, and an unknown thrill curled up her spine.

She's still scared on the rides, thrilled to death.

•

"And mammoth, now-extinct animals roamed the land, and our ancestors, prehistoric humans, crawled on all fours, on hairy limbs. They didn't have tools or fire. Foliage blanketed the ground. Forests and mountains and lakes and oceans and rivers and valleys were mighty. The hot yellow sun and the cool silver moon and the white nighttime stars generated life, and there was no time. The strange, naturally occurring objects made the world for the creatures below them. They determined the activity of all the incipient or simple humans and the large and small creatures."

Jeff, Rose, and Kelly sit in the darkened theater. The voice-over rolls along as dinosaurs, winged mammals, pterodactyls, and hunched over, crawling, or standing early humans move like ghosts across the 3D screen. Kelly is a butterfly mounted on her seat. Jeff considers the magnitude of prehistory, first as myth, then as fact. He thinks about evolution, those first human baby steps, the laborious move to stand upright, creatures crawling out of the water onto land and adapting. He wonders if humans are still adapting or if humans are finished, soon to be extinct. He looks at Kelly. She fills him with hope.

Rose has her own hopes. Maybe a life in the country or a life with Jeff, though that might be a bad idea, just a fantasy, and then there's mixing business with pleasure, but none of those rules really matter to her, deep down. Jeff wonders if Rose is in love with him. His wife used to say that, but he thought she was just giving him grief. Rose thinks maybe she loves Jeff. Kelly doesn't like Rose. She wants her mommy and daddy to be together again. Actually, she wants her daddy all to herself.

In the darkened theater, all three discover that wearing 3D glasses is uncomfortable. Rose is disoriented, agitated. She can't shake an uneasy feeling. Then the show's over and they walk outside. The bright sun hurts Jeff's eyes. Rose squints, too. Kelly asks, Daddy, Daddy, go carousel?

Paige wanders through the sprawling carnival, the playground—massive tents, quaint, small buildings, golden facades, enormous terrifying rides, food booths, staged acts, video and computer games, interactive Gothic houses of horror. Waves of brilliant color rise and splash over her. A tide of electricity carries her away from shore, from herself. Startling neon signs glare and blink naughtily. Light encases her as if it were a gaudy gown.

Paige strolls slowly up one ramp and then down another, she follows the twists and turns of the road. She's in a labyrinth. She wants to absorb everything. She doesn't want to know where she is. She doesn't want to be herself. Unconsciously she smells perfumes and underarms and hair spray and young and old bodies. The smells of food are memory ridden. Smell is the sense closest to the center of memory in the brain, a psychologist once told her. Even when Paige doesn't remember what is evoked by a scent or aroma, the smell lingers, tantalizingly. Paige believes memory is in every cell of her body.

Steve Whitehurst sees Paige Turner. Her long, curly red hair. He's always had a thing for redheads. Steve notices Paige while standing behind his uncle's shooting gallery; it's one of his uncle's concessions. Steve wonders if she'll come to his booth. He sets his mind to it, to drawing her closer to the theater of rifles. But she walks away, toward the fortune teller. A couple of Black kids pick up rifles. Steve tells them, You have to pay first. One says they don't have money. Steve nods, Okay, and they go ahead. But just one round, he cautions. Steve hopes his uncle doesn't spot him doing this. Everyone in his family is in the carney business. Steve's not made for the life.

•

Grotesque advertisements for horror fan Paige's spirits. I have no soul, she whispers to no one. And I don't want one. But I want something. Maybe I'll run away and join the carnival, call myself Dahlia and paint myself purple, I'll think purple thoughts, and be the purple lady in the sideshow. She wonders if, without the idea of a soul, she can think about beauty lasting, or of anything lasting, of goodness living on after death, of anything of her continuing, or of anything at all in her, or anything that might survive the death of her body. She didn't want the thoughts. A friend told her that's why people have children.

Paige is transfixed by the swirl and rage of the raucous action around her. No one has planned it all, it's not plotted, it's not a plot. She can do whatever she wants. But Paige sometimes finds it hard to choose.

The shocking pink-striped facade of the fortune teller—the Cabinet of Dr. Joy—entices Paige. A poster picture of the fortune teller is dramatic. He's an old man with a white beard and wire-rimmed glasses. He looks serious, Paige thinks, as she takes the plunge and parts the heavy curtains. Though Paige doesn't believe in it, she always has her fortune told. Cards, tarot, palm readings, tea leaves, handwriting, crystal balls. The old man doesn't work that way.

Frank and Lily Lee are riding on the Wonder Wheel. It stops. They're stuck at the top. Frank cracks a joke about there being room at the top for the likes of them. He calls himself legal lowlife. Lily Lee tells him to stop ragging on himself. The little carriage shakes back and forth. Frank takes Lily Lee's hand. I have a secret, he says soberly. Lily Lee looks at him hopefully. You can't tell anyone, he goes on. Only my partner knows, and he's a tomb.

Lily Lee listens, waits breathlessly. I murdered a guy, Frank says.
They're both silent, the little carriage jolts back and forth. In the
line of duty? Lily Lee asks. No, he says, not in the line of duty.
I was a kid. It was an accident. They are on top of the Wonder
Wheel a long time. Frank stares ahead. He's not frightened. Lily
Lee is, but Frank's stoicism infects her. Frank asks, Do you think
you could marry a man like me? Lily Lee swallows and coughs
nervously. Is he serious? Frank goads her: But since you're half
inscrutable, I'll never know what the real deal is . . . Lily Lee bites
her tongue. She says, If you keep on this half business. Then she
breathes in and out. I know my mother's family will love you,
anyway. So that's a yes, Frank says. If we live, Lily Lee answers,
looking down, her heart in her mouth.

Paige Turner instantly and inexplicably comes under the spell
of the fortune teller. A charming mind reader, she decides. The
fortune teller stares calmly at Paige. He takes her into his inner
sanctum. He motions that she sit down. He wants to hypnotize
her. Does she mind? When he looks at her with his peculiarly
intense eyes, she says, No, go ahead. Then she adds, What have I
got to lose? Your inhibitions, he answers serenely. But he continues, I don't predict the future. You don't? Paige asks. No, he says,
I predict the past. Predict the past? Paige repeats. He dangles a
silver object in front of her eyes and speaks in a warm voice and
her eyelids grow heavy, as he says they will.

Steve Whitehurst's uncle returns and tells him to take tickets at
the sideshow. That's more your line, he adds, to Steve's annoyance. In an uncanny way, his uncle's right. He's more at home
in front of the Odditorium than behind a counter where people
shoot at targets with ugly brown rifles. The Odditorium is out

of date, the name was used a long time ago, but the sideshow business—there's no business like the sideshow business—is having a comeback, he reassures himself. Steve walks over to the ticket booth. He doesn't really like the current freaks who are bringing sideshows back, but at least they don't want the life to disappear. We're up against soap operas and daytime talk shows, his uncle complained all the time, freaking talk shows, freaks for free, but they're just talk, blah blah. People come because they still want the real thing, live stuff, live exhibits.

But not as much as they once did, Steve knows. He smiles at the posters around him, relieves the other guy in the booth, and remembers the redhead nearby. Live exhibits, Steve thinks.

Nothing dies here, everything's alive, vital, the old man chants. You're in a carnival. You're in the fun house. But it's not a fun house. It's also a tragic place, a cemetery for things that aren't dead. A home for the hidden, the driven, the obscene, and sometimes something leaps out, but it's not what it seems. What arrives wears a costume, and an event is a mask. It may be something else. It may be light or dark and really be its opposite. But there are no simple opposites.

Paige, you will encounter your contrariness and bare it boldly. Your ambivalence will concoct dreams beyond your wildest wishes. Here, your contradictions may be honeyed and bitter.

Paige tastes bittersweet chocolate in her mouth.

Paige, here you can be anything. Where are you now?

Paige listens to something, maybe it's the fortune teller: Where are you?

I don't know. I can't tell.

Do you see a window?

Yes, I see it.

Go through it. What do you see now?

Ropes, funny china, people in costumes, neon lights, monkeys on trees, crates of fruit, my mother, a stack of orange books, and so many colors, and there are three ways to go, paths . . .

Take one.

Where am I? Paige asks herself. This is corny. Maybe I'm having a near-death experience.

Where am I? she asks aloud.

You are not yet. You are not I.

I know that. I don't want to choose a path.

Then you'll stand in one place.

I'm at a standstill, Paige thinks. How did the fortune teller know?

Jeff Brown carries Kelly. She's a drowsy bundle in his arms. Rose and Jeff walk to the sideshow. Signs proclaim exhibits and acts—a bearded lady, a tattooed man, a sword swallower, the largest rat in captivity. I don't want to see a giant rat, Rose announces, disgusted. Her lip curls. Jeff hates that. And as her lip curls, and she says this, an amplified voice blurts: See the incredible rat. Come, look at the largest rat in captivity. Look at the giant rat. They see a poster for a hunger artist. That, I have to see that, Rose says. They pay their money to Steve Whitehurst. Jeff's glad Kelly's asleep.

They enter a room and pass the giant rat in a glass case. Rose ignores it. There's another glass cage with hefty cockroaches and, in its own separate section, a furry tarantula. A man-eating snake rests, coiled, in its box. Then they approach the hunger artist. She is a woman in a large cage sitting on a stool next to an empty refrigerator. A doctor's scale is next to her. A sign I WILL EAT NO FAT hangs behind her head. She is emaciated, so weak she can't stand. Is this a joke? Jeff asks. Rose points to a smaller sign at the hunger artist's bony foot:

> I have to fast, I can do nothing else . . . because I could not find the food I like. If I had found it, believe me, I wouldn't have made a fuss but eaten my fill like you and anyone else.
>
> ——FRANZ KAFKA

Paige chooses a path, under protest. Now she doesn't really have words for what's happening, or isn't actually happening, and she can't make it conform to logic. It has its own logic and is indifferent to reality. She's moving and she's not, she's talking and she's not. Nothing dies here, she hears again.

Maybe something's dead in me, Paige says mournfully.

Nothing's dead in you, it's only unavailable. Behind one object lies another, nothing is lost. Life is a veil . . .

A vale of tears? Paige interrupts.

Life is a veil of self-consciousness, there are many . . .

Many lives? she asks, hopefully.

You have many possibilities, positions, and poses.

I'm a fake?

There are no disguises. Everything reveals you.

Paige struggles with the riddle and the eccentricity of the riddler. Finally she speaks, but her voice cracks, and she doesn't really have control over it. She thinks it's not hers.

"I want to go where I'm not supposed to go. I want to see what I'm not supposed to see. I want what I'm not supposed to have. I want to have everything, before I die. I want to be everything. I don't want life to end, and I don't want it to be for nothing, at the end. I want something about me to live forever.

I want death to lose, I don't want to reach an end. I don't want to come to a conclusion. I want to continue. And I don't want anything in my way."

Steve sells tickets for another freak show, it's hard-core, underground, more expensive. In a back room, people slash and cut themselves with razors and hang weights from their nipples or scrotums or both. There's a bondage and whipping act. Marrieds with children don't usually know about this show. It's word of mouth. Steve wants to have his nipples pierced, but he's afraid of blood and disease. He might do it anyway. Della, the dominatrix in this sideshow, knows how to pierce skin antiseptically and without pain. Yesterday, she told him, "Unless you want pain. My slave did." Steve asked, "How can you stand to watch his pain?" Della the dominatrix fixed her eyes on him and answered sternly, "It's not my pain." Steve was rocked by her frankness, her brutality.

Today he sways with abandon to the beat of the inside-out world he frequents. He doesn't think he wants pain or punishment, but he always feels guilty.

Lily Lee and Frank buy tickets to the back room show. Steve thinks Frank looks familiar. But is he a mark or a narc? Frank figures if Lily Lee can accept him, if he lets her know the worst about him, he can marry her without feeling like the pig he is. Frank's lied all his life and thinks everyone's a liar. Besides, he's good at it, and it's an occupational hazard. Lily Lee looks at Frank. She likes his paunch. His excess. Lily Lee wants nothing more than to live dangerously. Frank's her ticket to ride. He's a dark character. But she has secrets she'd never tell Frank. She has more sides to her than he could guess.

Lily Lee's mouth drops open. A guy is pounding a spike through his penis. Frank gapes at a man hanging from the ceiling by his tongue. Surprisingly, Frank is sick to his stomach. Lily Lee remembers, with a pang, that she had another dream. In it she handed a hard-boiled egg to Frank. But the yolk wasn't very hard. Maybe she'd tell Frank. He'd probably laugh and say it was a bad dream or bad yolk, that he's a rotten egg. Maybe she does want children.

The Imperfect Pretense

Paige isn't sure if she's babbling, in a trance, or daydreaming.

I shouldn't be telling you this, she says aloud.

I may or may not stop you, the old man says. Though you're the one who does that. You may want me to stop you.

No, I don't.

There's no no here.

This is crazy.

You imagine there's something else.

Paige is falling. Like Alice. She refuses to be Alice. She's falling anyway.

She is nowhere she knows. She may lose hope and lose hopelessness, abandon innocence and find her guilt, speak lies and truth, know reason as unreason, discover thoughtful thoughtlessness, and meaning's meaninglessness, be good and bad, and she may uncover things or bury things, forget to forget or forget to remember, and she may deny the dead, embrace hate and love murderousness, she may rage and covet. All her passions are allowed. She may repeat herself, endlessly. She can hold on and hold on, resist nothing, everything, and defend herself constantly.

Paige grips the arms of her chair.

Paige, the old man says, ugliness turns into beauty the way grapes turn into wine, and beauty may be ugly in a bad light.

Grapes aren't ugly, Paige answers, feeling dumb.

Paige is crestfallen, downcast suddenly, and Dr. Joy lifts up her chin. She doesn't know he's doing this. She hears him say: If you don't look for confirmation of your beliefs, you'll have an interesting life.

Now Paige imagines he's opened a fortune cookie.

Jeff, Rose, and Kelly emerge from the Odditorium. Rose can't get over the emaciated woman. She's starving herself to death. Kelly awakens and cries out, Carousel, I want carousel. Jeff smiles at his demanding little daughter. They follow the signs and walk in the direction of the carousel. Secretly Jeff wishes there'd been a snake woman and a fat man.

The sun is going down, it's cooler, but it's also warm, too, balmy, and far above, a mirror to the carnival, the sky is flecked with pink, orange, red, and gold. The sky's on fire. Brilliantly decorated and brightly colored vans and trailers are converging into the center, where the carousel acts like a magnet.

Suddenly Jeff and Rose are energetic. The pounding in Jeff's head evaporates, Rose stops worrying about a case she's handling, about the argument she has to make in court the next day, she stops fretting about Jeff.

Paige, wake up, you'll be as awake as you can be. You may remember that you are alone and not alone and that something lives you can never know or grasp fully. This is yours, but it's not yours alone.

Paige, wake up.

Paige opens her eyes and senses, weirdly, gravely, that she is awake, that she wasn't completely asleep. She shakes her legs and arms. She imagines she's a dancer and a dance. She knows she's dancing around herself. That's strange, she thinks, I'm not a very good dancer.

Her eyes are wide open.

Paige asks, Am I alone?

Paige, you've come late to your vanity.

What does he mean? she wonders.

I can't see it, she says.

Dr. Joy smiles, then he responds in such a low voice, she can barely hear him. She thinks he says, How can you see all of what's indefinitely, even infinitely, unfinished, with or without you? He pauses and chortles. You and I are easily undone, Paige. And, anyway, seeing isn't believing.

Paige doesn't believe her ears, either.

With Kelly still in his arms, Jeff and Rose keep walking to the carousel. Kelly's beside herself with joy. Streams of people are going their way. Everyone's drinking and eating, giggling and shrieking. Thousands of people are marching in time to organ music. Maybe it's piped in through a public address system coming from the carousel. Jeff isn't sure.

People are wearing silly clothes. People are walking on their hands. People have stockings pulled over their faces as if they're bank robbers. Women are dressed as outrageous men, and men as sensible women, and children are wearing oversize evening gowns and tuxedos. In a sideshow parade, that's what Rose calls it, a carnival king and queen are crowned, and then their crowns are stolen from their heads. They're throned and dethroned in a bizarre celebration. Their chairs are pulled out from under them again and again, as they're mocked and they mock each other. People shout, Death to the Dead. Death to the Dead. Death to the Queen. Death to the King.

Rose knows if they yelled Death to the President, they'd all be arrested.

Then Jeff and Rose buy tickets for the carousel from a woman who claims to be president. President of what? Rose asks the old woman. Had she penetrated Rose's mind? Of these disunited states, the old woman answers. The elderly ticket taker smiles wickedly and turns a cartwheel. I'm eighty, she claims with glee. Jeff guesses the woman's a gypsy and touches his pocket, unconsciously. The old woman watches him do it.

Lily Lee and Frank eat hot dogs and drink beer. When the cotton candy melts in her mouth, she knows she's on earth again. Terra firma, Frank says, nothing like it. Frank has mustard on his lip, and Lily Lee wipes it off with her hand. Maybe she really loves him. It's hard to tell. She's always been romantic, ever since she was a kid and fell for her first movie star and dreamed about him every night. Rock Hudson. Every night she prayed to God that he'd bring her Rock.

Paige is ready to leave. She turns to the old man once more.

"You didn't read my mind," she says. Paige is perplexed.

"Mind reading isn't my field. I told you I predict the past."

"That doesn't make sense," Paige objects.

"It doesn't," the old man agrees. "You were reading your own mind. I was listening."

The Future of History

By now Kelly has climbed out of her father's arms. Rose, Jeff, and Kelly linger at the base of the antique carousel. It's red, blue, silver, and green; the sturdy old wooden horses are white, pink, and black. The carousel goes round and round, round and round, round and round so fast, the whirling structure is a blast and blur as the colors whip into one. But then it slows down, goes slower and slower, and figures appear and shapes become objects, and the colors separate again.

Now the three walk on, Kelly and Jeff choose a pink horse, Rose a black horse. The music starts up and the carousel begins to move, and slowly it gains speed. The sturdy horses ascend their poles and descend, they go up and down, up and down, up and down, in time to the music. Kelly is ecstatic. The carousel turns round and round, faster and faster, the music is loud and familiar, people reach for the gold ring, and Rose is floating above herself, above the world. She's flying. She feels she can do anything. She wishes she were still a kid, but not the one she was when she was a kid.

Suddenly Rose notices a man with a gun. She always sees things like that, evidence like that. He's packing, she says aloud, and reaches across her horse to touch Jeff's arm.

His act is magic, Paige decides. Aware and unaware, and reluctant, she leaves the fortune teller's pink-striped tent just the way she came. She's not sure it's the same passageway. Does he have a license to do this? Paige wonders. She's a little dizzy, almost nauseated. What's magic? she thinks. Maybe nothing really happened.

Steve Whitehurst asks to be relieved. He wants to leave the

booth. He doesn't want to work anymore. He wants to be part of the crowd. Besides, he just saw the redhead leave. He has to find her. He wants to drift with her through the Soul Tunnel of Love. Steve follows Paige. She's unaware of him, she's still in another world. To Steve she looks blissed out. What if, he thinks, I kissed her, the way the soldier kissed the woman in Times Square? That famous end-of-the-war photograph had impressed Steve when he was a kid. It happened on your birthday, his mother told him proudly. Why not? Steve thinks.

In the distance people scream on the roller coaster. Steve realizes his life has been one long ride on an emotional roller coaster.

Lily Lee and Frank stroll along Lovers' and Others' Lane. She has agreed to marry him. She agreed one time before, but she left the man standing at the altar. The morning of the wedding, she awoke and couldn't move. The doctor called it temporary paralysis. Her mother said, You didn't want to marry him. Lily Lee prays that doesn't happen again.

They walk aimlessly and arrive at the carousel. Lily Lee wants to grab a ride. Frank reluctantly nods yes. To him it's silly. They buy tickets from the woman who claims to be president. Now her clothes are on, inside out.

So many people are around, more and more of them. It's working my nerves, Frank tells Lily Lee. He hates crowds, crowds worry him, the possibility of danger and disaster. Frank touches the gun under his belt, the bulge on his right hip. His gun never leaves his side.

Just then a huge float passes by. It's painted red, draped with shiny red satin, and lit by Chinese lanterns adorned with crystal spangles. On the side of it is a sign: HELL. Frank nudges Lily Lee: See, baby, now we can go to hell together.

•

Paige drifts and weaves through the crowd. Steve is near her, following her, but he's also caught up in the makeshift parade. Some acrobats join the throng and turn cartwheels. Dancers in pink tights and toe shoes stand on their toes. Everyone glides along to the canny rhythm of the organ music. The red float named Hell passes Paige, too. Comic red devils leap up and down on the top of the float. They stick their tongues out and cry Death to the Father. Paige touches her red hair. Nothing ever dies, she remembers. The devils point at each other ironically and shout: Death to You. Death to You.

Steve gathers up his courage. He moves closer to Paige and introduces himself, and no, he doesn't kiss her, he simply says, Isn't this weird? Paige nods.

Then she sees Dr. Joy. She thinks it's him, anyway. He's dressed as a clown, with a fright wig, red lipstick dotted on his cheeks, and an enormous, painted-green mouth. Dr. Joy spots her, signals, and stands on his head. Everything's upside down, Paige exclaims to Steve. Steve puts his arm around her, as if to steady her, but really he's steadying himself. He wants her.

Rose, Jeff, Kelly, Frank, and Lily Lee are going round and round on the carousel, round and round and up and down. Turning and turning, even Frank is subdued, nearly content. Things seem possible and unpredictable. Kelly grabs a ring, Jeff kisses Rose, Frank starts to get emotional, and Lily Lee cries for no reason. There seems to be no need for restraint.

Then, suddenly, there's a noise, a huge roar, an explosion, and the float named Hell goes up in flames. The fire rises and burns wildly, grandly, it's out of control, it's not being controlled, and the red satin cloth, the Chinese lanterns, everything is immolated in its glorious blaze. No one's afraid. People cheer, joke, dance, and laugh, as if tomorrow will never come.

Paige is ready for anything. Craziness has erupted, and she's carrying weird, anarchic instructions. Don't look for confirmation, you can't see, you're undone . . .

Steve's almost naked with his longing and lust stains his blue eyes. Paige wants him to want her. His desire is a delicacy on her plate for her. The heat in his eyes turns them liquid and silky, empty of everything. He has an illusion of her, of what she could be. She sees that. He might be disappointed. There's always disappointment and regret, and Paige wants regret less than she wants to want anything. His heart beats under his shirt. Paige likes that.

Later, when Steve and Paige ride through the Soul Tunnel of Love, she relishes the anonymity of being a stranger, the fantasy of being strange with a stranger.

Eventually, though the fire still burns and the shouts and laughter continue, Frank becomes aware of the man with the gun. It pulls him from one world into another. The man touches his gun, so Frank draws his. He shouts: Police officer. The man fires, and they exchange shots. Rose is hit in the shoulder by the round of bullets. She isn't seriously hurt, but the dramatic event will change the course of her life. Kelly's in shock, startled by the sight of blood, the sound of gunfire, the confusion around her. She howls. For hours she's inconsolable.

In what seems only a few breathless seconds, Rose is rushed to the hospital, and Jeff, with Kelly crying in his arms, accompanies her in the ambulance. Frank and Lily Lee are escorted by two cops, who know Frank, to the nearest police station. The unknown man, the assailant with the gun, gets away. He loses himself in the carnival crowd. The cops pick him up later. His gun's registered to his brother.

The Past Is Tense

Lily Lee didn't leave Frank at the altar. One night, though, shortly after their marriage, Frank went berserk and threatened to kill himself. Lily Lee insisted he get counseling or she'd divorce him. They never had children. She wanted a dog and finally bought one.

Rose dissolved her partnership with Jeff, gave up law, and moved to New Mexico. She fell in love with a dancer named Gwen and, one day, opened a storefront law office. She couldn't stay away from it.

Jeff reunited with his wife for a while, then they separated again for good. He became an expert in DNA, and in his spare time read about extinct forms of life. For years he worried about Kelly's future.

Kelly wanted to be a musician and played in a few groups around town. For a couple of years she had a drug problem. Jeff thought it was the result of the divorce, even the trauma of the gunfire at the carnival. Kelly thought it was about being the child of a mixed marriage in a racist country. She overcame her drug problem and studied art history. Kelly focused on color, its meanings and interpretations, aesthetic and cultural, in contemporary theory and history.

Paige and Steve had a torrid and occasionally torporific relationship. They played in ways she and he had never before tried or done. To both of them their involvement was extreme, exhausting, but it was an accomplishment, achieved against overwhelming odds.

•

Out of the blue, Paige broke up with Steve. By way of explaining, she wrote him a letter:

"I liked your following me. Ordinarily I wouldn't have, I don't think. That carnival deranged me, rearranged me maybe. It was a good and a bad start for us. You don't know where you're standing when you're with me, you said. I didn't know where you stood in my scheme of things. I know I shouldn't have a scheme of things, but I do. Dr. Joy was a joke, you said, but he wasn't funny. I couldn't take it all in, and I couldn't take in you and your scene, and my decisions along the way made it hard for me to deal with yours. There's no way to apprehend or appreciate everything about anyone else. I'm selfish or just limited like everyone else, or both. I didn't see the end coming, I couldn't. Then one day I didn't feel for you. I'm giving you my version. I don't want to defend myself, and I know I am. It was chance. I'm just what you met that day. This is what I made of things. You kidded me about how it was bigger than both of us. It was. You and I nearly believed and then I stopped believing. I want to believe in what can't be seen in the moments I'm not there. But I don't have confidence. Maybe we were just hanging out. And in the end there was my ambivalence, my mixed feelings, as you used to say, always there, and where we started from and what I brought with me . . ."

Paige never finished the letter. In her mind she addressed it to Steve, but it wasn't really for him. What she had told him, the last time they met, was: It was a fantasy, and now it's not anymore. I don't know what it is. I'm sorry.

The next day Steve had his nipples pierced and for about a year was one of Della's slaves. Then he lost interest in Della, quit the carnival, and wistfully thought about becoming a priest and taking a vow of celibacy. But he didn't. Instead, Steve learned the computer software business. To his good friends Frank and Lily Lee—they'd met at an S&M party—Steve cracked inside jokes about hardware and software, of the hard and soft wear and tear on his life.

Once upon a Time Again

Forever after, Paige Turner pondered the wonderful and disquieting events of the strange day and night at the carnival. It became a turning point for her, one she never completely understood. She couldn't explain it to herself or anyone else. She often dwelled on the sensations of losing herself, and not losing herself, or being herself and not caring who she was, of having been in a trance or hypnotized, of standing in a place out of place, of not seeing and seeing, of being frightened and calm, and all this was familiar and mysterious. She never forgave herself for the way she broke up with Steve and worried, long after his face was a dead letter, whether she'd used him.

Over the years Paige discovered she'd memorized the day and night at the carnival. The details were kept in her mind, like precious objects in a box. She mentioned the day more and more, at odd moments, too. Occasionally she embellished it, and sometimes she chose new words to describe it. Sometimes she said it was indescribable and indefinable, but she never believed that. And sometimes a detail imposed itself, one that she hadn't remembered the last time. The telling of the tale came to have the character of a fable or myth, whose truth or falsehood was hers to cherish.

And much, much later, when years had passed, many years, and she was very old, and her red hair was white, and not long before she died, when the events of every day and every night merged together, when every thought was liminal, and every conversation the remnant of a hypnagogic dream, Paige strained to live the day and night again fully, even to read her mind. Her mind wandered. It might never have happened. Not that way, not that way, that way, yes, that way, I believe, yes, yes, I think it must have been that way, it might have, yes, like that, yes.

And so, to the end, Paige held the thrill close, like an old friend.

AFTERWORD

by Lucy Sante

I first met Lynne Tillman in the mid-1980s, and I picture us talking on Thirteenth Street as I walked my dog. We'd have casual NYC conversations. Then I moved out of the neighborhood, and we'd see each other at events; we had dinner a couple of times. And now I'm pleased to be writing this afterword for her short story collection, *Thrilled to Death*, a selection of work from the 1980s to the present.

No one would mistake Lynne Tillman's prose style for anyone else's. Her sentences glide from concrete to abstract and back again, in flotillas of phrases connected by commas, every observation proudly subjective and disdainful of the assumption of authorial transparency.

Her writing sometimes seems conversational, in the way that unshaped speech will interrupt and contradict itself.

> Another love like this could shatter him, he'd crack
> up, go mad, or be forever changed, and he wanted
> that, to be out of himself, to believe ideas he abso-
> lutely never had, suddenly, and he also wished for

stability and hardly any—no—he wanted no more
sad surprises.

Every story is different. The variety of Tillman's work is
mind-bending, surprising, tantalizing. A critic might be flum-
moxed expecting more similarities. And there are some, of course.
Her stories are secrets. Some have the texture of gossip, especially those written in the third person. They read as if they
are being related in low tones in the shadow of the garden wall.
Her voice remains steady even while constantly interrupting itself, never breaking high or low, because doing so might attract
unwanted attention.

"Life is a dream" is the motif that informs "The Shadow of a
Doubt," which shows Tillman at her most oneiric and cinematic.
It wouldn't be made by Hitchcock, though, but maybe Germaine
Dulac. Her engagement in psychoanalysis is often present—as in
the title story, "Thrilled to Death," but the writing is never di-
dactic. Instead, events and characters are subject to the irrational,
when, for instance, several protagonists visit a wild carnival and
one of them speaks with a fortuneteller, Dr. Joy—*Freud* means
joy in German—who foresees the past.

Many are tales of daily life rendered uncanny, because to Tillman no one is ordinary. She can be no less of a surrealist of the
daily than Jane Bowles, whose vividly real accounts of intimate
drama seem to be taking place on a Punch and Judy stage. Like
Bowles, Tillman manages to lift the daily out of its nest and into
strangeness.

Tillman's zoological eye renders all creatures, animals and
people, without judgment. In her story "That's How Wrong My
Love Is," her character's observations of mourning doves, who
live near her windows, are not entirely anthropomorphic, but are

seen as another kind of family. And she watches with fascination how the female and male birds parent the egg and then the new-born chick. Her character also knows herself as an animal, perfect and deeply flawed:

> I love animals, I am an animal, I'm a mammal, a human being, I like most people, love many, despise one person, though I don't want to hate anyone. I am also selfish and want what I want. My greatest and most enduring problems in life are ethical . . . Not feeding the mourning doves regularly is wrong, but I generally give myself a pass . . . I love animals but discriminate among them and eat some.

Tillman opens the door just enough to turn her readers into potential voyeurs. And from time to time, Lynne Tillman, the writer, like all of us, can't resist dining on her human compatriots.

ACKNOWLEDGMENTS

To and for the many people who helped, encouraged, edited, or published the stories in this collection; and to people who invited me to give a reading, a lecture. I cannot mention everyone, I'm sorry. With their attention, over the last thirty-five years during which these stories were written, I've had great support.

Some people have died: Susan Hiller, David Rattray, Craig Owens, Jim Haynes. They encouraged me early on, when I needed every bit of love I could get. Later, Paula Fox and Peter Dreher. I need to mention their names, to keep them as alive as possible.

MacDowell, where I was a resident fourteen times: Without those weeks when I could shut out almost everything but my work, a lot of writing wouldn't have happened. It's true. That time was precious.

I have been beyond fortunate to be asked to write for, to, and about contemporary artists, their artist books, and by scholars, and curators for museums and galleries for catalogs and monographs. These places and people have been essential to my work, my survival as a writer. When there's a collection of my art and culture essays, I hope to cite everyone.

Now, specifically for this book, I want to thank my editor Mensah Demary and his assistant editor, Cecilia Flores, for their tremendous work on my and its behalf. And their patience. Wah-Ming Chang, who is the unwobbling pivot for this book's completion.

I want to thank, especially, my stalwart, excellent agent and friend, Joy Harris. And Richard Nash, who saved my career by publishing *American Genius, A Comedy*, and then other books. For this collection of stories, Richard's acuity and great literary sense helped carve out what is included here.

My gratitude expands daily. I have a lot to be thankful for.

© Craig Mod

LYNNE TILLMAN's latest novel is *Men and Apparitions*. Her most recent book, *MOTHER-CARE*, is an autobiographical essay on caregiving. Her essays and stories appear in *Aperture*, *Bookforum*, *Frieze*, *n+1*, *Granta*, *Tank*, and in art catalogs, artist books, and other magazines. Tillman has received a Guggenheim Fellowship, an Andy Warhol Foundation Arts Writers Grant, and the Academy of Arts and Letters Katherine Anne Porter Prize for contributions to literature. She lives in New York with the bassist David Hofstra.

CHRISTINE SMALLWOOD is the author of the novel *The Life of the Mind* and a short book about Chantal Akerman's film *La Captive*. She is the recipient of the 2023 Anthony Veasna So Fiction Prize from *n+1*.

LUCY SANTE is the author of *Low Life*, *Evidence*, *The Factory of Facts*, *Kill All Your Darlings*, *Folk Photography*, *The Other Paris*, *Maybe the People Would Be the Times*, *Nineteen Reservoirs*, and, most recently, *I Heard Her Call My Name*. Her awards include a Whiting Award, an award in literature from the American Academy of Arts and Letters, a Grammy (for album notes), an Infinity Award from the International Center of Photography, and Guggenheim and Cullman Center fellowships. She recently retired after twenty-four years teaching writing and the history of photography at Bard College.